Where is Stephanie Lawrence?

Richard J Coley

DEDICATION

I dedicate this, my first book to my "Nicole",
my wonderful daughter, Chloe, and my father, David,
my real life heroes.
Now I can say, "I did it."
Thanks, Love you all.

CONTENTS

ACKNOWLEDGMENTS

I want to thank my team of proof readers and whip crackers that were invaluable in helping me write this. Nikki, Chloe, and David, Massive thankyou to you all.

Cover photography: Chelsea McCulloch
Cover design: Clarke Wardle & Richard Coley
Cover artwork and creation: Clarke Wardle

And lastly, just a mention of two writers that captured not just mine but millions of readers minds all over the world, Dame Agatha Christie and Sir Arthur Conan Doyle, you inspired me to want to write, I salute you both, thank you.

Chapter one.

"You're moving in together? Wha..? How? I mean, how long have you known each other? How? When did you meet?" Quizzed a befuddled Matthew, with a wry smile on his face.

Matthew was questioning Ryan, his childhood friend of over thirty years. They were sat in a small London pub called "The Old Soldier" on Baker Street. The pub was clean, with hard wooden floors, dark tables and chairs and a few benches upholstered with dark red leather. Although the building itself was old, the interior had a fresh modern décor and furnishings masking the age of the establishment. On the outside it was the freshly painted glossy royal blue wooden frontage that showed the building's character and age. "The Old Soldier" had been professionally hand painted, in large gold letters across the top on a black background, that went the whole length of the pub. As with most pubs in London it was the ground floor, with three floors of apartments or flats above it. The front of the flats were painted a clean, bright white, only lending to make the Royal Blue colour of the pub more vibrant and bold.

"So, come on, tell all, geeze I go away for ten months, not so much as a whisper from you and not only have you met a girl, you're telling me you're moving in together; that's so unlike you. What did you say her name was again? Is she pretty? What's she like?" Pressed Matthew.

"Okay, Okay, enough already" Replied Ryan, laughing at his friend's quick-fire questioning, asking the next question before allowing him to answer the first.

Ryan looked down into his pint, feeling a little

embarrassed for not having made more of an effort to keep in touch with his best friend over the last ten months. Though it wasn't all him to blame, Matthew could have sent the odd email, he'd landed a lucrative contract in Saudi setting up an I.T. infrastructure for a large financial institution out there. Great weather, no income tax and a hefty pay-check with a large bonus if he finished ahead of schedule, all made it an opportunity he couldn't resist.

Ryan looked up and smiled at his friend.

"I've missed you mate, I really could've done with having you around the last ten months. It's been somewhat of an adventure and a bit hairy here and there. Could've done with a wingman ya know?" said Ryan, calmly and softly.

"Really? She that scary?" Joked Matthew.

"Not at all, to answer some of your questions, her name is Nicole, she's thirty two, she's of Caribbean descent, absolutely stunning, she's intelligent, dresses impeccably, has a great job, can cook, has a great sense of humour and has the most beautiful hair ever. It's better than you see on those models in those L'Oréal adverts on the telly" Ryan said, finishing with a chuckle.

"You can judge for yourself soon, I asked her to join us, she should be here any moment. I've told her a lot about you and she can't wait to meet you. I suspect you should be prepared for being questioned yourself, about me and our antics as kids." Continued Ryan.

Almost on cue, as Ryan finished his sentence, the door opened and in walked a beautiful women with long, dark, soft, curly hair that she was wearing down. It was flowing over her shoulders and down the back of her white, wool blend trench coat. The coat looked expensive, with wide collars and a belt that was fastened, pulling the coat in to hug her great figure. She was wearing black trousers and black high heeled stiletto shoes. Her entire outfit looking so immaculate you would have thought she just bought it and put it on two minutes before entering the pub.

"No way." Matthew said, almost shrieking.

"Yes way." Laughed Ryan, as he stood from his chair and took a step toward the woman.

Matthew also stood, as is the gentlemanly thing to do. Putting his hands down by his sides, almost looking like a soldier on parade waiting to be inspected by his commanding officer, but for the silly nervous grin he had adorned across his face.

"Hey Beautiful." Ryan said, to Nicole.

"Hey Baby." She replied.

"Matt, I'd like you to meet Nicole, Nicole, this is Matthew, Matt, my oldest friend and by that I mean all my other friends are much younger than him." Laughing, as Ryan finished making the introductions.

"You're such a git Ry" Matthew said, humorously with a big smile on his face as he stepped forward extending a hand to greet Nicole.

"Hi Matt, ignore him he's trying to put you down so I don't get any thoughts of running off with you or something, and what's with the handshake nonsense? Ryan's told me so much about you I feel I know you already, you're practically brothers, give me a hug." Nicole said, excitedly.

Nicole pecked Matthew on both cheeks which made him blush a little. Matthew was a great guy and once he felt comfortable around you, he came out of his shell, but at first he was always quite conservative. For Nicole this was quite a big thing, this was the closest to meeting any of Ryan's family as she'd gotten over the last nine months. Ryan's parents had emigrated to Spain over five years ago. As of yet they, nor Ryan and Nicole had made the trip to get to meet, but it was planned to happen soon. Ryan's only sister was living in Scotland and again they had not yet met. Ryan gave his chair up to Nicole, grabbed another chair from a nearby table and pulled it over to theirs. As Nicole sat, so did Matthew and Ryan.

"So, I expect you have lots of questions Matt." Said Nicole, smiling at Matt as she did so.

"Can I get you a drink?" Interrupted Ryan, as he stood and looked at Nicole, "Same again mate?" he asked Matthew.

"Yes please Ryan, Cap'n Morgan's and coke would be nice." Replied Nicole, as she leant back and undid the belt of her coat.

It was cold outside and she'd kept her coat on for a few minutes until she was sure the pub was warm enough to remove it. She undid the three buttons, shrugged the coat off her shoulders, slid it off her arms and then hung it on the back of her chair.

"Yeah go on then, I think we might be here a while." Chuckled Matthew, as he finished the last drop of lager in his pint glass.

Ryan took his and Matthew's empty glasses from the table and headed for the bar to order the round of drinks.

"So, I know a little about you but Ry still hasn't explained how you both met." Questioned Matthew, almost sounding big brotherly to Nicole.

She could see Matthew held a lot of affection and concern

6

for Ryan and she thought it touching.

"Nooooooo? Ryan hasn't told you that story yet? Oh my goodness. Well I guess you haven't had much time. I should let Ryan tell you, as it's quite a long story but I will say it's nothing like an average guy meets girl tale I can tell you." Exclaimed Nicole, "Let's wait for him to come back with the drinks, you'll probably need one, it's like something off an episode of Luther or some other gritty T.V. drama. Have you seen Luther? Ryan is a real life hero, no joke."

"Really? I'm intrigued and yes I've seen Luther, that's with that Idris elbow fella right?" Replied Matthew, who really was most intrigued.

Nicole Laughed and corrected him "Elba, and yes that's the one."

Ryan came back to the table carrying the three drinks in his hands and carefully placed them on the table.

"You should've asked for a tray darling." Nicole said, as she smiled and thanked Ryan.

"Oh no, I hate trays, I don't trust myself with them, things have a tendency to slide and fall off them when I try using them." Ryan retorted.

"Yeah remember that time? I think we were about thirteen, your mum had made us a Sunday roast and we were taking them up to your room on trays?" Asked Matthew.

"Yup, that was the reason I've hated trays ever since. My door handle was a round door knob, so you couldn't use an elbow to open the door, you had to use your hand, take hold of the door knob and turn it to open the door. As I balanced my tray in one hand and went to open the door with my other, the plate started to slide forward on the tray towards the door, my natural reaction was to quickly tilt the tray back towards me and flipped the whole damn plate of food at the door. Matt and I ended up laughing as we saw roast potatoes, peas, Yorkshire puddings and brussel sprouts rolling down the stairs like some sort of food avalanche. Mum wasn't best pleased as there was gravy all up my door and food all over the floor. I wasn't too happy either because I was starving. Luckily there was enough food to make up another plate and we cleaned up the mess after we ate but yup, since then I avoid using trays." Explained Ryan.

"You poor thing." Nicole said, "Anyway, we've been waiting for you to come back so you can tell Matt the story of how we ended up meeting, I've warned him it's not your average run of the mill kind of meeting."

"Ok matey, I swear to you what I'm about to tell you is all true, you'll understand why I said there's been a few hairy moments and I could've used a wingman by the time I'm finished." Ryan said, with a serious tone in his voice, one you don't often hear, so Matthew sat forward and was prepared to take this all very seriously indeed.

Chapter Two.

Ten months ago………

It was a cold morning, cold enough for you to see your own breath. Steam rose up from the gaps in man-hole covers offering more proof of the low temperature. It was early February and winter had out stayed its welcome like the un-liked weird uncle at a family party.

Ryan was up bright and early, he'd showered, shaved and put on his best suit as today was the day of his first interview. He'd been out of work for the last three months since being made redundant from his last firm. He was actually kind of pleased this had happened as he absolutely hated his job, but as he always answered his friends when they asked;

"Why don't you look for another job", "It's better the devil you know."

Ryan had worked at the last place for fifteen years and actually got quite a decent severance. Even though he had quite some time before the money would run out, he wanted to get back to working sooner rather than later for fear of losing his discipline of getting up in the mornings. His job was that of a security software developer, creating software to guard against hackers and malicious cyber-attacks. This also involved trouble shooting issues with the software, providing consultancy to the customers who bought it and trying to win new customers by giving demonstrations at exhibitions. He had kind of fallen into the job after college as he was himself a hacker back in the day and a pretty good one. A friend of his had landed a role at a software company creating all kinds of software as a software support engineer, and had recommended Ryan to his manager when another similar role came up. Ryan had only been there two months, when he'd been caught hacking into the payroll system to give himself a raise. The only reason he was caught was because it was a closed system and even though he'd covered his tracks by creating a user on the system that had nothing to do with him, he was the only person in the building at the time. He cursed himself for making such a school boy error, but as it turned out the system was protected by the company's own security software. Rather than fire him or involve the police, the managing director was so impressed he'd managed to hack in, he instead had a meeting with Ryan and after a stern talking to, which had Ryan sweating, he told Ryan;

"I think you're wasted in support and I want to ask you if you would be interested in becoming a tester of our software for vulnerabilities? We had a team of six looking for weaknesses and they couldn't find a one."

Ryan, feeling as though he didn't really have much of a choice, as it was made pretty clear this was his, "Get out of jail free card", he accepted the job. Ironically enough the new role came with a substantial pay increase, so Ryan got what he was after, albeit in a round-about way. Ryan had worked his way up from tester to test lead within a year and from there he moved into developing the software. He came up with a radical new encryption algorithm methodology that far surpassed the industry standard levels of encryption that had his manager overcome with excitement at the breakthrough. This change alone catapulted the somewhat medium sized company into the big leagues. They made Ryan head of development for the newly named "Alcatraz secure." security software, the position in which he had remained, until the company was bought out in an aggressive take over by one of the largest American corporate I.T. companies. Their reason for letting Ryan go, was that they already had a team of developers in China and so ended his, "oh so hated job". He was pleased, excited and a little anxious all at the same time, as this was forcing him to seek new pastures. An opportunity to try and find a job that he could enjoy. He had money that afforded him the time to really look for an ideal role. He didn't have much in the way of criteria that the new job would have to meet. Somewhere close to home so the commute wasn't too bad. An established company but not too big. A reasonable salary not necessarily having to match what he was on, but enough to keep him comfortable. A role that didn't involve travel, going to customer sites or doing exhibitions and finally the people he worked with had to be congenial.

"Not too much to ask for." he thought.

Ryan had been searching the internet for the right job, fitting his desires. He had found a company, a financial institute looking for an I.T. director with a strong development back ground, especially in security. It was a decent salary advertised for the right candidate, with good benefits and only five stops on the Bakerloo line. Ryan figured it would be about a fifteen minute tube ride from his home on Baker Street, to the company situated not far from the Embankment tube station. He imagined an office with a view of the embankment in one of the tall buildings down there by the river. Although he'd never been a director before, he felt confident he could do the job. As head of development, he reported directly to the I.T. director at his last place. He had even stood in for him for a month when he was off for medical reasons. So far this position ticked most of the boxes of Ryan's short list of wants. All he needed now was for the other employees to be nice to work with and he was sold. Then all he'd have to do is get offered the job. It was a short walk from Ryan's flat to Baker Street tube station. He'd left his flat and pulled up the collar on his blue, wool mix, over coat as he stepped off the kerb to cross the street to walk to the corner and the entrance of the station. The cold nipped at his ears and he pulled his scarf up higher to try and protect them from the bitter chill. He reached the station in just a few minutes and went down the steps heading for the platform that stated "Southbound" and showed the list of stops that included his destination. This was his favourite station, the chocolate brown painted trimmings around the place only helped to raise the brightness of the beige coloured ceramic tiles. Of course there was also the pattern on the tiles that showed the head and shoulders of the greatest fictional detective, Mr Sherlock Holmes. Ryan was a big fan of Sherlock Holmes and was so pleased when he managed to purchase a flat on Baker Street, the street where the famous detective lived according to Sir Arthur Conan Doyle. Of course anyone who is a true fan of Sherlock Holmes knows that, not only was the detective fictional but so was his address, for there is no 221b, Baker Street. For Ryan though, the street address that contained his flat was something to be proud of, probably one of the most famous street names in the world, rivalling New York's 5th Avenue, Miami's Ocean Drive, Paris's Avenue des Champs Elysees, Rome's Via Del Corso and so on. The tube train came bustling down the darkened tunnel toward the platform, it could be heard long before it could be seen and the gush of wind that preceded even the sound gave away the fact a train was approaching. Because of the size of the tunnels, a train moving along them causes air pressure to build up ahead of the train. Air is forced along the tunnel into the greater open space of the platform areas. Because of this, if you were stood on the platform, you could feel the gush of air with almost explosive force against your face. The rattling of the train, the screech and squeal of the brakes grew louder as it approached the platform. The train stopped, the doors opened, the usual announcements were heard over the public address system including the well-known, "Mind the gap". Some passengers alighted from the train and quite a few, including Ryan boarded. Seemingly just before the doors closed and the train hurtled off into the darkness of the awaiting tunnel and its next destination. Ryan leant against the glass panel near the doors instead of choosing to sit down. Even though he knew where he was going, he looked up at the map of the Bakerloo line and mentally counted off the stations to his destination. Next stop, Regent's Park. Having lived in London all his life he knew the underground very well, but he always had this thing to check the next station to ensure he was going in the right direction. Within moments the train started to slow as it entered the next station, which was of course Regent's Park. Looking around the carriage there was the usual mix of people. Mostly workers heading to their place of work. A small group of probably Spanish school kids Ryan guessed just before it was confirmed, as one of the students turned to reveal the Spanish flag on his back pack. An elderly couple sat stoically looking forward not wanting to catch anyone's eye. Ryan felt a little sad at seeing this but understood. This is what the world had come to, even he himself often felt uncomfortable travelling across London at times. There is just an uneasy feeling about it these days and not just because of the terrorist attacks. Sat next to the elderly couple was a young woman with a baby. The baby was at this moment in time peacefully sleeping, blissfully unaware of its surroundings and most probably the fact it was on a journey. The baby was wrapped in a white woollen blanket and wore a white hat. Its little cheeks were a rosy red colour, suggesting it was cosy and warm. The train pulled into the next station, Oxford circus. The woman stood up holding her baby close to her in one arm as she adjusted the handbag and baby bag over her other shoulder. As she moved towards the doors, one of the baby's cotton booties fell from the youngster's foot. Ryan stepped forward and stooped to pick it up as he said,

"Excuse me.", to the young woman.

She turned to look in his direction as he held out the tiny, white, cotton footwear. She smiled, took the booty, and departed the train onto the platform before attempting to reunite the baby's foot and item of clothing. The train's doors closed and once again lurched forward to continue on to the next station. Only two more stops before Ryan would reach Embankment, his station to disembark. He closed his eyes for a moment and leant back against the glass. He could hear the muffled sound of music coming from the young guy's ear phones who was stood on the opposite side of the doors, leaning against the glass panel that was there. He could hear the Spanish students conversation getting slightly more excited sounding and guessed they were probably heading for Piccadilly Circus. The train slowed and Ryan opened his eyes. The young guy standing opposite him moved towards the doors, as did the Spanish kids. The elderly couple also stood and shuffled forward a little to be closer to the doors. The tube train doesn't give you long to get on and off, before closing its doors and zooming off again. The train stopped at the platform of Piccadilly Circus and the doors once again opened. There were a few people waiting to board the train as the Spanish kids all bustled out of the doors on to the platform. The young guy stepped from the train closely followed by the elderly couple. A couple of teenage boys tried to enter the train as the elderly lady was about to step from the train onto the platform. The young kids almost barging into her. The young guy with the headphones turned and grabbed them, then said,

"Wait a moment, let the lady off the train."

The young boys looked embarrassed and turned crimson uttering, "Sorry", almost under their breaths as they stepped away from the doors. The young guy held out his hand, the old lady took it and stepped from the train with the old gentleman following close behind.

"Thank you." the old couple said in unison and the young

guy smiled, nodded and turned to continue on with his day.

"Maybe there is some hope for humanity with the younger generation." Thought Ryan and he smiled to himself.

The teenage kids, along with a few other people, boarded just before the doors closed and the train pulled away from the platform. The train stopped once more before arriving at Embankment and Ryan exited on to the awaiting platform. He checked his watch,

"Yep, fifteen minutes, just as I figured." He thought to himself.

He worked his way out of the station up to street level and came out where Embankment Place was on his left. There were a group of shops and cafes on both sides of the road under the bridge. He chuckled to himself, never before had he seen a Costa coffee shop and a Starbucks right next door to each other. He walked straight passed them and up Villiers Street. He cut through Victoria Embankment Gardens, onto Watergate Walk, then up the steps and through the gate onto Buckingham Street. Ryan walked up the road passing The Strand Gallery. The building where he was heading to was just opposite on the right. He entered the building through a revolving glass door. The reception on the ground floor was sparse, almost clinical looking. White tiled floor, white and grey marble tiled walls. A solitary glossy white desk was placed to the right of the entrance. The ceiling was high and from it suspended a single light fitting. It was modern looking with many rectangular pieces of white glass hanging from it vertically, in what at first glance looked haphazard. Only when you studied it more closely you could see some symmetry in its design. Ryan walked up to the desk where behind it, sat a pair of security men. Both men wearing matching uniforms of grey trousers, grey jumpers with black epaulets, with "Security" embroidered in white on them and black peaked hats.

"Look like traffic wardens." Thought Ryan.

"Good morning sir." Said the security guard on the right, "How can we help you?"

"Good morning, my name is Ryan Clark, I have an appointment with Mr. Edwards at nine forty five." Replied Ryan.

"One moment sir." Said the security guard, as he typed something on a keyboard hidden from view because of the high front of the desk.

"Have you any I.D. on you sir?" Asked the second security guard.

Ryan reached inside his overcoat and pulled out his wallet and from within it, he drew out his driving license.

"Will this do?" he asked.

"Thank you sir, that all seems in order." Replied the guard, after inspecting it and then handing it back to Ryan, who returned it to his wallet and stowed his wallet back in his inside pocket.

"Please face the camera on the wall over there." Said the first security guard, as he pointed to his right behind the second guard.

Ryan's gaze followed the direction of the man's finger and he spotted a round black ball, with a glass front and a small red light fixed to the wall by a bracket. He turned so he was face on to the device and he heard the security guard click a key on his keyboard.

"Thank you Mr. Clark." Said the guard operating the keyboard.

A low humming sound followed by a couple of clicks emanated from behind the desk. The second guard leaned over reaching for something behind the desk. He straightened with a visitor's credit card sized plastic badge with Ryan's picture and name on it. He slipped it into a clear plastic badge holder that had a crocodile looking clip on it.

"Please make sure you wear this so it is visible at all times while in the building and return it to us on your departure sir." explained the second guard, as he handed Ryan the badge in its holder.

"I'll be sure to, thank you. Do you need me to sign in or anything?" Quizzed Ryan.

"No, that won't be necessary." Said the first guard, "It's all on the computer."

The guard stood from his chair and pointed to his right.

"Turn right at the end of this wall sir, in the alcove there, you will see the elevator. Hold your badge up to the red plastic part then push the button just below it to call the lift. Once the lift arrives step into it, hold your badge up to the red plastic strip above the numbers panel and then press the button for floor number twenty three. Your card is programmed to give you access to floor twenty three only, if you try any other floor it won't work and it will trigger an alarm on our board down here."

Ryan thanked the guards and followed the first man's instructions.

"Wow." Thought Ryan to himself. "It's like Fort Knox around here.", as he held up the card to the red plastic strip and pressed the button for number twenty three.

The doors closed and the lift started to ascend. The interior of the lift was smoked mirrored glass. Ryan checked his hair, made sure his tie was straight and checked the corners of his eyes for sleep, even though he'd showered in the morning. He checked his teeth were clean and finally looked up his nose to make sure nothing embarrassing was hanging around up there. Just as he'd finished checking himself over, out of the corner of his eye he noticed in the mirror, the same looking red light of the camera in the lobby. He turned sheepishly around and sure enough, up in the corner was one of those black ball shaped cameras pointed down into the lift.

"Okay, that was my embarrassing moment, glad to get that out of the way before the interview." Chuckled Ryan to himself.

He looked up at the floor indicator above the doors and twenty one had just lit up followed very soon after by twenty two. He took a deep breath and exhaled slowly, he took another, held it, counted to ten then let it out slowly. He was following a calming technique once suggested to him by a trainer for delivering speeches at conferences. Do the process four times and it calms the nerves, it's more about the exhaling of carbon dioxide than oxygenation evidently. The lift stopped suddenly followed by a "Ping." and the doors opened just as Ryan exhaled for the fourth and final time of his exercise.

"Once more unto the breach dear friends." Ryan thought to himself, as he exited the lift.

Chapter Three.

Ryan walked out of the lift and saw a sign on the wall opposite with an arrow pointing to the right. The word "Reception.", in large green letters just above it. He followed the direction of the arrow as he walked along the corridor. The walls were white and completely bare. The floor covered with a grey and black mottled carpet. There were no doors and no windows in this part of the building, which gave the place an almost claustrophobic feel. The corridor turned sharply to the right, just a few paces further took Ryan to the reception area. A young red haired girl sat behind a brown desk.

"Finally some colour." Ryan thought, as he smiled at the young receptionist.

He was about to introduce himself to her when she perkily said,

"Mr Edwards is expecting you Mr Clark, please go down the hall to your right and knock on the third door on the left."

"Thank you." Ryan said through his smile, as he nodded his understanding of her instructions. He turned to his right and headed along the hallway.

The first two doors were blank and he noticed everything looked freshly painted. He came to the third door and took another deep breath, exhaled slowly and knocked three times on the white wooden door. This door had "Mr J. Edwards" painted on it in black lettering.

"Enter." in a loud authoritative voice came the response.

Ryan turned the handle to open the door and entered the room.

"Do come in, there's a good chap." Said the silver haired gentleman in a grey pin striped suit, sat behind a large wooden desk.

This room was vast. Half of it had walls covered with wood panelling, this half was where the desk was situated. The wood of the desk matched that of the walls. The same grey and black mottled carpet from the hall had flowed into here too. The other half of the room was all windows along the back wall opposite the door that Ryan had entered through. There were three two-seater black leather couches arranged in a horse shoe configuration in that half of the room. On the far right wall which was white, a large painting hung. It looked like the image on the painting was an artist's impression of a sun setting over some plain in Africa. It was a modern piece, the likes of which Ryan didn't usually care for, but for some reason actually quite liked this. Maybe coming through the almost clinical white and grey corridors his brain and eyes were enjoying the extravaganza of colour bursting from the painting. Either side of the painting stood two, three feet wooden carved statues that looked African also. Maybe these had subconsciously influenced Ryan into thinking the painting depicted what he thought it did. Ryan closed the door behind him as the gentleman stood from his chair but remained standing behind the desk.

"Welcome, welcome, nice to meet you, punctual I see, that's a good start, Jon Edwards, please call me Jon." The man said, in a voice not unlike Edward Fox thought Ryan, as he extended his right hand to shake Ryan's.

Ryan stepped closer putting his right hand out ahead of him to grasp Jon's and shake it. He had a strong firm grip, especially for a man of his senior years, extraordinarily so, thought Ryan. Mr. Edwards sat and beckoned for him to do the same. The interview lasted a little over two hours. Ryan was a little confused and perplexed with some of the lines of questioning, mainly concerning his parents and grandparents. He thought that some of the questions were a little unusual but he answered them anyway and soon forgot about them. The rest of the interview centred on Ryan himself and it seemed like the gentleman wanted Ryan's life story. He felt he had nothing to lose by being honest and told Jon the whole story of the hacking incident. He left the building and headed back to the tube station the way he had come. Instead of going home, Ryan decided to stop off at Oxford Street and do a little shopping. While browsing at the latest movie releases on Blu-ray in one shop, an old work colleague had snuck up behind him and startled Ryan by pretending to hold him up with a gun. There was of course no gun: it was Justin's finger. Justin was a few years younger than Ryan and the office practical joker. He was harmless enough, some people found him to be nothing more than an annoyance in the office, but he was friendly enough and a likeable character. He and Ryan had gotten along quite well. They chatted for a while about ex-work colleagues, then Justin asked him what he was up to that evening. He went on to explain that a friend of his who played in a band, had just gotten their first gig in a bar in Leicester square. He explained that he was looking to bolster the audience to give his friend some moral support. He also added it would be great to catch up as they hadn't seen each other for a while. Ryan agreed to meet up with Justin later that evening at the bar. The bar was called, "The Best Bar None".

"Great name." thought Ryan, as he said his goodbyes to Justin and left the shop without purchasing anything.

"I could do with a bit of a night out; I'll consider it a bit of a quiet self-celebration for getting the interview today." Ryan thought to himself.

He headed home. It was getting late in the afternoon and

he thought he should get home, prepare an early dinner and relax a little before getting ready to go out and meet up with Justin. Justin had said the band were due to start at eight PM but they should meet at seven thirty, to get close to the stage. The time went quickly. By the time Ryan had cooked and eaten his steak dinner, cleaned up the kitchen and loaded the dishwasher, he barely had time to watch a bit of news before he had to shower and get ready for his evening out. He met Justin outside the front of, 'The Best Bar None', they headed inside to get a drink and situated themselves near the front of the make-shift stage, where the band were already setting up. A quick sound check and before you knew it the band had started playing. They had a sound like the Foo Fighters, which appealed to the crowd and Ryan alike. Justin had been jabbering away in Ryan's ear most of the evening, updating him on who had left the company since Ryan's exit. Who was left and what had happened to the cute girl from accounts. Who, as it turned out had gotten herself pregnant by one of the directors who was married. It was rumoured he'd offered her a large sum of money to get an abortion and seek employment elsewhere. She'd been scorned, she had expected the guy to leave his wife and live with her happily ever after. Once she'd made those thoughts of hers clear to the guy in question and been rebuffed, she'd gone to HR claiming sexual harassment. They had both been suspended pending the outcome of an investigation. The guy's wife of course found out and kicked him out of the marital home. When the guy tried to get back with the girl from accounts and turned up on her doorstep, he found she was already living with another guy and ended up in a scrap with the boyfriend. Evidently he'd received a broken nose, a bloodied lip and several fractured ribs, because the girl said she had never slept with the guy and he'd been stalking her at work.

"Geeze what a bitch." Ryan had shouted back in Justin's

ear.

"Yeah lucky she never took you up on your attempts to take her out huh?", was Justin's reply, "She was after bigger and better mate but you were lucky there, that could've been you. Talking of that, you got a girlfriend yet?"

"No not yet: with women around like that it's a little off putting right? To be honest though mate, I haven't actually seen anyone that has peaked my interest." Came Ryan's response.

The band played their last track and the audience all clapped and cheered. They had been pretty good. Due to the difficulty in getting to the bar, Ryan and Justin hadn't actually had that many drinks. They said they're goodbyes and Ryan headed back to the tube station in order to get home. It was gone midnight by now, the streets were full of party goers and Ryan couldn't wait to get home.

"It would be nice to have someone special." He thought to himself, as he wandered back to the station, "I just haven't really seen any girl I like the look of enough to want to talk to her to see if I like her. Next girl I see that I think is cute I promise to myself, right here and now, I'll make the effort to talk to her and find out a little about her to see if there could be something. Some kind of relationship worth pursuing."

He turned into the station and headed down the stairs leaving the sounds of the street above behind him. He swiped his Oyster card over the sensor, passed through the turn style and headed to his platform for his homeward bound train. He went down the stairs to the platform and noticed how much quieter it was down there. There was a soft sound of a saxophone being played in the distance, a lone busker trying to make a few more pounds from drink induced generosity of the people also heading home from bars.

"Good luck pal." Ryan thought, as he continued to his platform leaving the sound getting fainter behind him. Ryan reached the platform and he thought it a little odd that he was the only one there.

"Must've just missed one." He thought.

He turned and looked at the sign hanging from the ceiling that showed the time of the next train. Twelve minutes to wait. His feet were throbbing from standing in the bar listening to the band, he turned and looked at the bench on the platform set against the wall. It was blue, uncomfortable looking but better than standing he figured and strolled over to it to take a seat. He was feeling tired now and looked down at this shoes, thinking he couldn't wait to get home to take them off and soak in hot shower. He felt grubby, sweaty and a little abused from the bar, as he had had at least one drink spilt over him by some young, over excited girl trying to get closer to the band. As he sat there staring at his shoes holding his aching feet in them, something caught his eye in his peripheral vision. Something white with a picture on it. At first glance he thought it was a credit card. It was just by the right front foot of the bench just tucked slightly behind it. His curiosity got the better of him and he looked around the platform, still no one else there. He turned back to the card shaped object and leant over to pick it up. He grabbed it and held it in his hand to look at it. It was an I.D. badge, on the side facing him it read

"If found please return to Ripley and Scott investment bank P.O. Box 1023"

There was a dark brown magnetic strip running the entire length of the card. Ryan turned the card over and on the front was a picture of a beautiful woman, a head and

24

shoulders photo of the girl was on the left. In bold capital letters next to the picture was her name,

"Stephanie Lawrence"

"Wow." thought Ryan, "I wonder how old this is." He checked it over and the card looked quite new. There were a few scratch marks on the card going the full length of it that indicated it had been used, at least a few times, to swipe through a magnetic card reader: the kind used for access to buildings or offices to gain entry. He studied the card a little more and noticed the picture was also bright and still maintained good colour, so he deduced it really couldn't be that old.

"She must've dropped it during rush hour leaving work." He figured.

The picture showed a girl with tight curly blonde hair, almost an afro. She had a coffee coloured complexion and stunning green eyes. A half relaxed smile was set in her full pink lips, which were parted just enough so you could see the brightness of her white teeth, making her smile look beautiful and natural, not forced for the picture.

"Wow." he whispered to himself, "Stunning girl. Okay, I did make myself a promise and if you can't keep a promise to yourself who can you keep one to?" He almost chuckled to himself.

He felt a little excitement creep into his belly at the thought of meeting this girl. He allowed himself to daydream a little and in his head the girl was sweet, softly spoken with an angelic voice to match her wonderful personality. She wouldn't be a pushover. Not a girl who allowed herself to be dictated to, but nor would she be a girl with her head up her own arse, like so many pretty girls who felt everyone was beneath her. She'd be intelligent, kind hearted, generous and single. Ryan smiled to himself.

"Yeah wouldn't that be great? And I'd be just the guy she's been looking for her whole life."

He looked under the bench again to see if there was perhaps the holder for the I.D card but there wasn't. There was however a lipstick, he reached down and picked that up too. This was a little further back, nearer the wall and he had to get off the bench this time to retrieve it. He pulled the cap off it, it was pink, the same colour as the girls lips in the picture.

"How bizarre." Thought Ryan.

He looked again but there was nothing else under the bench. He felt the gust of air against his back giving away the fact a train was approaching the platform. He stood again and turned to face the oncoming train. He slipped the lipstick and the I.D badge into his inside coat pocket and waited for the train to arrive. The tube train arrived at the station with the usual bluster and screeching of brakes, as they all did. The public address system crackled into life, a female voice announced this was the last train to the final stop that night, and everyone should alight the train at its final destination, or any of the stops preceding it. Ryan stepped into the carriage nearest him once the doors opened. He looked up and down the carriage only to see he was alone in this one.

"Quite odd to be so quiet this time of night." Ryan thought to himself.

As he sat down he checked the card and lipstick were still in his inside coat pocket by feeling for them through his coat. They were still there. The carriage lights flickered as the doors slid shut. The train jerked forward a little as it started off before settling down to a steady forward momentum, trundling off into the tunnel and leaving the brightness of the platform and station behind. Once at Baker Street, Ryan exited the train, made his way up the stairs from the platform and out on to the street where he made the short walk home back to his flat.

His thoughts of his aching feet and taking a shower took a back seat for the moment, as he put the kettle on and powered up his laptop. The kettle was in full rumbling mode by the time he could open up a web browser to do a search. His online search page loaded just as the kettle clicked off to state it had boiled the water sufficiently to make tea. Ryan made himself a tea and turned his attention back to his laptop.

R-I-P-L-E-Y A-N-D S-C-O-T-T I-n-v-e-s-t-m-e-n-t - b-a-n-k-e-r-s, he typed into the search bar and hit enter.

First result was exactly what he was looking for and hoping to find. It was the home page of Ripley and Scotts investment bankers. He clicked on the link and up came their web page. It was the usual type of corporate web page, full of jargon and bold headings, with quoted captions regaling the reader of their great achievements in the world of investment banking. Up the top of the page in small letters just to the right of "FAQ's" was just what Ryan was looking for.

"Our office locations."

He excitedly clicked on the link and within seconds another page loaded with information on their office locations. There were three in total. One in Belfast, Northern Ireland, one in Edinburgh and one in London, all three had phone numbers and full postal addresses.

"Awesome." Shouted Ryan, to no-one and everyone in the world.

"She has to work in the London office, but oh no. Knowing my luck she probably works in Edinburgh or even worse, the Belfast office and is just here on training or something daft." Ryan thought negatively, "No, she must work in the London one and tomorrow I'll go there and find out. I'll return the I.D. card in person and that'll be my excuse to meet her. I'll make out I found it that morning and just happened to be passing."

Ryan grabbed the note pad that was stuck to his fridge door by a magnetic strip. He took a pen from the drawer to the left of the cutlery draw and scribbled the address down. He tore off the page, placed the pad back on the fridge door and put the pen back in the drawer. He clicked on the small map icon next to the address on the web page and it pulled up a street map showing the location of the office in Canary Wharf. Tomorrow was Friday, he had to go there tomorrow as he was sure they'd be closed for the weekend. It was gone one thirty in the morning and Ryan was tired now. Especially after his little burst of adrenaline at the excitement of discovering the card, and the location of the office of this beautiful girl he hoped he'd meet. Hopefully she would live up to his expectations and have all the qualities his daydreams gave her. He powered down his laptop, grabbed his mug of tea, turned off the kitchen light and headed up to bed with a myriad of thoughts racing through his mind. Tomorrow was a new day, tomorrow was a day he'd hopefully find the one. He laughed at himself a rueful chuckle,

"Yeah right." He said aloud, "We'll see."

Chapter Four.

Ryan woke early. He showered, dressed and was now sat at the breakfast table with a tea and two slices of jam on toast. There was no point rushing over to Ripley and Scotts: Ryan had noticed their hours of business were from 9AM to 5.30PM and it was still only eleven minutes past eight. He decided it wouldn't look too much like the behaviour of a stalker if he were to arrive there between ten and quarter past. It wasn't long before Ryan had left his flat and had caught the correct train to take him to his destination. He exited the train and headed up the stairs from the platform. All sorts of thoughts were running through his head.

"Is this mad what I'm doing? Should I have just posted the I.D. card as it suggested on the back of it? Too late now" he thought to himself, "I made a promise to myself, I wouldn't shy away from opportunities."

It was already ten twenty five so in his mind he was on schedule. It would appear he was already out taking care of some other business before turning up at the offices of this woman. He walked along the embankment. The sun was out but having little effect on warming what was a chilly morning. The river was busy as usual with boats carrying goods into the heart of London. There were ferries ferrying tourists and commuters from one side of the river to the other. There was the usual throng of walkers and joggers getting their morning exercise, making the most of the wide path that ran along the side of the river.

Ryan headed towards the building that was home to the company on the I.D. badge. He walked up the steps and entered the building through one of its three revolving doors. The lobby had a marble floor and there was a cleaner sweeping around one of those cloth broom like dry mops. There were two security guards standing at their posts either side of the reception desk. The reception desk itself was a crisp bright white and silver trim ensemble. It was wide and had four women and a man sat behind it. Several were talking into their headsets while tapping away on their keyboards in front of them, obviously fielding calls and putting them through to whomever the callers had requested to speak to. Ryan pulled the I.D. badge from his inside coat pocket and read the name on it again just to be certain in his moment of nervousness that he hadn't forgotten her name. He approached the reception desk and walked up to one of the women who didn't appear to be on a call.

"Good morning." Ryan said, with a friendly and positive tone.

"Good morning sir and how may I help you?" came the pretty young woman's reply.

The woman was mid-twenties Ryan guessed, with dyed blonde hair, recently done he thought as there was not a hint of dark roots. She had perfect make-up finished with bright red lipstick, her hair pulled tightly into a bun on the back of her head: a perfect image of what a company would like its visitors to be presented with when entering the building.

Ryan smiled and said,

"I'd like to see Stephanie Lawrence if that's possible please?"

"Have you got an appointment?" the woman asked politely.

"Errrrmm no", stuttered Ryan, "I was just passing and I thought I would pop in on the off chance."

Ryan felt a little awkward at that point and considered just passing the badge over and saying, "I found this.", but scolded himself at the thought as he had gotten this far, he must see it through.

The young woman had been tapping away on her keyboard and looked up at Ryan and said,

"Oh, she's not in today, I am sorry."

"Is she on holiday?" Ryan asked.

"No, it looks like she is out on sick leave, on the screen it says she's been out for the last two weeks. Are you a friend?" Asked the receptionist.

"Yes." Lied Ryan, "I do hope she's ok, I guess I'll try again another time, thank you."

Ryan's mind was racing now.

"That's just typical of my luck." he thought, "I seriously do hope she's okay though, been out of the office sick for two weeks already and this is taking it in to the third week. There's not many things that would make you sick for this length of time that is not serious."

He smiled weakly at the receptionist with an honest look of concern on his face and turned to head toward the door.

"What do I do now?" he thought, "I guess I just have to try again maybe next week, I don't want to keep coming back if she's not in, it'd look weird."

Just as he reached the revolving door another young woman came up behind him and touched his arm.

"Excuse me?" She said, in a very sexy sounding voice.

Ryan started a little, he felt his lie of being a friend had been seen through and he was going to be questioned on his reason for being here.

"Hi." He replied as calmly as possible.

"Did I just hear you asking for Stephanie? Stephanie Lawrence?" Quizzed the woman, "Sorry, I'm Nicole, a friend of Steph's."

"Yes, yes you did, I was told she's off sick, do you know if she's ok?" Asked Ryan.

"Can we talk?" Asked Nicole, "Outside I mean?"

"Certainly." Ryan said, feeling more awkward now.

He gestured toward the revolving door for Nicole to lead the way. He followed her through the door and into the street outside. Ryan remained in tow, as she walked to the left of the building once she had exited the confines of the revolving door. Ryan couldn't help but notice she was very nicely dressed and could tell she had a rather nice figure too. Her hair was dark and hung in loose curls, as he followed her, he could smell the fragrance of her perfume. For just those few seconds he'd almost forgotten what his reason for being there in the first place was.

Nicole reached the corner of the building and stopped and turned to face Ryan.

"How long have you known Steph?" She asked.

Ryan felt himself blush and made a sudden decision to just be completely honest with her. Apart from sounding a little crazy what did he have to lose? He could just hand her the I.D. badge tell her the story of how he found it and never see her again.

"Well, I... I'm sorry, I have a confession to make to you. I don't know what it is about you but I feel I just have to be completely honest with you. I don't actually know Stephanie, I'm not a friend of hers at all. Please don't think I'm crazy or some sort of stalker but this is what happened."

Ryan went on to tell her how he found the badge and how he had made a promise to himself if he saw someone he liked the look of and so on, and how he ended up being here.

Nicole's face had stayed the same throughout Ryan's explanation, giving away nothing as to her thoughts about this stranger's tale of events that lead them to this point. What happened next surprised Ryan, as he had no idea how she was going to react.

"Awww, I actually think that's really kind of sweet, could almost be considered romantic if you had met her and something came of it." Nicole was smiling an innocent, endearing smile that caught Ryan completely off guard.

"So you don't think I'm a loony?" Ryan chuckled, to himself more than anything, a nervous chuckle he often found himself doing when in an uncomfortable situation.

"No. Not at all, I guess it could be considered a little different, but when you explained your reasons I do understand." Replied Nicole, "And you do seem like a genuinely nice guy. So what are you thinking of doing about all this now?"

"Well I'm not sure to be honest, before you and I spoke I was thinking I would just maybe try coming back next week to see if she is back at work. Perhaps if I gave you my number, you would be so kind as to text me when she is back at work, but I'd understand if you didn't feel comfortable doing that. After all she is your friend and I am a complete stranger, but I assure you, I have no ill intentions and would just like to meet her." Said Ryan, "You also said you wanted to talk to me before we left the building and my confession, did you still want to talk to me about whatever it was?"

"Hmmm I'd have to think about that with regards your number. When I believed you were a friend of hers I wanted to talk to you about her and her not being in work. I don't know any of her other friends or family so I was glad to hear you knew her. I'm very concerned about her and her whereabouts." Explained Nicole, "But now you've been honest and told me you don't even know her, I don't know what to do. I do feel I need to tell someone though, maybe I should just take a chance on you and tell you my concerns."

Ryan looked at Nicole quizzically,

"Please, do go on, if nothing else I'm intrigued. This whole thing is turning out to be a little weird. It might help you feel a bit better for getting it off your chest."

"Okay, okay," Nicole started, "You're right and maybe I'm just being paranoid and you being impartial can give me your opinion."

"Of course." Ryan interjected.

"I'm worried about Steph, we are friends out of work you see, not just work mates, but I haven't heard from her for over two weeks. The last time I saw her or even spoke to her was over two weeks ago. I've had no phone calls, no texts and when I've tried calling her, her phone just goes straight into voicemail. I have left messages of course and still nothing from her. This is very unlike her, we would normally speak out of work at least every other day, that's how close we are."

"Have you been to her house?" Ryan asked.

"Yes of course, by the end of the first week of no contact from her I popped round there to see if she was okay. It was early evening and there were no lights on in her flat or any sign that she was actually there." Came Nicole's response.

 "And you say this is totally out of character for her to just disappear and not let you know where she is?" Questioned Ryan.

"Well yes. Most definitely…Oh hang on, there was this one time she went away last minute with her boyfriend, well her ex-boyfriend now. But they went away, he'd surprised her with some long weekend trip to Amsterdam. I only knew about it when I got a text from her on the Sunday asking if I'd cover for her at work. She asked me to make out to her boss she'd had a close relative taken ill suddenly, and she had to go up north to see them in hospital. She didn't get back until the Thursday." Nicole corrected herself.

"Ok, so is it possible something like that has happened again?" Asked Ryan.

"The ex-boyfriend is no longer on the scene and she's shied away from meeting anyone else because her ex is a little…er…well, not a nice sort if you get my drift?" Nicole replied, "Actually I wonder if he has got something to do with her disappearing. Now that I think about it, the last time we did talk she sounded a little nervous about something. I asked her if she was okay and she just said she'd been watching a scary movie on T.V. and that she was just a little jumpy in the flat on her own."

"Well, have you thought about going to the police?" Asked Ryan.

"No, what would I say to them? If she has per-chance gotten back with her ex and is having a sneaky get-away with him, she wouldn't want the police contacting her boss or anything. I just don't know what to do." Nicole said, sounding desperate.

"Alright, what if I were to say I want to help you? See if I can find her?" Asked Ryan.

"Well I guess that would be great but why would you want to do that?" Questioned Nicole.

"I'm curious as to what has become of her and I can hear and see your genuine concern. Besides I'm not working at the moment so I have time on my hands. Apart from that, I guess I'm a good guy." Explained Ryan, with a coy smile.

"Okay, where do we start?" Nicole said, with a hint of a smile.

"I want to start at her home, do you happen to have a spare key?" Quizzed Ryan.

"I do." Replied Nicole, "But to be honest it's at home and if I did have it on me I'm not sure I'd hand it over to you, please understand I don't doubt your intentions but I have only just met you."

"No, no offence taken, I understand completely. Okay, so we should go there together, when are you able to go?" Came Ryan's response.

"I finish at four o'clock I could meet you somewhere after then?" Nicole replied.

"Ok sounds good. What sort of area does she live, maybe we could meet on the way. I live on Baker Street, not far from the underground station." Said Ryan.

"Wonderful, she's lives in Willesden Green, I live near Regents Park so I'll pop home first, get her spare key and meet you outside Baker Street station at say five pm? Does that work for you?" Nicole said, as she started to turn and head towards the revolving doors, "I have to get back to work, what's your number?"

"Yes, yes, that works for me, here, here's my card." Ryan replied, hurriedly following her whilst trying to take one of his business cards from his wallet, which he'd pulled from the inside pocket of his overcoat, "Call or text me your number when you get back to your office so I have it, just in case I need to contact you."

Nicole took the card from Ryan and placed her hand on his arm and said,

"Thank you, I will, as soon as I get to my desk. It was nice to meet you Ryan, until later." She smiled and turned for the door.

"Oh one more thing," Ryan said after her, "What's the ex-boyfriends name?"

"I only knew him as Ollie, short for Oliver, I guess." Came Nicole's reply, "See you at five." And with a cute smile she turned, entered the revolving door and disappeared into the building.

"Bye." Ryan said, almost under his breath and stood there for a moment or two watching after her.

"I came here to try and meet one girl yet I feel captivated by this one, I can't work myself out at times." Thought Ryan and he finally turned and headed for the station to catch a tube to take him home.

Just a few minutes into his walk his phoned beeped, he pulled it from his coat pocket. It was a text from a new number.

"Hi, Nicole here, now you have my number." The text

finished with a smiley face.

Ryan smiled and hit reply,

"Thanks, see you later, it was nice to meet you too."

Chapter Five.

It didn't take long for Ryan to make it home and once there, he went up to his room and fired up his computer.

"Ok, let's see what we can find out about Miss Stephanie Lawrence." He thought to himself.

First thing he did was an online search for her name and there were many hits. First on the list was a Wikipedia entry for an English musical actress who died in two thousand, at the age of fifty from liver disease. There were many hits for her. Finally after much searching, he found a hit for a Facebook entry that looked like it could be her. He clicked on the link, it opened his Facebook page and took him to her page. He was lucky: after the last update from Facebook, it discarded your privacy settings and he was able to view her page including her posts and pictures. Her last post was about a new coffee shop she'd discovered not far from her place of work, just over two weeks ago. He could tell she was an avid Facebook user and tended to like or post something almost daily. More often than not she'd post something more than once a day, so the inactivity over the last fortnight did lend credence to Nicole's concerns. Her relationship status still showed "Single" and there seemed to be no "coupley" looking photos of her and the mysterious Ollie. He had to go quite a way back on her wall to eventually find something that was "liked" by an Oliver Marshall. Could this be the elusive Ollie? He clicked on Oliver Marshall and it tried to take it to his page but there was nothing there. Either Ollie had closed his Facebook account or his privacy settings were blocking Ryan from viewing it. Ryan decided to do a search for Oliver Marshall and though there were many hits, including a Wikipedia page it was clear it wasn't the right Oliver as this one was born in eighteen fifty. Ryan decided to call in a favour and phone an old friend. He took his mobile off the desk, opened the contacts list and scrolled down to Ray.

"Ray? It's Ryan" He said into the phone.

"Oh Ryan, how are you buddy you okay?" Came Ray's response.

"Yeah, yeah, I'm fine thanks and how's you? I'm after a little favour mate." Ryan continued.

"I'm good, sure what's up?" Ray asked, sounding a little concerned.

"I'm trying to trace someone, all I have is a name and I'm not even sure it's the right name or his full name. Could you do a favour for me and run him through the PNRDB?" Asked Ryan.

Ryan met Ray when they were younger. Ryan used to work in a café on weekends when he was still at school and Ray worked in a tyre fitting place just around the corner. Ray used to pop in for a coffee every weekend, they always said hello and often chatted about this and that. Even after Ryan had entered full time employment having left school and his part-time job at the café, they'd often bump into each other and always asked how life was going. One day Ryan saw Ray in a police uniform and commented on it being a big change of career from the old overalls he used to wear. Ray was a big guy, tall and muscular, just a few years older than Ryan and always towered above him. A gentle giant but a mean looking guy. Ray had explained at that time of meeting how he felt he wanted to do more, to give back to the community. He was of mixed race descent and the police were on a drive to encourage a more ethnically broad police force, so it served Ray well when he applied. Ryan had left that meeting with a comment about criminals had better watch out now which had made Ray laugh. The PNRDB was the Police National Records

Database, anyone that had ever been in trouble with the police, or even had a parking or speeding ticket would appear on that database.

"Okay, but you know I could get in trouble for this?" Came Ray's hesitant reply.

"Thanks Ray you're a gent. The name I have is Oliver Marshall." Replied Ryan.

Ryan could hear a few taps on a keyboard and Ray humming quietly to himself, an obvious sign he was waiting for the computers to do their search and spit out their results, but also a sign he was nervous and hoping not to get caught.

"Right, there's two hits on here. A one Oliver James Marshall: last known address Northampton and one Oliver Terrance Marshall in the London area." Ray said, almost in a whisper.

"I guess we could probably rule out the guy from Northampton do you have an address and date of birth for the second one?" Ryan asked.

"Mate I could get in serious trouble if anyone knew I was doing this, I'll give you his date of birth but I honestly daren't give you the address, data protection act and all that, you know how it is. I'm sorry mate. D.O.B sixteen, twelve, eighty three, okay? I better go now. Hope that helps. Speak soon, maybe meet for a beer some time yeah?" Came Ray's hurried voice over the phone.

"Yes mate, definitely and I really appreciate it and sorry to put you on the spot but it's important." Retorted Ryan.

There was a click as Ray hung up the phone.

"Okay, date of birth, a name confirmed and an address

somewhere in London. Sounds like it could be our guy. Time to do some good old fashioned hacking. DVLA I hope you haven't increased your security any." Ryan thought to himself.

Ryan got up from his desk and walked out onto the landing. He reached up and pulled on the cord that brought the loft hatch down. As the hatch opened a ladder started to lower from inside the attic. Ryan reached up and pulled the ladder down so he could access the loft. He climbed the ladder and as he entered the loft he clicked on the attic light switch. He crouched as he entered the attic space, walked over to the far opposite corner and lifted a board panel from the floor, moving it to one side. Underneath the panel was a cavity, and in there lay two laptop bags. He grabbed both and placed the panel back in position. He climbed back down the ladder turning the light off as he did so. Once back on the landing he pushed the loft ladder back up and closed the hatch.

He went back into his room and placed both laptop bags on his bed. He unzipped each bag in turn. One held a metallic encased laptop, the other some communications equipment that didn't look like a standard modem or Wi-Fi router. All the cables, power cords and power packs were in the pockets of the lids of the two bags. Ryan carefully took everything out and before long had connected everything up as it needed to be. He opened the laptop and pressed the power on button. A soft hum followed by a whirring of a fan sound emanated from the laptop and there was a green glow from under the keyboard.

"Hello my old pal," Ryan said to the laptop, "let's get busy."

Ryan waited for the login prompt on his laptop to appear and logged on. It had been a while since he had used this laptop and done any hacking, but remembered the password as if he had used it just yesterday. Ryan double clicked on a file on the desktop and it opened in a text editor. In the file were three lists: the first contained letters, the second a series of numbers separated by dots and the third more numbers. The initials were abbreviations of company names or governmental departments, the second were ip addresses and the third port numbers. Ryan scrolled down the list and found the DVLA entry. (Department of vehicle licensing agency) he minimised this program and with a few more clicks of the mouse button, he had a terminal window open. He checked he had connectivity through the router to the internet and thus the outside world by pinging the ip address of Google. Once he had confirmed this worked he then opened a connection to the DVLA using the information from the text file he had opened. After just a couple of seconds the terminal window went blank and he was presented with the word "Password?" and a flashing square cursor. He typed the password from memory and was rewarded with the words, "Password accepted." and a list of directories on the server. Within moments he was looking at the DVLA's database that stored every drivers' license owner's details. He started a search using the information he had acquired from Ray,

"Oliver Terrance Marshall, sixteen, twelve, eighty three."

The cursor sat there blinking back at him. He waited. After a few minutes, "One record found." Came the response on the screen. Ryan issued another command to display the information from the record on his screen.

NAME: Oliver Terrance Marshall

D.O.B: 16.12.1983

SEX: Male

ADDRESS: Flat 2 Berkshire House

       Kenton Road

       Kingsbury, Greater London

That's it, he now had an address for Stephanie's estranged ex-boyfriend, as long as it was current of course. He logged out of the DVLA server and exited the terminal window. Ryan had successfully hacked into the DVLA and gotten the information he needed. It was easy to do so, because any customer Ryan visited and installed his company's security software on, he had created a secret backdoor into their server. The hacker in him had never gone away and always thought to himself,

"Never know when it might be useful to have access."

Luckily DVLA was one of the first clients to have contracted his previous company to install security software. Ryan shut down the laptop and disconnected all the equipment, packed them neatly back in the laptop bags and hid them back in their hiding place in the attic. He looked up the address on his normal laptop and found it was an address based in Northwest London. Now all he had to do was wait for his meeting with Nicole. It was only early afternoon so he made himself a sandwich and a cup of tea. His thoughts turned to his interview and the fact he hadn't had any news from them yet as to how his interview went, or if he had been successful or not in his application. He then realised it really hadn't been that long since his interview, they were sure to have other applicants and interviews to conduct, so he put the thought out of his head. The next couple of hours passed quickly and Ryan left his flat to be on time for his meeting with Nicole. He stood and waited at the entrance of the tube station. At one minute to five Nicole tapped him on the shoulder from behind.

He turned to face her, "Hi, how was your afternoon?" Ryan asked.

"Pretty slow to be honest, I guess it was because I was watching the clock the whole time, I'm anxious to see if we can find any clues as to where Stephanie is. How about yours?" Nicole replied.

"Not bad to be honest, in fact quite productive as long as it turns out to be necessary. I did some digging and came up with a full name and hopefully address for Ollie." Ryan exclaimed.

Nicole looked at him a little wide eyed. "Impressive." she said, "And how did you manage to do that?"

"I have my methods, probably best you don't know about them." He replied, "Shall we go?"

"I guess we should, I have Steph's key in my bag." Nicole replied.

They headed into the tube station to take the tube to their first stop. They headed for the platform that serviced the Jubilee line heading north. It was just a short ride that didn't take long at all as it was only six stops to Willesden Green from Baker Street. The pair exited from Willesden Green tube station and hailed a cab. During the ride on the tube, Nicole had explained that it was a fair walk from the station to Steph's flat, so a cab made more sense. The journey only took ten minutes. Ryan paid the cabbie and they both got out onto the street. It was starting to get dark now but the street lamps had started to come on. The street was lined with terraced houses that to Ryan all looked the same. They were three story town houses but it looked like many had been converted into flats, as was the case with Stephanie's. They stood on the pavement directly outside the address that Nicole had told Ryan was

Stephanie's. They looked at each other and both shrugged their shoulders. The silence between them was broken by Ryan,

"Ready to do this?" He inquired.

"Yes." Came Nicole's response.

They started up the five, white marble stairs to the front door to Stephanie's flat. To the right of the door was a large bay window. On reaching the top step Nicole tried to peer through the window.

"See, no change, curtains are open but I don't see any lights on in there." Nicole almost whispered to Ryan.

"I guess she's not home then, it's dark enough for there to be lights on if she's home." Ryan replied.

Nicole opened her hand bag and reached in. After a little rummaging, she pulled her hand out holding a set of two keys on a key chain that had a little green frog on it. She inserted the first silver key into the lock and tried to turn it. It wouldn't turn.

"Ughh wrong key, I always do this, it's the other one for this main door." She said, sounding a little annoyed.

She pulled the key out and inserted the other one. This time the lock turned and she pushed open the door. They entered the building. It was a small hall with white walls and a white tiled floor. The tiles were tiny rectangle ones, not unlike those you see in the public toilets in the train stations Ryan thought to himself. On the left was a narrow staircase with a dark wooden bannister, obviously going up to the floors above. On the right was a white door that served as Stephanie's front door. A silver letter "A" was screwed to it. Nicole inserted the first silver key into the lock.

"Wait, wait, shouldn't we try knocking first?" Enquired Ryan, "What if she is home, we'll scare the pants off her if we just let ourselves in."

"You're right of course." Nicole replied and without taking the key out of the lock, she knocked loudly three times on the door. They waited but nothing happened.

"Try once more." Ryan said.

Nicole knocked again even louder and again they waited, but nothing stirred from within. Nicole turned the key slowly, she wasn't sure why but it seemed to be the thing to do. The lock turned and she pushed the door slowly open. She called in through the gap.

"Steph? STEPH? It's Nicole, are you home?"

Silence, no answer, no TV or music playing. The room the front door lead into was the living room, and though it was dark there was some light creeping in from the street lamp outside. It cast a yellow haze through the net curtain that didn't really lend itself to help illuminate the room. Nicole pushed the door further open and reached her hand in. She ran it up the wall to the right of the door, feeling her way for the light switch. She found it and flicked it on. The room burst into light. They entered and the place was a mess. The couch had been sliced open the whole length of the back upright, the cushions had been cut diagonally and half their stuffing was hanging out of them. The glass panels that once adorned the coffee table in the middle of the room were smashed and laying in pieces around the base of the table. There were two bookshelves with almost all of the books laying haphazardly on the floor around the base of them, like someone had swiped them off their shelves in one violent action. The arm chair had also been slashed, as was its cushion but the chair itself was also upended and laying on its side, showing even the bottom had been cut open. A side table was still standing at one end of the couch, but the lamp that was probably once sat on it was laying on it, with the shade all askew from being pushed over.

"OH MY GOD." Nicole almost screamed, "What's happened? I knew something was wrong. Ryan, what the hell happened here?"

Nicole turned to face Ryan who was looking around the room, taking it all in with just as much of a shocked expression on his face.

"I'm no expert but from the cop shows and movies I've seen I would say that someone was looking for something. Let's take a look at the rooms, shut the front door and you stay here, I'll go look. Don't touch anything" Ryan said, as calmly as possible to try and settle Nicole.

He Turned to Nicole and put his hands on her upper arms and squeezed, more to try and reassure her. She looked back at him and he could see tears welling up in her eyes.

"I'm sure she's okay, maybe she came home found this and went to a family member's house and has been hiding out there or something." He said, in an attempt to calm Nicole and offer some explanation.

"No, no, no, she would have contacted me somehow and told me." Nicole responded.

"Who knows, maybe she doesn't have her phone, I don't know anyone's number anymore without looking it up in my contact list on my phone." Ryan retorted, again in an effort to find a reasonable explanation, but really he was worried just as much that something sinister had happened to Stephanie.

"Maybe you're right, I'm the same." Nicole said, sounding

calmer and even with a hint of a smile.

"Okay, stay here, remember, don't touch anything and I'll go check the other rooms." Ryan repeated.

Nicole stood there, just looking around the room fixed to the spot.

"Where are you Steph?" She thought to herself.

Ryan headed for the only other door in the room which was on the far wall in the left hand corner. He called out "Hello", before opening the door and seconds later Nicole saw the light go on in the room. It was a small kitchen and it was worse than Ryan had expected. All the cupboard doors were open, a couple hanging off of one hinge and all the contents that once existed in the cupboards were strewn all over the floor. Pots, pans, broken plates and mugs. The cutlery drawer had been removed and its contents dumped on the work surface. The fridge and freezer doors were wide open and something from within was creating a stench.

"That's not a good sign." Thought Ryan, "For something to be smelling up the place this bad this must've happened a while ago."

He looked in the fridge and who knows what it once was, but there was a green furry looking thing, sat on a small plate on the middle shelf of the fridge. The washing machine had been pulled forward, away from the wall and even the base shelves in the cupboards had clearly been pulled up in an attempt to see under them. Ryan went through another door that was opposite the one he had come through. He found the light switch and flicked it on. This led into a small bathroom that just contained a sink, a toilet and a shower in the corner. The cabinet on the wall was open and most of its contents dumped on the floor.

There was another door to the right of the shower that Ryan guessed led to the bedroom. On entering that room and turning on the light he was proved right. This room hadn't faired any better either. The wardrobe was tipped forward so it was resting on the bed. The contents again all over the floor. The bedding had been torn off the bed and thrown in a heap in the far corner. The mattress, like the couch and arm chair, had been slashed open and you could see stuffing and springs through the gaping slits. The mattress was not aligned with the bottom of the bed and had obviously been slashed then lifted to see the bed base, then just dropped again. The chest of drawers that should've had five drawers in it only had three of its drawers still half in place. The other two were also now on the floor upside down with their belongings scattered about the room. The three drawers that were half in their places had most of their items missing from them and were probably in the same scattered piles covering the floor of the room. No sign of Stephanie though and nothing to give any clear clues as to her whereabouts.

Ryan made a quick but fairly thorough check around the room to see if he could find a mobile phone that would most probably belong to Stephanie, with no luck. He returned to Nicole, switching the lights off in the rooms as he left them.

"The whole place has been turned over. No sign of Stephanie though and I couldn't see her phone anywhere." Ryan reported to Nicole.

"I just don't understand." Replied Nicole, "If she is unharmed why hasn't she contacted me? I think something terrible has happened to her Ryan."

"Well look, there's no sign of blood or anything in any of the rooms and just because I haven't found her phone it doesn't mean she has it on her. Maybe the battery is dead?" Ryan exclaimed, "Do you want to go to the police now? I think we should."

"No, what if she has been kidnapped and she has got family I don't know about and the kidnappers are asking for a ransom? You always see in the movies the kidnappers say, and no police, or the victim dies." Nicole responded, with a little desperation in her voice.

"Ok, we'll leave them out of it for now. Nothing more we can do here but it has told us that she definitely isn't here." Said Ryan.

As they headed for the front door Ryan asked, "Where does the postman deliver the flat owners' post?"

"There are boxes on the wall in the hall, I think the postman just shoves the post through the front door and whichever flat owner sees the post first they stick it in the addressee's box on the wall. Why?" Nicole replied.

"Well it might give us a clue as to how long she's not been home." Came Ryan's response.

They turned the light off in the living room and left the flat via the front door. Nicole pulled the door shut and made sure it was closed. They then turned their attention to the three individual post boxes on the wall opposite her front door.

"Steph's is the first one." Nicole pointed out.

"Okay, let's take a look." Ryan said.

They were grey metal boxes fixed on the wall at about chest height. There was a wide slot at the top where post could be inserted. Unfortunately they were lockable and each one had a small chrome lock about half way down, on the right of each door.

"I don't have a key for it." Nicole said.

"Do you have a hair pin?" Ryan asked, as he inspected the lock.

"As it happens I do." Nicole replied. "Are you going to try and pick the lock?"

"That's the plan." Replied Ryan, "I used to be fascinated by locks when I was younger and I had one of those small cash boxes. I used to practice picking the lock on it, I got quite proficient at it."

"Oh okay, I thought you were going to admit to a life of crime or something." Nicole said, jokingly as she took a hair pin from her hair and passed it to Ryan.

Ryan slowly inserted the hairpin into the small silver lock. Just as he did, a rattling of keys and the sound of a key being inserted into the main door to the building made them both jump with a start. Ryan pulled the hair pin from the lock just as the main door swung open. A large man came through the door way. He was wearing a flat cap, a roller neck jumper and a black jacket that was open half way. As he came through the door he too was taken aback by the presence of Nicole and Ryan and looked a little startled himself. Ryan could feel his heart beating faster in his chest. Nicole took a step back. The man got a hold of his senses much quicker. He took a step toward them.

"Oh Hello. You must be Stephanie from flat A?" The man enquired, in somewhat of an effeminate voice.

Both Ryan and Nicole let out the breaths they hadn't even realised they had been holding.

"No, sorry, I'm Nicole, a friend of Steph's." she said as she smiled, "We were just in the area and we thought we'd pop by and surprise her but she doesn't appear to be in."

"Oh I see, I guess Michael buzzed you in through the main door did he? I'm Roger, Michael is my other half, ha-ha some say better half. We live on the second floor, just moved in about two weeks ago. Well I say two weeks it's a little over two weeks. We've met Caroline and Martin on the third floor but still yet to meet Stephanie, though we had an evening of wine and chatting with Caroline and Martin and they told us a lot about her. She sounds like a sweet girl. Oh listen to me going on. I expect I'm holding you up. A right chatter box I can be, Michael's forever telling me off about it. But we've been cooped up in the flat for the last two weeks redecorating. Hardly spoken to a soul other than each other. Oh the taste of the previous owners, shocking darlings let me tell you. Well nice to meet you, I must get the shopping upstairs before things start defrosting on me. Toodleoo" Said Rodger and with that turned around to the main door reached outside. He picked up the three bags of shopping he'd put on the door step while he opened the door and headed upstairs to the second floor flat.

Ryan and Nicole heard his door open and close on the floor above them, they both breathed out a sigh of relief and laughed at each other. Ryan handed Nicole the hair pin back.

"Don't you want to pick the lock? Or you afraid Rodger will come back down and catch us?" Nicole questioned but also teased.

"No need." Exclaimed Ryan.

"Why ever not?" Nicole quizzed.

"Well thanks to Rodger we know Stephanie hasn't been home for a little over two weeks. He said he and his better half haven't been out of the flat for that time because they've been decorating." Ryan replied.

"That doesn't mean Steph hasn't been here, maybe they've just been busy and not bumped into her." Nicole stated flatly.

"Honestly, you think they wouldn't have rushed down the moment they had any inkling their other neighbour was home? Rodger at least seems to be rather social butterfly kinda guy if you ask me." Ryan said, with a smile.

"Okay you're right, I'm sure they would have." Conceded Nicole, "Okay let's go."

They left the building and walked to the corner of the street before hailing a cab to take them back to the tube station. During the cab ride Nicole turned to Ryan and asked, in a hushed voice,

"What now? Do you think whoever tore up the place like that took Stephanie?"

"I'm almost certain of it. My guess would be that if she has indeed been taken, she was taken for a reason and whoever took her didn't get what they were after from her, so guessed they might find it at her flat." Replied Ryan, "Later this evening I'll return to the tube station platform where I found her I.D. badge and see if there are any more clues there. I'll also see if I can check out any CCTV footage from the platform, see if that gives us any clues."

In his head Ryan already figured that the reason the I.D. badge and lipstick were laying on the floor under the bench was because there was a struggle there. Maybe there were more clues on the platform that he missed. The lipstick colour matched that of Stephanie's in the photograph adorning the I.D. badge, so it was highly likely it was hers. He didn't want to mention this to Nicole just yet as it was still pure speculation on his behalf.

"How will you get to look at the CCTV? You're not a cop

or anything, are you just going to walk up to someone and say you need to watch the CCTV footage from a fortnight ago?" Quizzed Nicole.

"Well actually I wasn't even going to ask." Smiled Ryan.

"What does that even mean?" Asked Nicole, sounding a little frustrated at his answer.

"Okay I guess you're going to wonder how I also got this." Ryan said, as he pulled from his coat pocket a small folded up piece of paper.

He slowly unfolded it in front of Nicole as if he were a magician about to perform a close up illusion. As she watched, he unfolded the paper one last time to reveal the details of Stephanie's ex-boyfriend Oliver in Ryan's fairly neat hand writing, she read out his full name, date of birth and current listed address.

"What? How did you get that? Are you sure that's Ollie?" She asked excitedly.

"I'm ninety nine percent sure it is her ex-boyfriend yes but whether the address is correct still, I don't honestly know." Ryan answered, in a less excited voice.

"Can I trust you? I mean can I really trust you Nicole?" Asked Ryan, with a sincere look on his face.

"Yes, yes, honestly you can. If either of us should have an issue with trust it should be me. You did lie to me when we first met about being a friend of Steph's remember?" Nicole replied.

Ryan stared hard into Nicole's eyes before saying,

"Okay, I'm sorry about that, but I want to be sure, now we are in this together we have an absolute understanding that we can and must trust each other fully. Some of the things I've done in my past haven't exactly been on the right side of the law and I still have the ability and means to do those things."

"Oh my god. Are you a gangster or something?" Nicole said, with a little fear in her eyes.

Ryan rolled his head back as he laughed,

"Good lord no, sorry I make it all sound more dramatic than it is. I was a hacker, am a hacker. I break into computers for information. I hacked into the DVLA's computers and got the details on Ollie from there. With regards the CCTV footage I'm just going to hack into the London underground's servers and search for the footage on their systems."

"Oh, oh ok, I guess that makes sense, you had me worried for a moment." Nicole said, as she slapped Ryan playfully on the arm.

"Don't ever scare me like that again. I thought maybe I was in a cab with someone worse than whoever might have taken Steph." Nicole spoke with a calmer voice.

"Okay I promise." Ryan said, still smiling at the thought of her thinking he was a gangster or some rough violent criminal with a shady past.

The cab pulled up outside the tube station and they exited the car after Ryan had paid the driver the correct amount plus a small tip. As they walked to the entrance of the station Nicole looked at Ryan.

"What now?" She asked.

"Now I think it's still fairly early, this address we have for our man Ollie isn't that far. I suggest we go take a look. At least a cursory check to see if we can tell if it's the right address or not. You've met Ollie right? I mean you would recognise him if you saw him again?" Ryan replied, thoughtfully.

"Yes, definitely, I'd definitely know him if I saw him again." Nicole replied.

"Okay, let's go then." Ryan held out his arm for Nicole to take, as they headed down the stairs into the station.

"Are you always such a gentleman?" Nicole enquired.

"I try." Replied Ryan, with a smile.

He looked over at Nicole just as she turned her head to watch where she was going, as they took the last couple of steps down the stairs into the station. Did he just catch her smiling to herself?

"She's quite cute." Ryan thought to himself. Then shook his head a little to clear the thought, "This all started because I was interested in meeting Stephanie. Must focus on finding her." He admonished himself.

They headed to the correct platform to take the tube to Kingsbury which was where the address for Ollie was. They didn't have long to wait before a train pulled up to the platform, they boarded and took a couple of seats to the right of the doors. As usual Ryan checked the tube map on the wall opposite, making a mental note of the next station so he could, once again confirm to himself they were heading in the right direction. The normal announcements were heard over the public address system in the station about, "mind the gap between the train and the platform", "remember to take all your belongings with you when leaving the train" and so on and so forth. The doors slid shut with a hiss and a bump, and the train pulled away from the station. It wasn't long before the train rolled into the next station and confirmed to Ryan they were on the right train. Dollis Hill station. Two more stations before they had to get off.

Ryan turned to Nicole and asked "Are you ok?"

"Yes, I'm fine thanks. I was just thinking about Stephanie and if she is okay." Came Nicole's reply.

They sat in silence for a short while before the train pulled into the next station. Ryan occupied himself by looking around the carriage at the posters, mostly advertising education courses in different colleges and all different types of insurance from home to pet insurance.

"What should we do if this is the right address and we happen to see Ollie?" Nicole was first to break the silence with her question.

"Well to be honest I don't know Nicole, I'm thinking we first need to at least confirm the address is correct but that might be difficult. I mean what if we don't see him? Neither of us can really go knock on the door and ask if he's there. I think we need to have a bit of luck on our side." Ryan replied.

"Oh my goodness." Ryan piped up out of the blue.

"Jesus. What?" Nicole almost screamed at him.

"You have Stephanie's number right?" Quizzed Ryan, who looked at her with an almost excited glint in his eye.

"Yes of course, but she wasn't answering when I called, and the last time I tried it went straight to voice mail, what good would her number do?" Nicole retorted.

"Her phone records, her texts, using my skills I mentioned before, I could see if I can get information on any calls she made, the time and dates of them and possibly even see her texts. Which mobile phone provider was her phone with do you know?" Ryan explained.

"Errmmm ermmm, I'm not sure to be honest, sorry, that's not much help is it?" Nicole's reply came in a voice that made Ryan think she felt she was a disappointment.

"Not to worry, I'll see if I can find a way to find that out too." Ryan assured her.

During their conversation the train had stopped and left the next station and was well on its way to their stop. It wasn't long before they reached Kingsbury and they exited the train onto the platform. They found the exit and Ryan used the navigation application on his smart phone to enter the address he had for Ollie. As luck would have it, it wasn't far and he suggested to Nicole they walk from the station. It wasn't far at all and within less than fifteen minutes they were stood across the street opposite the address. It was dark now and they stood on the pavement between two street lamps that fortunately weren't all that close as to make them obvious in the gloom of the night. Also in their favour was a fairly large green van with gold lettering painted on the side advertising it was a painters and decorators van. They both took quick glances across the road trying to determine if there was any sign to indicate this was the correct address. The building itself was an apartment building, not a large one, only three stories high and built from a dark brown brick. It was wide though and Ryan guessed it probably housed six apartments, two on each floor. In the middle of the building was its front door, a rather solid looking dark brown door to match the brick work. Around the edge of the door was a bright, white door frame and sand stone coloured decorative bricks. To the front of the building either side of the door were two large, white, wooden framed sash windows. Two to the right and two to the left.

Above this floor there were five large matching windows, the fifth in the middle above the door and the same on the floor above. Nicole and Ryan stood there, each taking it in turns to glance across the road at the building, nothing was moving.

"Which flat is it?" Asked Nicole, as she looked over again at the building.

"Number two." Ryan replied, as he stole a peek over at the building, "So I'm guessing it's on the ground floor."

"There's no lights on that I can see in either of the ground floor flats, that's assuming there are two flats on the ground floor." Nicole added.

"I wonder if we can get round the back for a look." Ryan stated, more thinking out loud than asking Nicole, "There is an alleyway to the right of the building, maybe we should go take a look. Actually you wait here and keep an eye out, see if our man shows up. I'll take a quick look down the alley, see if I can see any lights on from the back of the building."

"Ok, don't do anything silly or risky." Nicole exclaimed, as she took another look over in the direction of the building.

"I won't." Ryan replied, "Back in a few minutes."

The pair of them had been stood by the back of the dark green van on the pavement. They were using the van to provide some cover so they wouldn't be easily spotted if anyone in the apartment block across the road had been looking out. Ryan stepped out from behind the van and looked up and down the street to make sure no cars were coming and strolled casually across the road. Nicole was watching him from across the street as he disappeared down the alley into the darkness. The air was getting colder as it was getting deeper into night. Nicole pulled the sleeve of her grey, wool blend coat back to reveal her watch. 8.35 PM, she could feel her stomach growl and because she was hungry she felt the cold more. Nicole pulled up the collar of her coat and nuzzled her neck into the soft material of it, then pulled the front of her coat tighter up around her neck. She folded her arms putting her hands under her arm pits and almost hugged herself. Her breath was visible as she breathed out, wisps of vapour leaving her mouth and dancing in the dimly lit night before dispersing and swirling into nothingness. It felt like it had been an eternity since Ryan had skulked off into the dark alley way. Just then, Nicole heard a car approaching from the left. From where she was stood she was unable to see it as yet and instinctively turned the opposite direction from where it was coming. She started walking, just slowly enough to not go too far but not too slow as to look suspicious. She saw the lights of the cars headlamps in her peripheral vision and seconds later the car drove past. She waited for it to reach the end of the road and make the turn before she turned on her heels and returned to the cover of the van. She checked her watch again, 8.46 PM, still no sign of Ryan, she was getting nervous. Just as she was thinking of crossing the road and following Ryan's direction he appeared out of the darkness. He scurried across the road to join her.

"Well?" she asked.

"There was a gate at the back that leads to a parking area that I assume is for the residents of the building. There was a keypad entry system on it but I guess it's on the blink, the gate had been propped open slightly with an old brick. I went in for a closer look. There was a light on, I could just see it through a blind in a small window in the apartment to the left looking at the building from the back but I couldn't see anything because the blind was shut." Came Ryan's reply.

"So we're still none the wiser." Exclaimed Nicole.

"We are a little to be honest." Ryan added, "The back door to the building was also slightly ajar, not sure if it's broken too or just doesn't shut properly. I went in and..."

"What? Are you crazy?" Nicole cut Ryan off in a harsh but whispered voice, "What were you thinking?"

"I went in and found our thinking was right, I was going to say. Flat two is the one on the right from this side and that's the one with a light on. I heard a noise coming from the apartment and didn't want to hang around in case someone came out." Ryan continued.

"Ok so that's the address but we still don't know if Ollie still lives there." Nicole said, in a calmer voice.

"Well actually I think there's a very good chance he does." Ryan said, with a rueful smile.

"Why? What makes you fairly sure of that if you didn't see anyone? Were there post boxes on the wall with names on them or something?" Nicole quizzed.

"No, nothing so obvious sadly." Ryan answered, "I noticed something as I was crossing the street though."

"What?" Asked Nicole.

"Take a couple of steps over this way." Ryan gestured away from the van to the other side of the pavement closer to the house they were stood in front of. Nicole side stepped away from the van following Ryan's instructions.

"Now turn and look." Ryan pointed in the direction of the apartment block.

Nicole followed his finger thinking he was pointing at the

building but actually he was pointing at the dark green van. She snapped a look at him then back to the van.

"You've gotta be kidding me." she said.

On the side of the van in gold lettering was painted;

"Oliver T Marshall's Painting and decorating services LTD." and a mobile number followed by an email address.

"Okay, so there is a pretty good chance this is the right address but we still need to confirm we have the right Oliver." Nicole added.

"Yes, short of knocking on the door and asking him if he used to go out with Stephanie I'm not sure how else we can do that. Are you sure you don't have any pictures of him? Maybe with Stephanie when you've gone out together? What about on her social media: Twitter, Facebook or whatever?" Ryan asked.

"No, when she split up with him she completely removed him from her life, especially on social media." Nicole responded.

"Ok well I guess another option could be for me to try pulling an image of his driver's license from DVLA and have you confirm if it's him or not." Ryan said, thinking out loud again.

"No need." Nicole whispered excitedly, "There he is."

Nicole pulled Ryan by the arm to be closer to the van and also to be a little hidden from Ollie's view.

"The guy in the black jacket, grey hoodie and jeans coming down the street on the opposite side of the road." Nicole added.

"You're sure?" Ryan asked.

He took his phone from his coat pocket and switched it to camera mode. The dark of night was not going to help but luckily across the road just where the guy was about to walk was a street lamp. Just as the man walked into the light Ryan zoomed in the camera on his phone, steadied it then pressed the button to take a photo several times, hoping to get at least one good clear shot of the guys face. He and Nicole snapped back to hugging the side of the van as it looked like the man was going to look in their direction. They could hear the man's footsteps now. He was crossing the road coming towards the van. Nicole and Ryan held their breaths. Ryan motioned for Nicole to move towards the front of the van a little so they weren't so close to the corner of the vehicle. It wouldn't make much difference anyway, if he came around this side of the van they'd be busted. If they were complete strangers to the guy they'd maybe have been able to talk their way out of it but of course Ollie had met Nicole and what possible reason could they have for being here? The footsteps got louder. Ryan looked around at the floor. He was hoping that the light from the street lamp over the road would be giving off enough light to cast shadows on the ground, so he might see the guy coming but it was too far. One of the reasons they stood by the van was to give them cover and it was pretty dark there. So what had initially been a benefit was now a hindrance. Nicole had hold of Ryan's hand. Her grip got tighter as she knew Ollie was just the other side of the van now. Ryan instinctively crouched a little. Feeling for some reason Ollie might not see them if they made themselves as small as possible. Nicole followed Ryan's actions and crouched a little herself. They were both pressed up against the side of the van. The footsteps stopped. Ollie was only a few feet from them now. Any moment he could step around the back of the van and the game was up. Ryan noticed his breath was coming in short rasps now, trying to get his breath back from unknowingly holding it. He tried to keep them calm and shallow so as to make as little noise as possible. Nicole's grip on his right hand was almost painful, she was holding it so tight. Everything seemed to go quiet. Not a sound could be heard. The darkness now seemed to have disappeared and Ryan felt like they were so visible they may as well be wearing high vis vests that the workmen wear. There was a scuffling of shoes on the ground just the other side of the van. Ryan and Nicole braced themselves. Ryan felt Nicole tremble a little as she continued to squeeze his hand even tighter. Just then they heard clunk, clunk of the vans central locking system open. Both of them were startled and jumped a little but made no sound. Then they heard the driver's side door open. Ryan moved a little toward the back of the van pulling Nicole to follow. As the door opened on the opposite side of the vehicle the light came on in the cabin of the van. Light poured out of the passenger side window and flooded the area in a swathe of yellow light where Nicole had just been. They heard some keys rattle and a couple of other indistinguishable bumps and scraping noises. They were braced now, expecting any second for the passenger side door to fly open and Oliver jump out at them. Nicole was now huddled behind Ryan's back. Her body was pressed up against his back but her head was turned looking expectantly at the passenger side door. Ryan's view was flitting from the door to the back corner of the van. He could feel his heart pounding in his chest as though any moment it would burst out and run off down the street of its own accord. He could feel the adrenaline building up in his knees. His fight or flight response was in full on mode now. He had no idea how he'd react if Ollie came round the back of the van and spotted them. There was another sound. A rustle like that of a plastic carrier bag. Then bang. The driver's side door was slammed shut. The light in the cabin went out slowly, getting dimer until the cabin was back in darkness and the area near Nicole was plunged back into shadow. Clunk, clunk. The central locking mechanism activated again as the doors locked. The indicators flashed three times then remained off. Nicole and Ryan crouched motionless waiting for whatever would happen next. They heard the rattle of keys again, the rustle of what was probably a plastic bag then silence. Then the scuffing of shoes on tarmac and footsteps. Instead of getting closer they were becoming more distant. The pair remained still. Another moment passed and the footsteps got fainter and fainter until they were unable to hear them. Ryan and Nicole stood up from their crouch and looked at one another.

"Pheww." Ryan finally let out, "That was too damn close. You are sure that was him?" He said, as he opened the picture gallery on his smart phone.

"Definitely him." Nicole replied, in a slightly shaky voice.

Ryan had pulled up the pictures on the phone and flicked through the six shots he'd managed to take. Fortunately there were two clearly visible ones of the guys face. He held the phone so Nicole could see the images.

"Yes, without a doubt that's Ollie, Steph's ex." Nicole confirmed.

"Okay, so we now have confirmation this is the correct address. Let's make a note of this mobile number, I have an idea." He added, as he opened the contacts menu on his phone and added the number with Ollie as the name of the contact.

"What now?" Nicole enquired.

"Now we go get something to eat, your stomach was rumbling so much I thought it was going to give us away." Ryan teased, "That is of course if you have no other plans, I'd like to take you to dinner."

Nicole chuckled. "Very funny but yeah I was worried about that too, could you hear it? Yes let's go eat I'm starving."

"Do you like Chinese?" Ryan asked. "I quite fancy some Chinese tonight after all this excitement."

"I love Chinese, I know this great place in China town, oh that is unless of course you have somewhere in mind already?" Replied Nicole.

"I feel I chose the cuisine so it's only fair I let you choose the place if you know of a good one." Ryan smiled in response.

They headed back to the tube station from where they came and it wasn't long before they were back on a train heading back to the west end of London.

Chapter Six.

It was gone nine thirty by the time Ryan and Nicole reached China town. They had taken the tube to Piccadilly Station and it was just a short walk from there into the heart of China town.

"Come on, it's this way." Nicole said over her shoulder to Ryan who was looking around at the different restaurants, wondering which of the brightly lit establishments she was taking him to.

"You do know where you're going right?" Ryan asked, stepping up his pace to catch up to her.

"Of course but it's a little off the beaten track, it's only a little place but I've been eating there for years. It's been owned and run by the same family for over thirty years. Isn't that amazing?" Nicole replied.

"I guess so, at this moment in time the thing I'm more concerned about is, how good the food is and the quantity. Now the adrenaline has worn off I could eat a horse. Though in this part of town I guess I should watch what I say." Ryan laughed at his own joke.

"That's terrible. I don't think Chinese even eat horse do they? Isn't that the French?" Nicole replied.

"I don't know I guess you could google countries that have the largest ovens because you'd need a pretty big oven to fit a horse eh?" Again he smiled at his own joke.

Ryan was feeling overly humorous and he put it down to the relief after the events of the evening.

"It's down here." Nicole said, ignoring his last comment but smiling all the same.

They walked down a side street off the main drag and a little way down was a rather understated restaurant. It had large windows and a red sign above the shop front with gold lettering on it. "The Yangtze" The letters were not painted on the sign but were nine inch, three dimensional characters that were sticking out from the sign on short posts. By the door was a small red Chinese lantern, glowing, rather than producing a lot of light. They walked past the windows to the door and Ryan took a peek inside.

"It's pretty empty." He whispered to her, "You sure this place is good?"

"Trust me the only reason it looks a little empty as you put it is because not many people know about it and how wonderful the food is." Nicole replied, almost sounding defensive.

"Okay, I'll take your word for it." He smiled at her, a conceding smile as he reached for the door handle to open the door. He pulled on the door and took a step back.

"After you my lady." He smiled what he thought was his most charming smile.

"Why, thank you dear sir." Came Nicole's reply, "Always the gentleman."

As Ryan followed Nicole in, a little old lady was waiting inside to greet them. She was all of about four feet nine inches and dressed in what Ryan considered traditional Chinese dress. Before he could say anything, Nicole piped up,

"Nǐ hǎo wǎnshàng hǎo" with what to him sounded like a flawless Chinese accent.

The old woman replied with something similar, smiled, took Nicole's hand and led her, with Ryan in tow, to a table near the window. Ryan pulled out a chair and motioned for Nicole to sit.

"There you go again, being all gentlemanly." She laughed.

"I honestly can't help it, it's just the way I am." Ryan said, "I can try and be an onerous pig if you like but I really suspect I'll fail miserably at it and then end up spending the rest of the evening apologising for trying to be so."

"I'm sorry I'm just teasing you because it seems so rare these days. Meeting anyone with manners let alone chivalry. It really isn't dead yet. Please, don't stop being the way you are, for all my teasing and comments I'm actually quite enjoying it." Nicole said, with a smile.

Ryan looked at Nicole as she looked down at her menu that had just a moment before been placed in front of her by a much younger but still just as short waitress. The restaurant was typically dimly lit. The furniture was all the dark red cherry wood that seemed to be a favourite in these kind of places. It was a small place with only about twelve tables in all. There was what looked like a bar over near the door where you came in that didn't seem to quite fit with the rest of the décor as it was black with mosaic tiny mirrors stuck to the front of it. The rest of the décor was plenty of the dark, red cherry wood ornate carvings. Red and gold wallpaper. Several watercolour pictures, obviously Chinese art that were beautiful. Several of them depicting willow trees with their branches hanging into lakes or rivers. Even the ceiling was quite a sight to behold. Ornate cherry wood beams that had been lathed to create beautiful curves in the wood were crisscrossing the ceiling. In between the wooden beams were what looked like red silk or chiffon draping from one beam to the next hiding what otherwise would've been a plain boring white, plastered ceiling. The carpet was again red with Chinese writing in black and dragons dotted about on it. Ryan continued to look at Nicole until she happened to look up and he quickly looked down at his menu. He felt himself blush a little.

"I must say, I do really like the feel of this place, I was just taking everything in. It's beautiful." He smiled bashfully as he spoke, he was sure she caught him looking at her.

"Thank you." Nicole replied, "Did you know they had all the cherry wood in this place imported from the first owner's home village back in China?"

"Wow. Really no, I never knew that but in my defence I've never been here before." Ryan said, with a smile to suggest his sarcasm was him trying to be funny.

"Of course, I've just been coming here so long I feel like everyone should know it. Sorry." Replied Nicole, looking a little sheepish.

The young waitress returned to the table and this time placed a pitcher of water in the centre of the table and then asked if they would like to order a drink.

"I'll have a glass of red wine please." Nicole asked, smiling and with a slight nod of her head.

"I'll have a Chinese beer please." Said Ryan.

The young waitress smiled, nodded and turned to go request the drinks from the bar.

"Anyway, impressive greeting when we entered, what is it you said? Knee high washing ho? Is that what you said?" Ryan said, with a silly grin on his face this time to show he was making fun of himself.

"Nǐ hǎo wǎnshàng hǎo, it means hello and good evening. I spent a little time in China during my gap year at university. For all its problems I loved China. Of course I did a lot of the touristy stuff, but I also went off the beaten track to try and find the real China. I spent a fair amount of time travelling the country stopping in small villages, sometimes for a few weeks, and of course when you get away from the tourist hot spots English isn't often spoken. I've gone back a couple of times for the odd holiday." Explained Nicole.

"That's really cool and interesting." Ryan said, now with a more serious face because he was being sincere, "Have you travelled much then?"

"Here and there, mostly for holidays, occasionally for work." Nicole replied, "What about you? Have you travelled much?"

"Yeah I've done a bit of travelling, mostly Europe, a bit of North Africa, some of the U.S. and some of the Caribbean." Ryan answered, "I love the heat, I also SCUBA dive so some of my destinations have been solely for the diving."

"That's awesome I did some too, I'm PADI qualified to advanced open water, I did most of my diving in the far east, Singapore to be exact and a little in Dubai. The sea is so warm over there." Nicole said.

"Wow, another diver that's cool. I am a qualified PADI rescue diver with a couple of specialities like Nitrox and wreck diver. I keep meaning to finish another three specialities then I'll be a master SCUBA diver, but I haven't had much of a chance really. I don't know about you but it's good if you have a friend to do the courses with, not that its necessary but I just think it helps motivate you to get them done. My best mate Matt and I did all of our courses together but over the last couple of years he's been off working abroad a lot so we don't get much chance to get together long enough to book a course and get it done. Ahh I'm envious of you, I'd love to go dive out there in that part of the world, I heard the diving is really good." Said Ryan.

"Yes it is really good. The water is warm and clear, there are some good wrecks and some big fish out there too." Nicole responded, "So where in North Africa have you been?"

"Well for the diving Egypt of course for the Red Sea. I also went to Tunisia and Morocco, but those were just for non-diving holidays." Ryan replied.

The waitress returned with their drinks and placed them on the table in front of them and smiled and said,

"Please. Are you ready to order?"

"Oh, sorry we've been talking too much and not enough menu browsing, can we just have a couple more minutes please?" Ryan said.

"Of course sir, I'll be back in a few minutes, please take your time." Replied the young waitress.

Ryan turned to Nicole and said,

"She's lovely, what great service, she genuinely didn't seem to mind we've just been sat here chatting away. I like that."

"They are lovely in here, she's the great niece of the old lady that greeted us when we first came in." Nicole responded.

"Nice. Bless. So what would you recommend Nicole?" Asked Ryan.

Nicole looked up at Ryan and said "Do you trust me?"

"Completely." Ryan said with no hesitation, "I'm allergic to sea food and fish though."

"Okay, got it." Replied Nicole, as she raised her hand slightly and signalled to the young waitress.

When the waitress arrived at the table Nicole said a string of words that Ryan had no idea what they were as she spoke so fast and in what he imagined to be flawless Chinese. As she spoke Ryan watched her intently, her eyes were bright yet dark brown. The lights within the restaurant glinted off them making the image captivating. He focused on her mouth to see if he could pick up any of the words she was saying but it just seemed to be one long illegible sound. Her lips were full and covered with red lipstick making them bold and bright against her soft caramel coloured skin. He watched her speak and it was as if time slowed down, he was almost entranced by the movement of her mouth, as she made certain shapes with her mouth to say certain words the smallest of dimples would appear in her left cheek and an even smaller one on her right. At one point during her speaking a lock of hair fell onto her forehead and over her left eye. She daintily brushed it to one side and over her left ear to hold it out of her face without even breaking her sentence. Finally she stopped talking and the waitress said something in return. She checked her notes that she had been making on her small pad and smiled at Nicole then Ryan in turn before taking the menus and retreating to the kitchen with the order.

"Oh my god, that was so amazing." Ryan said, as Nicole took a sip of her glass of wine.

She smiled and said "Thanks, I hope you like it all, I ordered a few of my favourite things."

"I'm sure I will." Replied Ryan, with a smile on his face.

Unbeknownst to the pair of them, a man in a dark overcoat, wearing a hat and a dark scarf was outside the window looking in, watching them.

Ryan smiled as he looked at Nicole, "I can't wait to see what you ordered." He said.

Ryan turned to look out the window, as he did he saw a dark figure of a man walk away from the window and out of view.

"Did you see that?" He asked Nicole.

"See what?" She quizzed.

"A man, outside, I'm not sure but I could've sworn he was watching us." Ryan said, with a little nervousness in his voice.

"No, don't be silly, whoever it was, was probably just looking in to see if they fancied coming in here. You're getting a little paranoid because of earlier this evening and sneaking around over at Oliver's place." Nicole suggested.

"Yeah, you're probably right." Replied Ryan, shrugging his shoulders and returning his focus to Nicole.

The waitress assisted by another young waitress and a young waiter shortly arrived at the table bearing several plates between them and commenced placing them on the table between the two of them. Any thoughts Ryan had of the man in the dark overcoat and being spied upon soon disappeared from his mind as his eyes feasted on the glorious looking dishes laid out in front of him. The aromas coming off of some of the dishes that laid before him soon captivated him, strong smells of garlic and ginger and some other more subtle fragrances danced a merry dance in his nostrils. Steam was rising from the food, a tell-tale sign everything was cooked fresh.

"Please, enjoy your food." Said the first young waitress, as the three servers bowed slightly and moved away from the table to leave them to eat.

Nicole picked up the pair of wooden chopsticks that were joined together at the top end and broke them apart with a small snapping sound. Then commenced to grab food from the different dishes and placing them on the small empty plate in front of her.

"You don't mess around do you, if I tried that there would be more on the table cloth than on my plate, if you don't mind I'll use my fork." Ryan said, impressed with her ability with chop sticks.

"Of course I don't mind silly. Do whatever you need to, just enjoy the food." Nicole replied, with a smile and sense of pride from Ryan's compliment.

"Ryan?" Nicole paused for a second just to be sure she had his attention, "I just wanted to say…well thanks, thanks for believing me when I said I thought something was amiss with Stephanie and her whereabouts. You are a veritable stranger to her and, well me if I'm honest and here you are doing everything you can to try and help find her. If it wasn't for you I'm not sure what I would have done. I certainly wouldn't have gotten as far as we have on my own."

Ryan looked down at his plate then back at Nicole.

"I guess it just felt the right thing to do. I should thank you too, for not thinking I'm a weirdo when I told you my reason for being at your place of work. I mean who does that kind of thing? Turn up to a woman's place of work in the hope of meeting her because he found a picture of her and liked what he saw? Once I told you the truth I'm surprised you didn't call the police, it sounds a little stalker-ish." He chuckled a little to hide his slight embarrassment.

"Actually I think it's kinda romantic to be honest as I said before. I guess I felt seeing as you were honest as soon as you had the chance to be so, it made me think you're actually a decent guy." Nicole replied, with a gentle look on her face, "Besides you have a kind and honest face."

Just at that second as she finished her sentence music started playing, it was a rather rambunctious version of "Happy Birthday" and all the waiters and waitresses gathered near a table towards the back of the restaurant to join in singing "Happy birthday" to one of the customers at the table. The little old lady that greeted them at the door emerged from the kitchen with a small birthday cake with one lit candle on it. The flame on the candle danced and flickered as she walked toward the couple at the back. Ryan half expected the candle to go out before she made it to the table but it didn't and the cake was delivered to a blonde woman who looked to be in her forties, with slightly heavy makeup, wearing a red dress. Her husband or boyfriend beaming from ear to ear sitting next to her thinking he did well to surprise her. The woman was smiling also but you could see she was rather embarrassed by the whole thing.

"What do you think?" Ryan asked Nicole, "Kisses and sex later or an argument?"

"What? Nicole's face was filled with shock, "What did you just ask me?" she carried on.

"Huh? Oh, good lord, I was talking about the couple over there, oh my god I'm sorry, I'm feeling a little embarrassed now." Ryan could tell he was blushing, his cheeks felt warm and the temperature in the place hadn't changed.

"Oh. Oh my god, sorry." Nicole said rapidly, "My thoughts were elsewhere and didn't make the connection. Oh I think, though she looks embarrassed now, the man did good and he'll be getting his rewards later. We ladies like to be made a fuss of now and then. We like to be made to feel important to the one who loves us and it's often the simple gestures that mean the most."

"Okay, making a note of that." Ryan pretended to scribble something down in an imaginary note book then carried on the pretence by making out he was closing the book and stowing it in his pocket.

"I'm sure you don't need tips, I bet you do alright with the ladies?" Nicole smiled and winked a jokey wink at him across the table.

"You'd be surprised, I'm actually really quite shy and I've never been very good at talking to women to be honest." Ryan replied, with a gentle smile only just making an appearance on his lips.

Nicole looked at him as he looked back down at the food in front of them.

The rest of the meal passed as they both ate and drank with little chats about different things interspersed with waiters or waitresses bringing more drink or just asking if everything was alright with the food.

After they had finished eating Ryan asked Nicole if she wanted anything else to which she replied "No" and he signalled to one of the waitresses for the bill. One of the young waitresses brought the bill over on a small, black plastic tray with the small paper bill folded in half so as not to show the amount openly. On the tray were two round mints that had been rolling around on the tray as she carried it to the table. As soon as the tray was placed in front of Ryan, Nicole reached over and grabbed a mint.

"Helps with the digestion." she said, and popped it in her mouth.

Ryan said,

"Okay, I thought it was to try and mask all the garlic and ginger in case you wanted to kiss your date after the meal." And he laughed.

He took out his wallet, unfolded the bill and proceeded to count out the cash. Nicole had reached for her purse and asked how much was her half, but Ryan dismissed her request with a slight wave of his hand and said,

"It's okay I'll get this."

"Are you sure? Thank you very much. But I should get half." Nicole protested.

"Seriously, my treat." Ryan said, smiling at her as he closed his wallet and handed the tray back to the waitress with the money folded inside the bill.

They both stood and headed for the door. They thanked the staff and the little old lady that was stood near the entrance to the restaurant. Nicole took the little old lady's hand, bowed to her saying something else in Chinese and turned for the door. Ryan opened the door and they stepped out into the cold dark night air.

"Thanks for a very interesting evening and thanks again for dinner." Nicole said, as she slowly walked backwards, heading towards the main street in China Town.

"You're most welcome. We both heading for the same tube station?" Ryan replied.

"Yes I think we are." Came Nicole's response.

They walked to the tube station and got on the correct train.

Just before Nicole got off the train she asked, "What's the plan then?"

"I'll text you tomorrow and let you know." Ryan replied and smiled.

Nicole leant forward toward him and kissed him on the cheek, "Thanks again." And she hopped off the train and headed for the exit.

Ryan felt a little something stir inside him as he watched her walk off. The doors to the train slid shut with the usual shhhhhhh thud sound and the train jerked forward and moved off from the platform. Ryan continued to watch after her until he could no longer see her. The ride on the train to his station was one of contemplation.

Chapter Seven.

It was early morning and Ryan woke to the sound of pigeons cooing on the window ledge outside his bedroom window.

"Bloody pigeons." He thought, as he opened his eyes and looked over at the alarm clock on his bedside cabinet.

Six minutes past six.

"Ugh, really?" he thought, "It can't even be daylight out there yet, why are you up you stupid bastard?"

He rubbed his eyes, threw the duvet off himself and swung his legs round to the edge of the bed and sat up.

"This is too early for a non-work day." He thought to himself, "But things to do, may as well make a start I guess."

He strolled sluggishly to the bathroom, lifted the lid and seat of the toilet and relieved himself. He turned to the basin and turned on the hot tap, reached back and flushed the toilet. He put his hands under the running water and felt it start to warm. He washed his hands then cupped them, scooped up some of the water and splashed his face. He rubbed his eyes with his wet hands then opened them and looked at himself in the mirror that was positioned over the sink.

"Geeze I look like I've gone five rounds with Tyson then slept rough on a park bench for a week." He said out loud to no one that was listening.

He rubbed his chin and cheek and heard the bristly sound of his stubble. He turned to the heated towel rail and grabbed the towel that was folded over a few of the bars. He dried his hands and then his face and placed the towel neatly back from whence it came. He headed down to the kitchen and filled the kettle with fresh water from the filter jug that was in the fridge. He made himself tea and grabbed a packet of chocolate biscuits that were in the cupboard above the kettle. He placed the biscuits and tea on the kitchen table and headed back upstairs. He once again retrieved his hacking equipment from its hiding place and brought everything down to the kitchen to set it up on the table. He took a sip of tea and opened the brand new packet of biscuits. He placed the edge of a biscuit between his teeth while he continued to work to connect all the cables and computer gear together. He took a hold of the biscuit and bit into it, the chocolate had melted slightly where it was in contact with his lips causing him to lick his lips as he could feel the sweet warm stickiness of the chocolate covering them. He finished the biscuit, took a swig of his tea and finished connecting all the gear up and powered it all on. He was sat in front of the screen waiting for the automatic login to the dark net he'd setup to connect him. Once it showed him as connected he tapped away on the keyboard and within a few keystrokes he was connected to the servers that host the police force's national database.

He did a search for Oliver Terrance Marshall and added the date of birth as a cross reference. Dots appeared one by one across his screen as the search commenced. He sat back in his chair and took another biscuit from the packet and proceeded to munch on it while he waited for the results to come back. He took another swig of his tea and waited.

"Come on." said Ryan, in no more than a whisper, "This is taking too long, I guess the police don't have much of a budget to keep their computers up to date."

Almost a third of his screen was covered in dots by the time the search had finally finished.

"That can't be right." Ryan said a little louder, staring at the screen.

In capital letters under the last row of dots showed:

"NO RECORDS FOUND (0)"

He got up from his chair and went over to the case that had housed his kit. From the pocket in the lid of the case he pulled out the little note book he'd made notes in from his conversation with Ray at the police station. He came back to his chair and checked the date of birth he'd put in. It was correct. He entered the details again but this time replacing the colons with slashes and set it off to search again. Dots started appearing across his screen again. The dots got almost to the same position again before they stopped and beneath the row of dots this time it showed;

"NO RECORDS FOUND (1/14):#OTM161283"

Meaning one record found with fourteen sub records. Another few commands entered by Ryan on the keyboard and he opened the record and started perusing through the entries.

"Aggravated assault"

"Domestic Burglary"

"Possession with intent to supply"

And several other drug and violence related crimes. For most of them he'd served a little time or had the sentences reduced to community service, or on house arrest having to report to a parole office.

"Hmmm what a charming chap." Ryan thought to himself, "How is this guy still out in society? Defies belief. Well it certainly makes sense that this guy could have something to do with Stephanie's disappearance and I wouldn't put it past him to have been the one that broke into her place but I mustn't get ahead of myself. Shouldn't let past crimes prejudice my feelings about this man, yeah right. With that record and the fact he knew Stephanie I think it's very likely he has something to do with it."

Just then his mobile phone beeped. It was now almost seven AM. He took his mobile off the kitchen work counter and unplugged it from the charger it had been attached to overnight. As he disconnected it the screen lit up and it showed he'd received a text message. It was from Nicole.

"Morning sunshine. Hope you slept well. Let me know what your plans are today. N x"

Ryan hit reply on his phone and composed a response.

"Well good morning to you and I hope you slept well also. I have some background on our mutual friend, I must say I'm surprised you'd know anyone of such character. Planning on going and watching the place to see if there's any sign of Steph. Ryan x"

He paused for a moment before pressing send wondering if she'd meant to end her text with a kiss or if she was one of those people where she does it out of habit and almost uses an x as a full stop.

Within a few seconds of him sending his text his phone beeped again and it was another text from Nicole.

"I could lie and say I slept well but to be honest I didn't really, too many thoughts going through my mind I guess. Interesting and how did you get this background info? Or shouldn't I ask? You do amaze me. Keep in touch and please stay safe. Oh and if you happen to want to take a break we could meet for

lunch, this time my shout and no arguing about that. Got it? Lol N x"

This made Ryan smile. "Is she flirting with me? Or am I imagining or hoping that's what it is?" he thought to himself.

He tapped away on his phone writing his reply.

"Oh dear I'm sorry to hear your sleep wasn't great, we will get to the bottom of this and we will find her. Ok let me know what time would suit you for lunch, we can do that I'll come to you if you let me know where. Thanks and I look forward to it. Ryan x"

Ryan stood there holding his phone in anticipation. Staring at the screen almost willing it to beep again and it be another text from her. The screen dimmed and no new text arrived. The screen turned off.

"Okay." He thought, "Maybe she's not being flirty and just being nice."

He put his phone down on the table next to the laptop, took one last swig of his tea from the mug and put the mug in the sink. He turned his attention to powering down the equipment and started disconnecting all the cables. He was just putting the laptop back in its case and his phone beeped. He leaped up from the crouched position he was in and grabbed the phone. He could see it was a new text and hurriedly pressed the button to see who it was from. It was of course from Nicole.

"Will do….me too. Go careful. N X"

The smile returned to his face. He finished packing away the kit and stowed it back in its hiding place. He came back to the kitchen, made himself another cup of tea and put the biscuits back in the cupboard. He took his tea upstairs and drank it as he got his clothes out that he was going to wear for the day, then proceeded to shave and shower. He'd pulled out some faded blue jeans, black t-shirt, a grey hoodie and had laid them on the bed ready for after his shower. He had cleaned his teeth, came back into his bedroom to get dressed. He pulled on some socks and then put on a pair of tan, buck suede caterpillar boots. He took his empty mug back down to the kitchen and placed it in the dishwasher. He went to the coat hooks just inside the front door, grabbed the black leather bomber jacket that was hanging there and put it on. He grabbed his keys, phone and wallet then left the flat, locking it behind him. Ryan headed down to the tube station and got on the train taking him north, to where he and Nicole had been just the night before. He left the train and exited the station and did the ten to twelve minute walk to the address they now knew to be Oliver's. He was back on the street and as he walked along it he could see Oliver's green van was still parked opposite the brown building they had staked out the night before. There were a few other parked cars but not as many as there had been. A few pedestrians walked either side of the street, some walking fast obviously heading for work. It was just a few minutes past nine now and Ryan figured the street would only get quieter and he felt like he was standing out but realised that was because he knew why he was there. To anyone else he was just another guy going about his business. He ambled up the street on the side of the brown building, as he passed it he took a sideways glance at the windows he now knew to be the right flat. Nothing stirred, and although the curtains were drawn open, there were net curtains so he couldn't see inside. He continued walking past feeling like he may as well have been twelve feet tall yet no one passing by gave him a second glance. He walked to the end of the road occasionally looking back in the direction of Oliver's residence. Looking over his shoulder as though he was about to cross the road trying to make it less obvious that he was on a stake out.

"I should've read more spy novels: maybe I'd have an idea how you're supposed to do this." He thought to himself.

He reached the corner of the street and on the opposite side of the road diagonally across from him was a little convenience shop. He crossed over managing to avoid nearly getting run over by the cycle courier that seemed to have come from nowhere.

"Idiot. Watch where you're going." The cyclist shouted back at him as he sped off down the road.

"Way to be inconspicuous Ryan." He scolded himself.

He entered the shop and a happy faced, slightly overweight Indian man in his forties, wearing a blue turban and black jumper behind the counter, smiled at him and said,

"Good morning."

"Morning." Replied Ryan, "Can I get a pack of Benson and Hedges gold and this paper please?"

On entering the shop the newspapers were laid out neatly in piles on the ice-cream freezer and Ryan had grabbed a copy of the Daily Mail as he walked toward the counter.

"Oh and a lighter or box of matches please?" Ryan added, "Oh and this pack of gum too please." As he took it from the small metal rack stand that was in front of the register and placed it on the counter.

"Would there be anything else?" The shop keeper asked, "We have matches for thirty eight pence or a lighter for fifty pence."

Ryan chuckled and said, "No, honestly that's it now. I'll

take the lighter in that case please."

The shop keeper rang everything up on the till and asked Ryan for the amount shown on the display. Ryan pulled out his wallet and handed the guy a twenty pound note. The shop keeper pressed a few buttons to enter the amount paid and with a ping the cash register's drawer sprang open and he passed Ryan his change.

"Thank you." The shop keeper said.

"Thanks, have a good day." Ryan replied.

Ryan stepped out on to the street and looked up the road toward Oliver's building. The green van was still parked where it was and the street was now pretty empty of people.

"Ok, don't have the cover of darkness and can't use his van to hide behind." Ryan thought to himself, as he tried to think of the best way to keep an eye on the building without looking too obvious.

He had folded the paper in half and had it clutched under his arm. He put the packet of gum in his jeans pocket along with the lighter. He pulled at the little cellophane tab on the packet of cigarettes and tore off the top part of the plastic cover. He opened the pack and pulled the top part of the gold foil covering the contents. That smell of a freshly opened pack of cigarettes caught Ryan's nose and he breathed it in. He'd quit smoking over a year ago but for some reason this seemed like a time to be a smoker once again. He pulled a cigarette out of the packet and placed it in his mouth. He closed the pack and placed it in his jacket pocket. He took the lighter from his jeans pocket and lit the cigarette. His first draw on it, the first for over a year stung his throat and burned in his lungs. He coughed a little like he'd never tried smoking before.

"Ughhh maybe this wasn't such a good idea." He thought but took a second pull on it anyway. Then a third. In between puffs he glanced in the direction of Oliver's abode, still nothing new.

By his fifth draw on the cigarette he started feeling that dizzy head rush you get when you haven't smoked for a while. He was half tempted to just throw the half smoked thing in the gutter but took another few puffs before doing that. He walked the length of the street again slowly, this time on the opposite side of the road. He got to almost the corner at that end of the road and decided to pause there for a bit. It was far enough from the building so as to not look obvious that he was interested in the place but close enough for him to see any comings and goings from it. He leant back against the black railing that ran along the front of the building he was stood outside of. He took the packet of gum out from his pocket, opened it and put one of the pieces of gum in his mouth. The mixture of the taste of tobacco and peppermint took him back to when he was younger and would try and hide the fact he smoked from his parents by chewing vast quantities of gum. He unfolded the paper and pretended to read as if he were waiting for a cab or a friend to pick him up in a car. He was stood there for about thirty minutes pretending to read and look out for his imaginary lift but using that as his reason for looking up and across to the brown building, always expecting to see Ollie appear but as of yet had not seen a single person leave the building.

He walked the length of the street up and down and returned to his original position again unfolding the paper and pretending to read it. It was almost eleven thirty and there had been no sign of Oliver, in fact no movement from the building at all. Ryan was starting to think this wasn't one of his best ideas. Just then he felt his phone vibrate in his inside jacket pocket and he reached in and pulled it out. It was a phone call. It showed Nicole was the caller. He smiled to himself and folded the paper with his free hand and shoved it up under his armpit as he pressed the button to answer the call. He instinctively turned away from Ollie's building and started walking to the corner of the street.

"Hello." He said.

"Hi." Nicole's voice came back over the phone, "I was going to text but then thought maybe it'd be easier to just call, hope you don't mind."

"No, that's great. It's good to hear your voice, feeling a little alone out here." Ryan chuckled.

"Oh okay, yeah I feel kinda bad you're out there on your own. I hope you're being safe and not doing anything risky?" Nicole said, with genuine concern in her voice.

"No, not taking any chances, trust me." Ryan exclaimed, "Just meandering up and down this street waiting to see if mister Marshall appears, as of yet nothing happening."

"So, I was wondering if you wanted to meet me for some lunch. Seeing as nothing much is happening there." Nicole stated.

"Sure, that'd be great. When and where?" Ryan questioned.

"Well, if it's okay with you why don't you come down to the embankment and we'll go find a place to have lunch by the river." Nicole answered.

"Yeah, that sounds really good, I guess I could be there in about forty minutes, does that suit you?" Ryan asked.

"Perfect, I look forward to it, go careful please. Oh text me or call me when you get out of the tube station. See you soon." Nicole exclaimed.

"Will do, you can count on it. Bye for now." Ryan said, with a huge smile on his face as he clicked the button to end the call.

He looked back towards the brown building, still nothing to report.

"I wonder if he has another vehicle. He could be out all this time and I wouldn't know it." Ryan thought, as he turned to head back to the tube station.

His mind raced, searching for an answer, how could he find out if he was in or out of the building, could he find a way to discern if Oliver had another vehicle? Ideas were starting to formulate in his mind. His pace quickened as he walked toward the station, his walking speed trying to keep up with his rapid firing brain now, ideas were coming thick and fast. He almost didn't want to go meet Nicole for lunch. Not because he wasn't pleased she wanted to see him, not knowing if it was right or wrong to feel what he was feeling but he was really quite fond of her. It was just that the ideas of a way forward were coming one after another, then almost immediately overridden by an even better one. He decided he would calm his thinking. Take a moment and put his thoughts in order. His walk slowed a little as he calmed himself mentally. He reached the tube station and took the train that would get him to his destination. He had to change trains once but that didn't add much time to his journey. During this time he managed to get his ideas all figured out and resolved to run them by Nicole for her thoughts on them. Ryan exited the tube station at Embankment and immediately took out his phone and called Nicole.

"Hey Ryan." Came Nicole's voice.

"Hey, I've just exited the tube station, where did you want to meet?" Ryan asked.

"Come down to the river, opposite Australia house, this side of the river though." Nicole replied, "I'll be there in five minutes."

"Okay, on my way. See you in a minute." Said Ryan, and hung up the phone.

Ryan walked down to the river. It was a fairly cold day but the sun was out and there was no breeze so it wasn't unpleasant to be out. He reached down by the river in just a few minutes and looked across the river.

"There's Australia house, still flying the smiley face flag I see." Thought Ryan.

He looked along the river side walk known as the Queen's walk. There were a few eateries such as Eat me and Giraffe and just past them was the skater's park all covered in graffiti: some of it quite artistic. He didn't know whether to walk along a bit further to see if he could see Nicole or wait where he was, in the place she told him to meet her. He decided to give it a few minutes then he'd text or call her. He stood at the concrete wall looking across the river at Australia house and tried to remember which building was the Savoy hotel. About fifty yards from where he was standing was a metal plaque that had the buildings opposite engraved on it, he thought he'd walk along to it to take a look and confirm which building it was, just to satisfy his own curiosity.

"GOTTCHA." Nicole said loudly, as she poked him in his rib cage from behind.

Ryan almost jumped a mile.

"Owww, oh my god, I could've landed in the river." Ryan

said, as he turned to greet her.

"I don't think I've ever seen anyone jump so high, you ever thought about trying out for the Olympic high jump team? I think with the right motivation you could do well." Nicole joked.

"My motivation being you scaring the crap out of me when my mind is elsewhere you mean?" Ryan retorted.

He looked her up and down, she was wearing a smart, pale grey, trouser suit, a sky blue blouse, just visible between the lapels of her expensive looking black three quarter length coat, a purple woollen scarf and black high heeled shoes.

"You look fantastic." Ryan said excitedly, then felt he'd been a little over zealous in how he reacted to seeing her properly.

"Why thank you young man, you don't look so bad yourself. You going for urban criminal or well to do hoodie guy?" She laughed, "I'm just teasing you. You look very nice. Nice jacket."

"Thanks." Replied Ryan.

Nicole hugged him and kissed him on the cheek. He hugged her back and the smell of her perfume was intoxicating.

"Oh my god you smell so good." He thought and nearly said it out loud.

"Hmmmm you smell nice." Nicole said, over his shoulder as they were still hugging, "I do like a guy that smells good."

Ryan didn't want to let go, this felt so good. He hadn't had this feeling for a long time. His arms around her slender waist, he pulled her in closer and she responded by hugging his neck a little tighter. He felt something move in his jeans and relaxed his arms a little.

"You're squishing our lunch." Nicole laughed.

Ryan let go and she did the same. He took a step back and looked down, Nicole loosened her coat and from inside pulled out a small white plastic bag.

Nicole open the bag and said, "You can have either chicken Caesar salad wrap or southern fried chicken salad wrap. I also got us both a packet of crisps, cheese and onion or ready salted?" She asked.

Ryan smiled at her, "I honestly don't mind, which would you prefer?" he asked.

"How about we share it all?" Nicole suggested, "The wraps are cut in two halves in the packets anyway and we can have half a pack of each of the crisps."

"Yeah sounds great to me." Ryan replied.

"I like this girl so much." He thought to himself.

"Shall we grab a bench?" Asked Ryan.

"Sure, let's sit at that one over there away from anyone." Nicole replied.

They sat on the bench and Nicole pulled the items out of the bag and stuffed the bag into one of her coat pockets.

"So nothing going on at Oliver's huh?" She quizzed, as she opened one of the wraps and handed half to Ryan.

"No, not a sign of Ollie or Stephanie. His van was still parked in the same spot so I was wondering if he perhaps has another vehicle or maybe he's not even there." Ryan reported, "I was thinking I might do a bit of research see if I can ascertain if he does or not." Then he took a bite of the wrap, southern fried chicken.

"Hmm worth a thought." Nicole replied, "Company van and all, maybe he has a car too that he uses." And she bit into her half of the wrap.

"So, I have been thinking and wondered what your thoughts are on my ideas." Ryan said, in between bites of his food.

"Okay, go on?" Nicole replied, as she continued to eat also.

"Well I was kind of feeling rather exposed and out in the open watching the place so I was gonna hire a van. I can park on the street with a good view of the place. I noticed there were a few there already so it wouldn't look out of place and it'd give me some cover. Also I have one of those digital action cameras, you know the ones, people use them as dash cams, or for extreme sports to video what they get up to. Well there's an app on the phone so you can see on the phone what the camera is seeing, I think the range is about fifty yards. I can hide the camera round the back of the property in case he's using that exit and sit out front, that way I'm covering both exits to the place." Ryan said, "Hopefully the range between camera and phone will be enough."

"Wow, look at you." Nicole said with a smile, "Mr Bond, spy gadgets and all. You're beginning to sound like a pro."

"The name'shh Bond, Jameshh Bond. Double oh sheven lishensh to kill." Ryan did a not half bad impression of Sean Connery.

They both laughed.

"That's pretty good." Nicole said chuckling, "Can I be your Miss Money Penny?"

"Of course." Exclaimed Ryan, "Actually going off topic, I was, err, gonna ask, err well, errm, If, err, if you are single?" Ryan stuttered to say and looked at her sheepishly.

"Would my answer to that be of interest to you then?" Nicole did the usual womanly thing of answering a question with a question of her own.

"Ughh this is hard enough." Ryan thought to himself awaiting her true answer.

"Yes, it certainly would." He replied.

"Yes, I'm single and I know you are." Nicole said.

"How'd you know I am?" Ryan retorted.

"Cos of what you told me as to your reason about coming to work with Steph's card." Nicole replied immediately.

"Oh yeah." Ryan said. "I almost forgot about that."

"Okay, so, sorry, I can see as you pointed out that you aren't the most forward of guys when it comes to us girls. Do you want to ask me out on a date?" Nicole questioned.

"Yes, Yes I do, I know we don't really know each other that well but what I've seen of you so far I really like." Ryan said, "In for a penny in for a pound." he thought.

"I feel the same." Nicole replied with a big smile on her face.

"Brilliant." Ryan beamed, "Okay let's find Steph and then go on a date, yes?"

"Yes, let's stay focussed on finding her and once it's

behind us we can go out and have fun." Nicole replied.

They had opened and finished the second wrap and the crisps, sharing them as agreed. Nicole looked at her watch.

"Ughhh I don't want to but I'd best get back to work, it's been lovely hanging out with you Ryan. You going to go hire a van now?" She asked.

"Yes, I'll go get a van for a few days then head home and see if I can find out if our friend Ollie has another car or something, might help us to track him and explain his whereabouts too." Ryan replied.

"Okay, please be careful and keep in touch, I'll be worrying about you." She smiled and stood.

Ryan stood also and gathered the rubbish from their lunch.

"Do you have that bag?" Ryan asked, holding out a hand.

"Oh yeah." Nicole pulled the plastic bag out of her coat pocket and passed it to him.

"Thanks." Ryan replied.

He placed the empty packets in the bag and tossed it in a nearby bin.

They hugged and kissed each other on the cheek, Ryan told her she smelt great too, another quick peck on the cheek, a hug and they said their goodbyes.

Nicole headed off to work and Ryan did an online search for "Van rentals" on his phone.

He found a place close to home and headed back to the tube station to take him that way. About an hour later Ryan pulled up in his hire van round the back of his place on Baker street, where there was off road parking for residents only. He entered his flat, got his hacking equipment down and set up once again to do some research on Oliver. Gaining access to the DVLA he'd soon found out that there was indeed a car, as well as the van registered to Ollie at the address he had been staking out. He texted Nicole his findings with the details of the car. Soon he was back in the van, heading to Willesden Green after putting away his equipment and grabbing his action camera, which he'd had on charge since getting to his flat. The time was getting close to five PM and as it was winter, twilight was already upon him. He parked not too far from Oliver's building on the opposite side of the road, affording him a good view of the front of the property. Using the diminished daylight to his advantage, he exited the van and went through the little alleyway to gain access to the rear of the building. He entered the rear of the grounds and placed the camera so it was pointing at the back door. He'd noticed last time he was there that there was a small pile of rubbish including an old sofa. Obviously some resident had just dumped it in the gardens of the place and it looked to have been there for some time owing to the state of it. There was an old rusty microwave oven sat on the sofa, along with a few black sacks of rubbish.

"Don't understand people." Ryan thought, but this helped him to conceal the camera.

He'd powered it on, checked the battery was at full charge and connected to it via the app on his phone. He had the live camera feed showing on his phone screen now. He adjusted the position of the camera slightly to get a better view of the back entrance. There was a security light above the door, which was perfect, as it was on permanently once it was dark and this gave enough light to produce a good picture from the camera. Ryan returned to the van taking glances at the phone to ensure he still had connection to the camera. He'd made sure not to park too close to any street lights and once inside the van, the cab of it was pretty dark. He was wearing dark clothes and suspected it would be pretty hard for anyone just taking a casual glance over at the vehicle to spot him. He'd checked in with Nicole to keep her appraised of his actions and position. She'd told him she was having to work late but would be in touch and he was free to text her any time. Ryan had propped his phone with the camera app up on the dash board of the van and was easy to keep flitting his sight from the front of the build to his phone to monitor the back of the building. It was now seven thirty and Ryan was getting restless. He'd gotten out of the van once or twice and walked the street checking for Oliver's other car but there was no sign of it on the street. He had even taken a walk round the back to check, no sign of the car there either. Ryan had returned to the van and was just sat there, watching, waiting. He had received a text from Nicole stating she was finishing work and heading home for something to eat and a shower. She went on to ask if he'd like her to join him on the stakeout. He'd replied that even though he would have loved to see her and have her company, he felt this could get a little dangerous and would prefer her to get some rest after her long day at work.

It was ten forty five and as Ryan was struggling with keeping awake because of the boredom. A white estate car that matched the description of Oliver's second vehicle, pulled into the road and parked right outside the building, not twenty yards from where Ryan was parked. This woke Ryan up immediately.

"Finally, you arsehole." Ryan thought to himself and he watched as Ollie got out of the vehicle carrying a large brown paper bag.

From where Ryan was sat watching he could just discern steam rising into the cold night air from the contents of the brown bag.

"Takeaway." he thought, "Too much for just one person."

Ryan continued to watch as Oliver locked the car and entered the building. Moments later he saw a light come on in one of the bottom flat's windows and then the curtains were drawn shut. The faint glow of the light from the room still visible through the curtains.

"Okay so now we know you definitely live here for sure and you do come and go here." Ryan thought affirmatively.

Ryan continued to wait and watch. About an hour later Oliver came out of the building again and got in the car and drove off.

"Now's my chance." Thought Ryan.

Ryan grabbed his lock picking tool set, exited the van and headed for the alleyway by the side of the brown building. He walked quickly as he didn't know how long Oliver was going to be gone for. He soon reached the rear of the building and entered the gardens. He retrieved his camera from its hiding place and stowed it in his pocket. He trotted up to the rear entrance of the building hoping the door hadn't since been fixed which would immediately thwart his plan. Luckily enough he found the back door was still slightly ajar and entered quietly through it. He walked slowly along the corridor to the front door of the building passing Oliver's flat. He opened the front door a crack and peeped out. No sign of Oliver or his car.

"Good." Thought Ryan and closed it again as quietly as possible.

He could hear muffled sounds of a television coming from the flat opposite Ollie's. He took a quick look at the door to the flat opposite confirming it was closed, and stood for a few seconds listening for any noises coming from up the stairs leading to the other flats in the building. Nothing stirred. Ryan approached Oliver's front door. He pressed his right ear up against the cold wooden door and listened. Not a sound. He removed the small black canvas pouch that housed his lock picking tools from his inside jacket pocket and opened it slowly. He looked at the lock on the door and chose two of the tools from the pouch. His hands were shaking slightly and his breathing shallow and rapid, he was nervous. Thoughts of what might be behind the door filling his mind. What if Oliver was not alone in there and had an accomplice or more. What if Stephanie isn't in there and this has all been a waste of time.

"No time to lose." He said to himself in his mind.

He inserted the two tools into the lock and slowly manoeuvred the top tool around feeling for the five spring loaded pins. In order to pick a lock, at least a standard Yale lock as this one was, you had to align the pins level so you could rotate the barrel. If even one of the pins were not level it barred the barrel from turning and thus keeping the door locked. It felt like an eternity was passing and with each second that ticked away Ryan became more nervous. A bead of sweat left his hairline just above his temple and he felt it snake its way down past his ear. He rubbed the side of his face with his upper arm, keeping the lock picks in place. It took just under five minutes before he felt a little give in the lock and slowly turned the second tool which turned the barrel. There was a tiny click and the latch retracted back into the door. A gentle push and the door opened inward to the flat. Ryan extracted the tools from the lock and placed them back in the pouch. He could see through the crack in the door, the light was still on. The front door entered straight into the living room. He paused for a second and listened. No sound, if there was someone in there, maybe they were not in the lounge or hadn't noticed the door open. His adrenaline was coursing through his body. Sweat was now running down the back of his neck. He could feel the uncomfortable streams of sweat pouring down his back. He wiped his forehead with the sleeve of his jacket and pushed the door open a little more. The door was now open about a foot, if anyone was in there they would surely have noticed it by now. Ryan pushed the door open even further, half expecting someone to be stood there with a baseball bat or a knife. The door creaked a little on its hinges. No one was there. He entered the flat and looked around the room. It wasn't really that nice of a place. There was a battered looking terracotta coloured two seater couch under the window. The upholstery had holes in it here and there and the seat cushions were sunken. There were newspapers and magazines strewn on the floor by the side of the couch. Empty beer cans lay next to a full to the brim ashtray on the floor at the other end of the sofa. On the wall opposite from where Ryan stood was a black, floor standing wall cabinet that was almost as tall as the ceiling and almost ten feet wide. Although it looked solid it was slightly at a tilt to the right. Letters and empty envelopes covered the main shelf. One of its cabinet doors was open and the contents were mainly half empty bottles of booze that looked like they had been there since the seventies. Cinzano, Pernod and a very dusty, almost empty bottle of Bells whiskey among them. There were a few old pictures hanging crookedly on a couple of the walls. An old print of a painting, again probably from the seventies of three elephants hung in a white frame at an alarmingly obviously un-level angle. The tar and nicotine stained wall paper, which was reminiscent of an era gone by, in most places was curling at the top corners, coming away from the wall. Just then Ryan heard muffled sobbing coming from another room. His heart skipped a beat at the noise as it has been deafeningly silent up to that moment. He turned towards the noise. There was a doorway to the left of the elephant painting, it was open and he could see there was another light on in there. He slowly approached it, the door was open about a third of the way. As he got closer he could hear the muffled crying more clearly. It was definitely a female. He pushed the door open fully. There in the middle of the kitchen floor was a chair. Upon it sat Stephanie. Her ankles were zip tied to the legs of the chair. Her wrists tied to the tops of the front chair legs so her hands were resting on the corners of the front of the chair by her knees. Her hair was a mess. Her cheeks had smeared black streaks of mascara where she'd obviously been crying. Above her top lip was crusty with a mixture of dried tears, makeup and mucus from her nose. She was wearing faded blue jeans with rips at the knees, a white tank-top type t-shirt that was now grubby and covered in all sorts of stains. She had no shoes on, only dirty white trainer socks covered her feet. She had a black-purple bruise below her left eye covering most of her cheek. She had bruising around her neck so defined that you could determine the size of the hand of the person who had clearly been strangling her at some point. She had ligature marks on her wrists and dried blood where she'd struggled against her bonds. In her mouth was what looked like a rolled up flannel which was then half taped in place with duct-tape, one end had peeled away a little from her cheek. As Ryan entered the room she had looked up, upon seeing him and not recognising him she tried to scream through the flannel. Her crying started with more gusto. Ryan put his hands out in front of him, palms facing her much like you would to quieten a dog or a toddler. He moved his hands up and down to shush or calm her down.

"My name is Ryan, Nicole sent me," without wishing to sound like Luke Skywalker, "I'm here to rescue you." Ryan said, in a firm yet sympathetic voice.

Once he'd finished his sentence, Stephanie started shaking her head frantically from left to right. She was trying to talk through the flannel and tape but her words just came out muffled. She rocked back and forth desperately on the chair as much as her bonds would allow. Ryan stepped forward and removed the gag from her mouth.

"YOU HAVE TO GO." Stephanie almost screamed at him, "He's only gone to get some milk and bread, he'll be back any moment. Oh my god he'll kill you if he finds you here. Go, get out."

"Calm down, I'm not going to leave you here." Ryan said rapidly, "Are you okay? Can you walk?"

"I don't know. I've been here for, I don't know how long, it feels like weeks." Stephanie replied.

She was shaking. Ryan noticed she smelt too. Poor thing probably hadn't been allowed to shower or even wash. A strong overwhelming smell of ammonia was coming off her. She'd obviously urinated several times while tied to the chair. Ryan looked around the kitchen. He moved quickly to the kitchen counter and pulled open drawers, he found a knife that looked pretty sharp and cut the zip ties that held her wrists and feet.

"We won't get out." She said frantically, "I know he'll be here, you should have just left me here."

"Do you know where your shoes are?" Ryan asked, ignoring her.

"No, no, I don't know." Stephanie replied, as she started to sob again.

Ryan looked hastily around the kitchen floor, no sign of her shoes.

"What were you wearing on your feet?" He asked her.

She was sat on the chair rocking back and forth sobbing. Ryan asked her again, this time with a little anger his in voice. He was aware of her threat about Oliver being back any moment and he was now acutely aware he'd been here some time already. He took hold of her hands. She was trembling.

"Look, I know you've been through a terrible ordeal but get it together, we need to get out of here." Ryan said, in a slightly softer but authoritative voice.

She stopped rocking and looked at him. There was a look of anger, fear and yet determination in her eyes.

"Okay, okay" She said in a more controlled voice than he'd heard from her yet.

"Let's see if you can stand." Ryan said, as he cradled an arm round her back and grabbing hold of her under her other armpit. She had her left arm around his neck and as he stood from his slight crouch she tried to stand.

"I can't." Stephanie said, in a desperate voice.

"Come on, I'll support you." Ryan said, getting a little desperate now.

"Oliver has to be back any second now surely, if what she said is right." Ryan thought to himself.

"Oh my god, what if he's just gone to the shop at the end of the road?" Came the uncontrollable realisation.

"No, no, he wouldn't have taken the car." Ryan's rational thinking returning.

He lifted her again from the chair. This time she managed to stand and he started moving towards the doorway which he had entered through. She staggered a few steps then her legs gave way and she almost crumpled to the floor but for Ryan having a hold of her. He pulled her up on to her feet again.

"Come on, let's go, I have a van out front, you can do this." He said, looking at her with pity in his eyes.

"I can't, just go, I'll make out I managed to get free somehow." Stephanie replied.

"No, come on." He said stiffly and pulled her up and closer to him. His adrenaline supplying him with added strength.

They entered back in to the lounge. He moved toward the front door half dragging half carrying an almost limp Stephanie now. As he neared the door he spotted a pair of ladies white trainers just under the edge of the couch. He moved her to the couch and plopped her down on it.

"Here put these on." as he reached under and pulled the trainers out from under it.

"I can't." She said, her sobs now returning.

Ryan stood and pulled the curtain back a little at one side and looked out into the street.

"No sign of Oliver thank god." He thought.

Ryan knelt down in front of her and anxiously started putting her shoes on her feet. He tied the laces hurriedly and stood to pull her up off the couch again.

"Right. Let's get out of here." Ryan exclaimed.

He grabbed her round the waist and she put her arm around his neck again. They both moved towards the front door. Ryan pulled the door open and trying to push any thoughts of Oliver being stood just outside the door out of his mind and exited the flat. He turned and pulled the door shut behind them. Stephanie was now able to walk a little on her own. Sitting on that chair for a little over two weeks had taken its toll, but she was generally a healthy, fit and active person so the strength was returning rapidly. Ryan opened the front door to the building and looked outside. Just a space in the road where Oliver's car had been. He looked diagonally across the road to his hire van.

"Almost there, come on." Ryan said to Stephanie, as he removed his arm from around her waist and took a hold of her hand.

Just as Ryan stepped out on to the top step heading down to the street Oliver's car came into view.

"Shit." Ryan swore. His sight flitting from Oliver's car to his van across the street.

Oliver was driving quite fast, almost as if he knew his captive was about to escape. Stephanie hadn't quite made it out of the door luckily so the door to the building was still open.

"Quick, back inside." Ryan said, almost hysterically and he turned and almost pushed Stephanie back inside.

"Why?" Stephanie asked and instead pushed past Ryan to look into the street.

As soon as she did that, she spotted Oliver's car.

"Nooooo." She said, almost screaming.

At that instant Oliver saw her and his eyes widened. His face taking on a wild look about it.

"Quickly." Ryan said, and pulled her back into the

building.

The pair ran back inside and pulled the door shut behind them. Oliver's car screeched to a halt outside the front of the building.

"This way." Ryan said, and pulled Stephanie by the hand towards the rear exit of the building.

Behind them they heard the car door slam shut and hurried footsteps heading to the front door. They started running. Stephanie's strength almost fully returned to her legs now and the adrenaline helped boost her. As they reached the back door they heard the beeping of the front door code panel as Oliver was trying crazily to enter the code to open the door and allow him in. Ryan barged the rear door open, turned and grabbed Stephanie by the hand again. He pulled her down the few steps in to the gardens and they headed for the back gate. Ryan's mind was racing, if Ollie was following them, could they make it round the side of the building and back to the van before he would catch them? They reached the back gate and ran out into the alleyway just as Ollie emerged from the back door of the building.

"GET BACK HERE YOU FUCKING BITCH." Oliver shouted after them.

This only helped to spur the couple on. They ran to the right, down the alley and Oliver started to give chase. They exited from the alley and ran across the road to the van. Oliver was close behind them and emerged from the alley as they reached the van just thirty yards or so away. Ryan fumbled in his jeans pockets looking for the van keys.

"Fuck." Ryan cursed, "Where the hell are the keys." while feverishly checking his jacket pockets.

"OIII DON'T YOU FUCKING DARE RUN AWAY

FROM ME." Oliver shouted at them and started to run across the road towards them.

Ryan gave up looking for his keys, there was not going to be time to get both of them in and start the van before Oliver would be upon them.

"Come on." Ryan said to Stephanie and again grabbed her hand and started running down the road away from Oliver. They ran. Stephanie doing really well to keep up with Ryan given her weakened state but the fear was driving her. Fuelling her escape. She was dirty, sweaty and stank and did not want to go back to the hell she'd endured for however long it was, she wasn't sure. Oliver was getting closer. The pair reached the end of the road and Ryan looked left and right. It was very late now, the middle of the night. No one was about and no shops or businesses were open. None of the houses on this road had any lights on. They took off, taking the turn to the right. Ryan didn't know this area and was running blindly hoping to escape. It started to rain, that fine rain that you can hardly feel but before you know it would drench you completely through. The couple continued to run. Oliver continued to give chase. They ran along the pavement, Ryan checking over his shoulder to see if Oliver was closing on them. Luckily Ollie wasn't in the best of shape and the gap seemed to be growing.

"I need to stop." Stephanie panted. "I can't run anymore."

"Ok take a minute to get your breath back but we can't stop for long, he's not far behind us." Ryan gasped back, trying to catch his breath also.

He turned back and looked to where Oliver was, he was a good three hundred and fifty yards behind them now and had himself stopped running but was walking towards them. Ryan could see Oliver's breath as clouds of mist through the fine rain and cold air. The vapour catching the light of a nearby street lamp making it almost glow as if it were breath from a fictional demon from a horror book. Stephanie was almost doubled over with her hands on her knees panting for breath.

"Is he close?" she asked, sounding desperate.

Ryan bent forward also and took in huge gulps of air trying to get his breath back.

"He's a little way away, we're okay for another moment but he's coming still." he replied, through gasps for air, "Let's go."

He took her hand again and they began to trot. They ran across the road and turned down another street, then crossed that one too to the other side. Ryan kept checking back over his shoulder, he'd lost sight of Ollie. The pair kept running at a jog. They seemed to be entering an area away from housing. Just a little way ahead Ryan could see a railway bridge going over the road as it turned left. At the end of the street it looked like a dead end. A car breakers yard was at the end of the road with large metal gates and a high fence with razor wire atop of it.

"Fuck." Ryan said under his breath, had he just lead them in a dead end?

He looked back over his shoulder again as they continued to run. Ollie had just come around the corner at a slow paced run. They were about six or seven hundred yards apart now. There was no way they could turn back and get past Oliver. They reached the railway bridge and there was an archway leading under the bridge. They had no choice, they ran through the archway and onto the street the other side. It was an industrial area for sure. There were different lock up garages with signs on the doors offering such things as tyre repair and replacements to engine tune ups and car servicing. There were a few large trucks parked up here, probably waiting for repairs from one of the establishments. There looked to be no way out of this area apart from back the way they came yet still they pushed forward heading to the far end of a line buildings.

"This way." Exclaimed Ryan and lead Stephanie by the hand behind a large articulated lorry.

They stopped running and walked towards the back of the truck.

"Get your breath back. I think this is a dead end, I think we're gonna have to hide and hope he gives up looking or I'm gonna have to fight him, he's not going to give you up easily." Ryan said to Stephanie, through a panting voice.

"He's a killer." Stephanie replied, "Have you ever had a fight in your life? You don't seem the type to have had."

"No, I've not, I've been hit and I've hit people but never had a real brawl." Ryan said nervously, "I did do martial arts when I was younger."

"Hope they help." Stephanie said, sounding defeated, "How long ago was that?"

"Too long to be honest." Ryan retorted.

Ryan took a sneaky peak from behind the lorry's corner. Oliver had just came out of the tunnel under the railway bridge and was looking around to see if he could spot them. He was panting heavily. Ryan had gotten his breath back and was thinking if he attacked him now maybe in his winded state landing just one good punch may enable Stephanie time to escape back through the railway bridge and keep running.

"Why try and punch him?" Ryan thought and he looked around the floor behind the lorry. There. There was an iron bar laying in front of one of the lock ups.

"What are you doing?" Stephanie exclaimed, "You don't want to kill him."

"What? No of course not but I do want to put him down and make sure he stays down long enough for us to get away. You said it yourself, he's used to fighting, I probably wouldn't stand a chance in a fair fight. Sorry, but now is not the time for gallantry or the gentlemanly art of pugilism." Ryan said.

He looked back toward Oliver. He had stopped and was getting his breath back while looking around still trying to find them.

"I need him to be closer." Exclaimed Ryan, "I don't want him to see me coming."

Just then a black, beaten up, old looking van came through the arch under the bridge with the lights glaring in their eyes. Ryan could just make out someone was half hanging out the passenger side window and it looked like they had something in their hand. Oliver turned to see the van coming and ran to the right to get out of its way. Something wasn't right. Oliver looked scared.

"NO. NO. I'LL GET THE STUFF BACK." He said, in a loud voice to the occupants of the van.

Ryan had ducked back behind the lorry out of sight. The rain had stopped now, everything was drenched. They were wet through. Steam was rising from the two of them in the cold night air. Stephanie was shivering now. Ryan took off his jacket and put it round her. She put her arms in the sleeves and did the jacket up flashing Ryan an appreciative smile. Ryan looked across the road from the rear of the truck. There was a street lamp on the opposite side of the road with a really bright, white light emanating from it. The light reflected off the wet, black tarmac like a silver streak of paint had been splashed across the road. Ryan peeped out again at the events unfolding between the van's occupants and Ollie. Ollie had his hands raised as if to surrender. He started to speak again to beg whoever it was for more time.

"THE BOSS IS BORED." came the reply from one of the guys in the van, "TIME'S UP, YOU'VE HAD TWO WEEKS."

BANG

The silence of the night was shattered into a million pieces. Ryan saw the explosive flare from the barrel of a gun that the passenger was holding out of the window. The sound pierced the night and the echo reverberated around the small area they were in, a second echo coming from the archway. Ryan couldn't believe how loud it was. Oliver was thrown back from the bullet hitting him square in the chest. He spun, and it was only then that he caught sight of Ryan peeping out from the corner of the truck. He was dead before he hit the ground and had no time to point or gesticulate to his murderers where Stephanie was. Stephanie was shocked, she covered her mouth with her hands to stifle the scream she was about to release. Ryan shuddered, shocked too and now incredibly frightened. The passenger of the van got out and kicked Oliver's body. From Ryan's hiding place where he'd now crouched low at the back of the lorry, looking between the large wheels of the vehicle, he could see Ollie wasn't moving.

"WE KNOW WHO YOU ARE STEPHANIE." Shouted the man holding the gun in to the night, "YOU'VE GOT THREE DAYS TO RETURN OUR STUFF OR YOU'LL END UP LIKE THIS PIECE OF GARBAGE

ALONG WITH YOUR FRIEND THAT'S WITH YOU. AND DON'T WORRY, WE'LL FIND YOU."

A second man got out of the van. He was large, a little overweight but a bit muscular too. He walked over to the first man holding the gun.

"Gerry, what the fuck have you done?" He asked, "Mack says we should get the fuck out of here before the cops show up."

"He knew what was coming to him Sean." Said Gerry, as he pointed the still smoking gun at Oliver's motionless body.

With that, the two men turned and got back in the van. It reversed back through the archway, turned and sped off back up the road.

"Fucking hell." Stephanie said, "We'd better get the fuck out of here too."

"Agreed." Replied Ryan, as he stood up from his crouched position taking Stephanie by the arm.

They walked along the pathway on the far side of the artic lorry, toward the bridge. They were level with Oliver's body that was laying stretched out on the cold wet road. Stephanie covered her eyes as she saw it and buried her face into Ryan's chest.

"Oh my god." she said.

"Don't look, maybe we should call the police and an ambulance?" Ryan suggested.

"No, we have enough to deal with, he was a piece of shit and maybe he didn't deserve that but we don't deserve to be in a lot of trouble over his death. Besides who'd believe we didn't do this?" Stephanie argued.

Just then, the sound of sirens could be heard approaching.

"Okay, time to go." Ryan said, and with one last look over at Ollie's corpse he turned, put his arm around Stephanie's shoulders and guided her toward the archway.

They trotted along the street and once back on the main road, started walking back to the hire van. They were just turning into Oliver's road when three police cars shot passed, sirens silenced now but the blue flashing lights lighting up the front of the buildings as they passed. They had walked back in silence to the van. Ryan found the keys to the van, they had been in his inside jacket pocket the whole time. He clicked the clicker that unlocked the van and they both got in.

"There's no going back to your place, I guess you'll have to come to mine for now, until we work something out. Do you want to speak to Nicole?" Ryan asked.

"Yes, Yes please." Stephanie said, after exhaling a very long sigh.

Ryan pulled his phone out, hit the call button for Nicole and handed it to Stephanie. He turned on the ignition, pulled away from the kerb and headed towards his home.

"Hello. Hello Nicole?" Stephanie said, then burst into tears.

Ryan could hear Nicole's voice coming through the earpiece of the phone. All he heard though was,

"Oh my god, Steph? Are you okay?"

Then Stephanie started talking, holding back her crying to just a whimper now.

"No, No, we're going to your friend's place." Stephanie managed to say.

She put the phone away from her ear and turned to Ryan.

"Sorry what was your name again?" she asked him.

"Ryan." He replied.

"Yes, Ryan." Stephanie said, back in to the phone.

She continued to talk to Nicole as Ryan drove them home.

Chapter Eight.

They were back in Ryan's flat. It was almost three AM. Ryan was exhausted from the events of the night and could only imagine how Stephanie felt. They were in the kitchen, Ryan had put the kettle on and made them tea.

"Do you want something to eat Stephanie?" He asked.

"No, I'm okay thank you, not long before you showed up Oliver had brought back takeaway. He did feed me, not always, sometimes it would be days before I'd get to eat." Stephanie replied, "I can't believe he's dead."

"What's this all about Stephanie?" Ryan asked, as gently as he could.

"It's a long story and I'm tired, could we possibly talk tomorrow?" She asked.

"Of course. I'm sorry. I know it's late but would you like a shower or a hot bath?" Ryan responded.

"Oh yes. I feel disgusting, I can't begin to tell you what I've been through." Stephanie replied.

"We'll talk tomorrow when you've had a good night's rest." Ryan said sympathetically, "I'll go grab you a fresh towel and start the shower for you. I think you'd probably appreciate a change of clothes too right?" and he smiled softly at her.

Stephanie looked herself up and down. She knew she looked a right horrible mess and that she was covered in all sorts of stains. Her clothes were grubby and smelly. Her face was covered in sweat, dried tears, smudged makeup and goodness knows what else.

"Yes, I would, have you got a bin bag or something I'm

just gonna throw these clothes out, or burn them." She smiled weakly and looked sadly at Ryan, "Thank you. From the bottom of my heart thank you."

"You're most welcome, drink your tea, I'll be back in a minute." And with that, he headed upstairs.

It wasn't long before Ryan returned to the kitchen, he took a black bin bag out from one of the cupboards by the sink and handed it to Stephanie.

"Would you like to follow me? I'll show you where everything is. You can sleep in my room tonight, I'll take the couch," He said.

"You're very sweet and very kind, you don't even know me. Why would you do all this for a complete stranger?" Stephanie questioned.

Ryan chuckled, "That's a long story too. We can exchange stories tomorrow yes?" and he gestured for her to follow him.

He took Stephanie up to his bedroom: he'd laid out a pair of grey fleece jogging bottoms, a baggy t-shirt, a pair of socks and a pair of boxer shorts on the bed. Beside those were a fresh towel and a fluffy, cosy looking bathrobe.

"I'm afraid I don't have much in the way of women's clothes." He laughed, "I hope they'll do you for now? I'll be in the lounge, give me a shout if you need anything, oh and please use anything in the bathroom, shower gel, shampoo, body wash etcetera. Oh and there's a spare tooth brush still in the packet on the shelf. Help yourself."

Stephanie's eyes welled up with tears.

"Ughhh I can't believe this happened to me. It was horrible. I don't know how I'm going to ever repay you."

She said, as she wiped the tears from her cheeks and sniffed loudly to stop her nose running.

Ryan took a step forward and offered his arms out. He didn't really know what else to do. Stephanie stepped forward, her hands, with fingers interlocked, pulled close to her chest. Her chin rested on her clenched hands, she stepped forward again and leant into Ryan's chest and he put his arms around her. She started crying, sniffing and mumbling some apology about being such a mess.

"Hey, it's okay, honestly, it's over now. You're gonna be okay." Ryan said, comfortingly and rubbed her back with his hands.

He let go of her and stepped back.

"I'll leave you to it." He said, "The shower's running, you don't want the water going cold."

"Okay." Stephanie replied, she sniffed again, gathered what composure and dignity she had left and stood up straight.

She grabbed the things off the bed and followed Ryan out of the bedroom. He pointed to the bathroom door, she smiled, opened it and went in, shutting it behind her. Ryan, headed down the stairs to the lounge. He texted Nicole to let her know they were safely back at his place and hoped his text didn't wake her, but would talk to her in the morning. He watched his phone for a few moments, waiting to see if he got a response and guessed she was asleep. He'd grabbed a blanket from upstairs, made up a makeshift bed on the couch. He had put the kettle on again before his phone beeped indicating a text had arrived. He checked his phone. It was from Nicole;

"I'm glad you're safe, you're my hero. If it wasn't so late I would come over. I'm just glad you were right

and you found her and you're both safe. I've been so worried about you both. I'm going to try and get back to sleep but I can't wait to talk to you tomorrow. N. X."

Ryan smiled to himself and texted back a "Thank you" and "Sleep well" He was so tired he could hardly type out those words, let alone a longer message and hoped she'd understand that was the reason behind such a short message. He plopped himself down on the couch. He'd removed his hoodie when they got back to the flat and was sat there in his jeans and t-shirt. He laid back into the couch and kicked off his boots. Ryan took a sip of his tea and closed his eyes. Stephanie came down the stairs and entered the lounge. She had on the socks, the jogging bottoms, the baggy black t-shirt and the bathrobe tied at the waist with the belt. She had a towel wrapped around her head in a make-shift turban. All cleaned up she looked cute and almost as beautiful as the picture on the I.D. badge that started this whole insane business in the first place. Ryan had opened his eyes on her entering and couldn't help but look at her. It was like she'd been transformed or had had one of those makeovers like on one of those t.v. shows. When he'd found her, tied to that chair covered in tattered looking clothing, all stained and with unkempt hair, her natural beauty was visible, like a rough un-cut diamond, but now, even with the bruise adorning her cheek she looked stunning.

"How could any human being do to another human being what he did to you? Let alone one as beautiful as you." Ryan thought to himself.

"Sorry I was so long." Stephanie said, looking a little sheepish, "I would've been in there longer but the water started to run cool. Sorry if you wanted a shower."

"It's fine, I'll grab one in the morning." Ryan replied and

smiled, "You feel a little better?"

"Oh yes. So much better, thank you again." Stephanie responded.

"Would you like anything a drink? Some tea? Some water? Or anything?" He asked.

"A glass of water to take up please if I may?" Stephanie replied.

"Of course." Ryan responded, got up from the couch, went to the kitchen and returned with a large glass of water.

"Here." He said, handing the glass to her.

"Thanks. I guess I'll go up to bed now. Do you need to get up for work or anything in the morning?" She asked.

"No, sleep as long as you can, you need it. We'll talk in the morning when you wake." He replied.

"I really can't thank you enough. Good night." Stephanie exclaimed and leant forward and kissed Ryan on the cheek, spun on the spot and headed off to bed.

"Night, sleep well." He said, after her.

He slumped back on the sofa, swung his legs round so he was laying on the couch. Pulled the blanket out from under him and half covered himself. He plumped the cushion under his head and promptly knocked out.

The ringtone on Ryan's phone jolted him awake from his slumber. He opened his eyes with a start.

"What the f… What time is it?" He thought to himself and reached down to the floor to grab his phone.

The display showed it was Nicole calling. He coughed a little to clear his throat then pressed the button to answer the call.

"Hey." He said.

"Hi, I hope you don't mind I'm at your front door. I didn't want to use the buzzer as I didn't want to wake Steph if she's still sleeping. I've brought you breakfast and coffee." Nicole's sweet sounding voice came over the phone.

"Ughh, oh great, sure, the code to the door is one nine six nine, come on up, I'll see you in a moment." Ryan replied and they both hung up the call.

Ryan sat up on the couch, his neck was stiff from how he'd been sleeping. He tried rubbing it and stretching it out a little but that only seemed to hurt, so he stopped doing that and stood up. He checked his phone, the time was 9.35 AM. He ambled to the front door of the flat and opened it. Nicole was already stood there with a cardboard tray holding three coffees and a brown paper bag.

"Hey, good morning." Ryan said, "Do come in.", he bowed a little and waved his arm gesturing her into the flat.

"Well good morning to you sir." She said, with a smile as she entered, "Such a gentleman."

As usual Nicole was dressed impeccably: pale blue denim jeans, roebuck suede pixie boots, a white turtle neck jumper and a grey three quarter length wool blend coat, pulled in around her waist with a matching belt. Her hair looked like she'd just left the salon and her face with a minimal amount of make-up was flawless. You couldn't even tell she was wearing any cosmetics, other than a little red lipstick. As she entered Ryan's flat she walked past him into the lounge. The scent of her perfume, not over powering, hung in the air like a soft breeze of spring, carrying with it the gentle pleasing smell of fresh flowers and something sweet that Ryan couldn't put his finger on. He was still stood by the door almost intoxicated by the smell of her perfume. He closed the door and turned to look at her. She was walking toward his kitchen, her long, black, soft curled hair bounced gently with each step. Watching her was as if time had slowed as he took her all in with his eyes.

"Where do you keep your plates?" Nicole said, over her shoulder.

"Oh." exclaimed Ryan, as he snapped out of his daze, "The cupboard to the right of the oven."

"Is Stephanie awake yet?" She asked.

"No, not yet." came Ryan's reply, "She's had a rough time, I wouldn't be surprised if she sleeps for a week."

"I know it's horrible, did she say much last night?" Nicole questioned.

Ryan had joined Nicole in the kitchen and she was bent over taking a couple of small side plates out of the cupboard.

"No, not much at all really, we were both pretty exhausted by the time we got back. I guess the adrenaline and shock of everything had as much to do with that as how late it was." Ryan replied.

"It's awful, I was so worried about you both." Nicole said, as she stood with the two small plates in her hand.

Nicole set them down on the kitchen counter top, next to where she had placed the cardboard tray holding the three coffees and the brown paper bag. She opened the brown bag, and from within pulled out two pains aux chocolates, placing one on each plate. She took one of the coffees from the tray and handed it to Ryan.

"I hope you like white chocolate mocha." She said with a smile, "It's my favourite but I know coffee is a personal taste thing."

"I have no idea to be honest I've never tried it but I do love mocha." Ryan said, as he took the coffee from her.

"Here you go." Nicole said and pushed one of the small plates towards him.

"Thanks." Ryan said, as he offered a weak smile.

He took a sip of the coffee, it was creamy and sweet.

"That's really nice, I like it." He exclaimed, "That's the best tasting coffee I've ever had, I feel I've been missing out all this time."

Nicole laughed, "Bit over dramatic but okay, I'm glad you like it."

"So, what happened?" She asked.

"Well, before I tell you that, you should know Oliver is dead." He said, with a serious look on his face.

"What? What? You killed him?" Nicole replied, shocked.

"No, no, no, it wasn't me." Ryan bleated out, defending himself.

Ryan then relayed the string of events that led up to Ollie's demise. The breaking into his flat after seeing him leave, how he found Stephanie and the state she was in. Ollie's return, catching them escaping and the chase. The dead end, the arch way, the black van with the guys in it, the gun shot, then the threat. Finally how the van left them without even looking for them and how they left the scene before the police arrived.

"Oh my god." Nicole blurted out after Ryan had finished, "I can't believe it, I mean you see on the news about shootings in London but I've never known anyone that's been shot and killed. Stephanie must've been in a mess. Yeah Ollie had kidnapped her, threatened her and goodness knows what else he's put her through but he's dead and she was there when it happened. They were going out at one point. That must affect her somehow."

"I imagine it will but last night I think she was just in shock. Probably not had time to process it yet. We'll see what she has to say today when she wakes." Ryan retorted.

"What are we going to do?" Nicole quizzed. "I mean they gave her three days to return their stuff."

"At the moment I have no idea. I have no idea about what the stuff is, or who these people are. All I know is they are serious people and Stephanie is in a lot of danger and she needs to start talking and telling us what the hell is going on." Ryan replied.

"And you." Nicole said softly, "They threatened you too."

"They don't know who I am, I don't think any of them saw me." Ryan countered.

"Yeah but they said they know who Stephanie is and if they get to her they'll make her tell them who you are. Aren't you scared?" Nicole said nervously.

"I haven't thought that much about it to be honest but thanks for pointing that out." Ryan laughed a nervous laugh, he realised how right Nicole was.

"Anyway, how come you're not at work? Also, how do you know where I live?" Said Ryan.

"I called in sick, I didn't sleep well last night, I wanted to come and see you to make sure you're okay, and to see Stephanie of course. And your address, err you told me, I think when we went to dinner, remember?" Nicole answered.

Ryan didn't remember telling her but she showed up first thing so he must have told her at some point. He was trying to remember when he might have told her. Nicole put her hand on his and looked at him with her beautiful eyes, the thoughts left his mind.

"I'm so glad you're okay Ryan." She said, "I really like you, you are an amazing person. Everything you've done, finding Stephanie, putting yourself at risk. There's not many people that would do that for someone they don't know. So thank you." She took a step toward Ryan and kissed him on the cheek.

"I feel like I've known you for ages and I forget how this all first started for you. That I.D. badge and the elusive beautiful woman you wanted to get to know. Now that you've met her what do you think? Did she match up to your expectations?" Nicole asked.

Ryan felt a little awkward. Stephanie was without a doubt a beautiful girl, even in the rough state he found her in you could see the undeniable natural beauty that lay beneath the dried tears, sweat, blood and grime. She too had a wonderful womanly body that was very pleasing to the eye.

"She's a very good looking woman, there's no denying that, but that was the furthest thing from my mind to be honest." Ryan stumbled over his words.

"Look at you squirm, I'm sorry that was very unfair of me,

I'm just teasing you and trying to lighten the mood."
Nicole smiled an infectious smile.

Ryan smiled back, a little forced smile as he was still feeling
uncomfortable with her line of questioning. Ryan was
attracted to both women but he felt he knew Nicole more
and this Stephanie seemed like a whole heap of trouble
waiting to happen. As it stood right in that moment, if
Ryan had to choose one of them, without any shadow of a
doubt it would be Nicole. He wondered if he should air his
thoughts, let Nicole know what was going through his
mind but his shyness prevented him. He instead lifted his
pastry and took a big bite on it.

"So, don't forget you and I have a proper date in the
pipeline once this is all over. Do I have competition now?
You're not gonna run off with Stephanie are you?" Nicole
asked, half serious, half joking.

Ryan smiled, finished chewing the mouthful he had, wiped
his lips with the back of his hand and said,

"No, of course not, I'm looking forward to it. Besides I
don't really know her yet, ask me again in a couple of
days." and laughed, as he put a guard up like a boxer
would when against the ropes.

He was right to do so, Nicole punched him on the upper
arm playfully but there was some power in it.

"Tread carefully sunshine, or this woman won't be going
on any date with you." She said and laughed too.

"Oh I see, it's okay for you to tease me, that's how this is
huh?" Ryan laughed, as he pretended to recoil from the
blow, "Wow, you hit hard even when playing, you do
karate or something?"

"I work out, there's power in these guns." She chuckled, as

she flexed her right bicep and pretended to kiss it.

Ryan squeezed her still flexed arm, "Not bad, I think I feel something in there. Hang on, is there a button under there? You got a little T-shirt on with buttons on the sleeves under your jumper?", he laughed and resumed his guarded stance.

"I'll show you buttons." Nicole responded and went to punch him again as she giggled.

This time Ryan grabbed her right arm by the wrist with his right hand and pulled her towards him. Pulling her punch across his body in front of him and to the side. This caused her to spin and she ended up with her back to him pressed up against his chest. He then moved his hand still holding her wrist so it was in front of her at her belly and then wrapped his other arm around her and took hold of his right wrist. He now had her in a tight hug. Even though they were just playing he enjoyed it, enjoyed the feeling of holding her so close. Instead of struggling she relaxed and leant back into him.

"I really like you Ryan." Nicole almost whispered.

Ryan put his mouth near her left ear and whispered, "I really like you too, Stephanie.", he increased his grip and laughed, waiting for her to act all mad and try to wriggle free of his hug.

"HA HA, very funny." She said, sarcastically and didn't react the way he thought she would, "I mean it Ryan. I honestly really like you."

"Okay, I'm sorry, I really like you too, I'm not sure what it is yet but I feel there's something very special about you." Ryan replied in just above a whisper in her ear.

The closeness of his mouth to her ear, she didn't just hear

what he said, she felt it, the warmth of his breath against her ear made her tingle. She felt Ryan's hold relax on her and she turned and hugged him. Just for a second Ryan thought he caught the glimpse of a tear in her eye in his peripheral vision. She put her chin on his shoulder and pressed her cheek against his and hugged him tighter than he'd ever felt a woman's hug before. They stayed in the embrace for a few moments. Ryan wondering what this was all about. Eventually Nicole relaxed and let go, Ryan did the same and she stepped back. She turned away from him and grabbed her coat that she had taken off on entering the kitchen and had placed on the kitchen counter. She pulled the coat on and wiped her cheek with the cuff of one of her sleeves.

"It was a tear." Thought Ryan to himself.

"You okay?" He asked concerned.

"Yes, oh hay fever, makes my eyes water." Nicole replied and smiled with a little sniff.

"Hay fever? It's winter, what are you allergic to? Holly?" Ryan asked trying to make light of it and break his uncomfortable feeling.

"Oh, yeah, maybe I'm pms'ing, can make me a little emotional, TMI right? Too much information?" She smiled and played it off.

"Are you leaving?" Ryan asked.

"Yes, I just wanted to check on you and Steph, make sure you're ok." Nicole replied.

"Where are you going? I thought you called in sick?" Ryan asked.

"Yes, yes I did but I told them I'd try and get in for lunch time and I need to go home and change." Nicole responded.

"Okay, well thanks for the incredible coffee and the pastry, it was good to see you." Ryan exclaimed. Utterly perplexed.

"Did I do something wrong?" He thought to himself as he followed her out of the kitchen.

He walked her to the door and they hugged again.

"Go careful." Ryan said.

"I will thanks. Keep in touch and let me know what you find out from Steph. Can I come by again later? This evening, after work?" Nicole replied.

"Yes of course. Maybe Steph will be awake by then and wanting to see you and talk to you anyway." Ryan retorted.

They hugged again and kissed each other on the cheek. With that, Nicole opened the door and left. Ryan scratched his head. He checked the clock on the mantel above the fireplace. Ten forty five. The time with Nicole had flown by. He listened at the bottom of the stairs, nothing stirred from up there and figured Stephanie was still out cold. Until she woke there was nothing he could do. He had no license plate of the van, he didn't even know what make it was. No names of the men in the van. Absolutely nothing to go on until he could ask Stephanie questions and even then maybe she'd have no information to add either. Ryan returned to the kitchen and tidied away the breakfast things. He put the coffee intended for Stephanie in the fridge not wanting to throw it out or knowing what else to do with it. He put the pastry in the bread bin and threw the empty paper cups, cardboard tray and brown bag in the bin under the sink. He returned to the couch and flopped down on to it and promptly dozed off.

Chapter Nine.

It was two thirty in the afternoon when Ryan woke to the sound of a young woman's voice.

"Ryan? Ryan? Ryan? Sorry to wake you. Ryan?" Said Stephanie, at first in a quiet voice that slowly rose each time she spoke.

Ryan opened his eyes and blinked a few times to clear his vision. He woke a little dazed and for a split second confused as to where he was.

"Oh, Steph, Hi, You okay? What's wrong?" Ryan eventually said.

"I'm feeling better today thanks, nothing wrong really, I just wondered if you could take me to my flat at some point?" Stephanie replied.

"I'm not sure that's wise to be honest." Ryan exclaimed, "Why do you want to go to your place?"

"Well those men gave me three days so I figured they wouldn't be after me and I'd like to go home and grab a few things then work out where I'm going to stay." She replied in a thoughtful tone.

"I can't argue with your logic but I wonder if they were being honest, they could be watching your flat just waiting for you to return because you think just that." Ryan commented.

"Hmmm, I can't just stay in these clothes you gave me and I have nothing with me, no money, no phone, no make-up no personal items." Stephanie said.

"Okay, let me think about it." Ryan exclaimed, "Nicole came over earlier to check on us.

"Oh okay, I suspect she was worried about us. How do you know Nicole? I don't think she's ever mentioned you." Stephanie replied.

"Hmmm, yeah she was, especially worried about you of course. It's a long and quite embarrassing story to be honest. Nicole and I haven't known each other long at all and we met because of you to be honest." Ryan said, somewhat sheepishly.

"How do you mean, you met because of me?" Stephanie asked with a quizzical look on her face, as she took a seat on the couch next to Ryan.

"Would you like a tea or coffee or something? Nicole brought us coffee and pastries this morning. I can heat up your coffee if you want or I can make you a fresh one?" Ryan said thinking she must need something, "Then I'll tell you everything. Then I'd like you to tell me what is going on, how this all started and why Oliver had you tied up at his place. And who the hell were those people in that van?"

Stephanie looked like she was going to break down and cry.

"It's okay, sorry I just want to help and in order to do that I need to understand what's going on. You can trust me, just as Nicole does. We'll talk about one thing at a time when you're ready." Ryan reassured her.

"Okay, did Nicole bring Mochas?" Asked Stephanie, holding back from crying, "And Pains aux chocolates?", A hint of a smile appeared at the corners of her mouth.

"Yes, she did, would you like them?" Ryan asked, as he patted her on the knee.

"Yes please." Stephanie replied.

She was sat on the couch looking like a sad, lost and lonely thing. Wearing the loose jogging bottoms tucked into the socks and baggy T-shirt Ryan had lent her the night before. She pulled her feet up onto the couch and tucked them behind her bottom. She then grabbed the blanket Ryan had used on the couch as a make shift bed and pulled it up to her chin turning to make sure her feet were also covered. Ryan stood and looked at her, his heart sank at the sight in front of him. She was a beautiful girl mixed up in an ugly situation, the full extent of which he was still yet to understand.

"I'll be right back." Ryan said, as he headed for the kitchen.

He soon returned with the re-heated coffee and pastry and passed them to Stephanie. He explained the story of how he was single and his friend badgering him about meeting a girl. How he found her I.D. badge at the tube station and ended up visiting her place of work in the hope of meeting her. How Nicole had overheard him asking to see Stephanie and had explained her concern over the whereabouts of Stephanie. Ryan was at heart a decent person and felt it was only right to try and help find her. Stephanie had sat there and listened intently only interrupting occasionally asking Ryan to explain in a little more detail certain things. When he'd finished telling the story she was sat there with a contemplative look on her face. Ryan also sat there in silence, now somewhat embarrassed and wondering what she must think of him, the lengths he'd gone to in order to meet her. The fact he'd been honest about how he thought she was beautiful in her picture and that that was the driving force behind the string of events that had unfolded and brought them to where they are now.

"I don't know what to say." Stephanie finally broke the silence, paused to gather her thoughts then continued, "I mean it sounds strange but honourable, I feel flattered yet a little awkward. For Nicole to trust you I know you must be trust worthy as she is a great judge of character. What you have done for me and how you have been since we met I can see for myself you are a good and decent man. I also feel terrible that due to me you are involved in all this. You could have been badly hurt or worse. I'm not sure how I should be with you or what you want from me."

Ryan looked at her. Her hair was now clean and not so wild looking. Her soft pretty face was cute yet beautiful. Her eyes were clear now, dry of tears and seemed to shine like polished diamonds, no, sapphires would be a better description because of the colour of her eyes. He sighed.

"I want nothing from you and I expect nothing from you, other than for you to trust me and tell me everything that led up to you being kidnapped by Oliver. If you know who those men are that killed him, I'd like you to tell me who they are and how they are involved. I just want to help you, I have no ulterior motives. I just need to understand the whole situation so I, along with Nicole can help you out of this horrible nightmare." Ryan said with sincerity and empathy.

Stephanie took a deep breath.

"Alright. Where to start?" she said to herself. "Well, I don't know how much Nicole told you about Oliver and me. We used to date, we met a good few years ago. He was sweet, he had his own business that he was partners in with his father. A painting and decorating company. He was a bit of a lad but charming with it you know? I had not long left uni and was working as a receptionist at a law firm and life seemed pretty good. Then one day on a job, his father fell from a ladder and the shock caused him to have a heart attack. Ollie was out having a break. That was his only failing really; he was a little lazy. He would start a job with his father and then disappear often for breaks and leave his dad to do the work. Well on this occasion like I said his dad had the fall, the heart attack from which he died. Oliver returned to find him dead. He called emergency services but of course there was nothing they could do and it was determined his dad had died about an hour before Ollie returned. Oliver went into a depression and blamed himself. His mother had passed when he was young so his dad was really all he had and he felt responsible. If he hadn't been skiving off, it's very possible that even if his father had fallen, he would have been saved. After that Ollie turned mean, ill tempered, bad mannered but I tried to stick it out, hoping one day he'd forgive himself and go back to the old charming loveable character I knew and loved. It didn't happen. He didn't work, he didn't bother to look for new jobs. His business got into debt and he started drinking. After a while the drink wasn't enough and he turned to drugs. Then one day his dealer had been killed in a gang war incident and he was approached to become a dealer. Can I have a glass of water please?" Stephanie asked. "This is pretty hard going over it all.

"Of course." Ryan jumped up from the couch and returned with a large glass of water. "Please, continue." Ryan said gently.

Stephanie took a few sips of the water and placed the glass on the small table by the side of the couch.

"When I found out he'd become a dealer, that was the last straw for me. I couldn't see him coming back from that and only getting worse or ending up…"

A solitary tear escaped her left eye and rolled slowly down over her well defined cheek bone. She paused, took a deep breath, wiped the tear from her face and continued.

"…dead. As indeed he has. I didn't want to be there when that happened. Ironic really that I was in the end anyway. But what I meant was I didn't want to be his girlfriend when that happened so that's when I told him it was over, I wanted out. He was angry, very angry, he didn't want to lose me as I really was the last thing he had in his life. Now due to his own actions he had pushed me away. We fought, he got violent, he smacked me about a bit and that made my mind up for definite as if everything else wasn't enough. So, I waited for him to leave the place to go do some dealing, I packed what little I could and just ran. I didn't really have much in the way of savings so I didn't know where to go. I ended up staying at a friend's place that I knew from work. He knew where I worked so I never went back to that job. I looked for and got a new job, that's where I met Nicole, eventually got my finances together and got a place of my own." Stephanie paused and took another deep breath.

Ryan could see this was hard for her but urged her to go on.

Stephanie sighed and continued.

"Nicole and I soon became very close friends and I eventually told her everything over a couple of bottles of wine one night at her place and since then she's been like a big sister to me. Anyway that all happened about three years ago and I hadn't seen Ollie or heard anything about him. Because of that experience I wasn't interested in getting involved with another man until I was well and truly over the whole thing. Then one evening walking home to my flat I bumped into him. Call it coincidence or by design of some higher being or whatever but I saw him, I felt pity for him. I guess in a way I still thought I loved him and wanted to help him. We talked for a bit. He was different again. It seemed he'd managed to forgive himself for his father and seemed more humble, less violent and calmer. He apologised to me for the way he had treated me and left it at that. He walked off. I waited a moment and followed him. I still to this day have no idea what compelled me to do so but I did none the less. That's when I saw him, he was still dealing. The way he had spoken and acted, I just thought he'd gotten out of it and had really gotten his life back on track. I was so angry. I wanted to do something about it. I continued to follow him home without his knowing. I discovered where he lived so the next day I went back there. I had called him in the morning and asked him to meet me way over the other side of London making out that I was living over that way and wanted to see him. He of course took the bait. I broke into his flat and it wasn't long before I had found his stash. There was a load of drugs, all different kinds of drugs: pills, powder, grass, all sorts. I shoved them all in the duffle bag I had taken with me and left. I guess when he returned home and found his place had been ransacked and the drugs gone he put two and two together. Obviously because I hadn't been at the place I told him to meet me at, he knew I had taken them. He called me, he started talking calmly at first then before long he got angry and aggressive. He told me the stash wasn't his and I'm going to end up getting him killed. I denied taking them of course and made out I didn't know what he was talking about and lied and said something had come up last minute so I couldn't make the meet and my phone battery had died and I only just got to charge it hence why I couldn't call and cancel or reschedule. I just wanted to get him out of the drug business. I figured if he didn't have anything to sell hopefully he didn't have the money to buy more and he'd have to get out. I guess I wasn't thinking clearly about the bigger picture. I just wanted to help him try and return to that sweet guy I once knew. I didn't want to be with him, just help him get his life back." Stephanie started to cry again.

Ryan said "I'm sorry, I'm sorry you had to go through all that. I understand why you tried to help, sometimes people just can't be helped. Like you wanted for him, you have to forgive yourself and move on from this. So I guess from all that, the guys in the van are the true owners of the drugs and that's what they meant by give them back their stuff, right?"

Stephanie had stopped crying again and looked at Ryan.

"I guess." She answered.

"So you don't know who these people are? Oliver never mentioned a name? Or said whose drugs they were?" Ryan asked, as gently as he could, pushing for an answer but trying not to frighten her or upset her in any way.

"No, not at all, he just kept saying they weren't his and the people who he was selling them for weren't the type of people you want to piss off." Stephanie replied.

"Okay, let's start with the stash, where is that now? What did you do with it? Is it at your flat?" Ryan quizzed her.

"Errr yes, I have hidden it at my flat." Stephanie responded sounding a little nervous.

"What were you going to do with the drugs anyway?" Asked Ryan.

"Well, I'm not sure to be honest." Replied Stephanie, "I hadn't thought that far ahead."

"Okay, so I think first things first, we need to get the drugs so we have them and know where they are. I guess you're going to get your wish, I'll take you to your flat. You can pick up a few things and we'll grab them at the same time." Ryan suggested after pondering the matter for a few moments.

"Great, when do you want to go?" Stephanie asked.

"Soon. I think even though you might be right and the guys in the van, whoever they are, may not be looking for you, it would be safer during the day I feel." Ryan responded.

"I'll go get ready." Said Stephanie.

"I'll call Nicole and let her know what we're up to." Ryan exclaimed.

While Stephanie went upstairs to get washed and ready to leave, Ryan called Nicole.

"Hi Nicole." Ryan said, after Nicole answered her phone.

"Hey. How's everything?" Nicole replied.

"Not bad. Stephanie seems a little better today. I'm going to take her to her flat shortly so she can pick up a few things." Ryan continued.

"Okay, are you sure it's safe to go there? Please be careful." Nicole said, with concern in here voice.

"We'll be careful. Do you want to come over later? Ryan asked.

"Yeah sure. Let me know when you're back and I'll come over as soon as I'm done with work if that's okay?" Nicole Replied.

"Of course, that'd be great, I look forward to it." Ryan said with more than just a hint of excitement in his voice.

"Okay I'll be there, looking forward to it too." Nicole replied and hung up.

Ryan put the kettle on and made himself a tea and a coffee

for Stephanie. He listened by the bottom of the stairs and could hear the shower was still running. He took a seat on the couch and waited for Stephanie to finish getting ready and come down.

"I made you a coffee while you were in the shower but it might be cold now. I can make you a fresh one though if you like?" Said Ryan.

"No, I'm okay thanks, but is it okay if I just grab a glass of water?" Stephanie replied.

"Of course, help yourself, glasses are in the cupboard above the kettle. I'll go shower and get ready." Ryan retorted.

It wasn't long before Ryan returned to the lounge fully dressed and groomed ready to go out. Stephanie was sat on the couch looking contemplative.

"You okay?" Ryan asked.

"Oh, yes." Stephanie replied. Ryan had obviously disturbed her thoughts that were running through her mind.

"You sure?" He asked again.

"Yes, honestly, I was just thinking about everything that has happened over the last few weeks. I just want my life to go back to normal. I would love to get back to work but how can I? At least until all this mess is sorted out with those guys from the van." Stephanie confessed.

"Everything will be okay, we just need to return their stuff as they requested and hopefully things will return to normal for you." Ryan said, trying to sound as reassuring as he could but really wondering if they would just leave her alone after this, after all she had effectively witnessed a murder. Would they just let that go? She was a rather big loose end that could cause them a lot of trouble. Ryan knew she was probably terrified but was impressed by how she was seeming to be keeping herself together.

"Okay then, let's go Stephanie, if you're ready of course." Ryan exclaimed.

"Yes, I'm ready." She replied, with a little tremble in her voice.

Stephanie stood, looked down at her feet then up at Ryan who was standing just a couple of feet in front of her.

"Do you really think everything will be alright?" She asked.

Ryan looked at her intensely, "We'll make everything alright, I promise." Then wondered how the hell he was going to keep that promise.

They left Ryan's flat and went down to the rental van. On reaching the van Ryan opened the door for Stephanie and held out a hand to help her into the cab.

"Nicole was right, you are a real gentleman aren't you?" Stephanie said, as she climbed into the van.

Ryan smiled as he let go of her hand.

"It's been said." He chuckled, "I just can't help it."

Ryan jumped into the driver's seat and started the van. It was three twenty five in the afternoon and given the time of year, they didn't have long before it would start getting dark. Ryan looked up through the windscreen of the van, checking for the position of the sun. Even though it was winter it was a clear day. The tall buildings around his location masked where the sun was, but he figured they only had an hour, maybe an hour and a half at best before evening would draw in and darkness would descend.

"Let's get to your flat, grab the stash and what you need and get back here okay?" Ryan asked as he turned onto the main road and headed for her address.

"Yes, yes of course." Stephanie replied anxiously.

"Although I think you're right and those guys probably aren't looking for you right now I'd rather be out of there before it gets dark, there's no point taking any unnecessary chances right?" He said just to reiterate his point.

"No, not at all, I totally agree." She replied.

Chapter Ten.

They pulled up outside Stephanie's flat just after four PM. They were lucky with the traffic, when they set off Ryan was nervous that it'd take longer than he wished it to.

"SHIT." Stephanie almost screamed.

"WHAT?" Ryan replied, shocked thinking she'd seen the guys in the black van.

"I don't have my keys to the flat." She replied, just a little calmer, "I lost them in the struggle when Ollie took me.

"It's okay, I brought my lock picks." Ryan replied, with a wry smile on his face, "You know, you never told me what happened when Ollie took you?"

"Can I tell you that later? When we get back to your place?" Stephanie responded.

"Yeah, it can wait." Ryan conceded, "Okay, let's get in and out quick smart."

"Definitely." Stephanie replied as she jumped out of the van.

They walked hurriedly across to the flat and up the few steps. Stephanie reached the door first and pressed the button on the entry system key pad for the gay couple's flat above hers.

Buzzzzzzzzzz

Crackle

"Hello? Who is it?" Came the recognisable voice of the man Ryan and Nicole had met when they broke into Stephanie's flat.

"Hi, it's Stephanie, your neighbour from downstairs. I forgot my main door key would you be a love and buzz me in please?"

"Ohhh hello. We've been dying to meet you." Said Roger, "Michael and I have been wondering if you had moved out or gone away on holiday."

"I've been unwell and staying with a friend." Stephanie replied, thinking on her feet to come up with an excuse as to her whereabouts.

"Oh you poor thing, I hope you're feeling better." Came Roger's response.

Ryan and Stephanie were both getting a little nervous stood out in the open by the front door. This was taking too long.

"Well I'm a little better but still contagious, my friend just brought me home to pick up a few more things then we're heading back to his place. Sorry Roger but we're in a bit of a rush can you buzz us in please? When I'm better I promise we'll have a proper party to welcome you to the building…okay?" Stephanie said, sounding stern.

"Ohhh that would be lovely, yes darling of course, hope you get well soon." He replied and a second later there was a click and a long buzz as he pressed the button to allow the main front door to be open.

Stephanie pushed on the door and it opened. They stepped inside and closed the door behind them.

"Geeze, that's the longest conversation I've ever had on a door intercom." Stephanie said, with a smile on her face.

"Yes, not the time huh?" Ryan replied, while fumbling in his inside coat pocket for his lock picking tool set.

Seconds later he was working on the lock and within a few moments they were entering Stephanie's flat.

Stephanie walked in first.

"OH MY GOD." She exclaimed as she saw the state of the place, "What the fuck?"

"Sorry, with everything else going on I forgot to mention the state of the place." Ryan said sympathetically, "We guessed it was Ollie looking for his stash."

"What a bastard. What a wanker. Look at this mess." Stephanie said, in almost a whisper, her eyes welled up as she looked at Ryan.

Ryan gave her a quick hug and while hugging, said over her head,

"Don't worry, once we get everything sorted with those guys, Nicole and I will come and help you get this place straight again. Like it never happened."

"You will? Really? You're so sweet. Thank you." Stephanie sniffed and wiped her eyes.

"Now come on, go grab what you need, quickly. Where's the stash?" Ryan said, getting anxious now.

"Yes, yes of course." Stephanie replied, "It's in the bathroom, behind the bath panel, under the bath. You'll need a screwdriver, the panel is held in place by two screws."

"Do you have one?" Ryan asked, a little annoyed she hadn't said anything before so he could have come prepared.

"Yes, kitchen drawer to the left of the sink." Stephanie

replied almost nonchalantly as she headed for her bedroom to grab a few things.

"Ughh." Ryan thought to himself, as he headed for the kitchen.

As he entered the kitchen he could hear muffled groans of anguish as Stephanie discovered yet more damages and mess as she had entered her bedroom.

"Poor thing, this is going to take her a long time to get over all she's been through." He thought to himself.

The kitchen was still in the state of disarray Nicole and he had found it in with half the drawers open or skewed across the floor. The drawer Stephanie had told him that was home to the screwdrivers was missing. One of the casualties thrown across the floor, its contents scattered around the room. His eyes darted from left to right as he searched for any screwdrivers. He saw, over by the fridge freezer, a red handled one and picked it up. It was a smallish, flat blade screwdriver with a rubber handle.

"This will have to do." He thought to himself, as he stepped back over the strewn objects in his path to the door.

He could still hear Stephanie swearing expletives from the bedroom as she busied herself gathering clothes and toiletries. Ryan went to the bathroom which of course had been turned over also. Luckily the bath panel was still in place and even luckier was the two screws holding it in place were slotted screws. The screwdriver would fit them. He knelt down in front of the bath and started unscrewing one of the screws. Stephanie appeared at the door. She was holding a largish black sports bag and was red faced. Ryan couldn't tell if it was from anger or exertion.

"You okay?" Ryan asked, not knowing what else to say,

"You got what you need?"

"Just need a few things from in here and I'm all set." She replied, sounding a little more together.

Ryan had removed one of the screws and was already a good way to getting the other out. Another few turns of the screwdriver and the screw came free of the panel. It slipped down from the under lip of the bath and Ryan hoisted it free away from the bath.

"Mind yourself." He said, as he turned and placed the panel against the wall by the door where she was stood.

Ryan knelt down again in front of the bath and hunched forward to look under the space below the bath. There, towards the tap end of the bath was a cobweb and dust covered large, dark blue duffel bag. He reached in, grabbed the bag and pulled it out from its hiding place.

"I presume this is it?" He questioned Stephanie.

"Yes, that's it." She replied, "Can we get out of here now?"

"Definitely." Ryan exclaimed as he stood holding the bag.

It was quite heavy and he wondered how much was in this bag and how much was it worth, obviously enough for someone to die over.

Ryan followed her out of the bathroom and back to the lounge. It was getting dark outside now. Ryan saw a few of the street lamps outside through the drawn curtains start to come on. Though there had been enough light in the back rooms of the flat for them to achieve what they came to do it was getting dark quickly in the flat. Ryan pulled back the edge of the right hand curtain and looked out through the small crack into the street. Just as he did that

Stephanie turned on the light in the lounge.

"Fuck. Turn it off." Ryan almost shouted in a harsh whisper.

"What? What?" Stephanie replied a little taken aback and moved to turn the light off again.

"The black van is outside. Parked right behind our van." Ryan answered.

Stephanie almost collapsed down on to the couch in despair.

"Well, how the hell did they know we are here?" She asked, looking confused and scared at the same time.

"I doubt they did. My guess is they just thought they would try here, they've probably been casing Ollie's place too. Who knows what they thought your relationship with him was." Ryan replied, while still looking through the slightest of gaps between the edge of the curtain and the window frame.

"We'd better get out of here." Ryan said, as he turned to Stephanie, "They're getting out of the van. Is there a back entrance to these flats?"

"Yes. Come on let's go." Replied Stephanie, as she gathered herself mentally and stood from the couch.

She grabbed her sports bag and Ryan picked up the duffel bag and headed for the door to exit her flat. They stepped out into the hall and closed the door quietly behind them.

Buzzzzzzzzzzz......Buzzzzzzzzzzz…..Buzzzzzzzzzzz

"Shit they're trying all the flats on the intercom." Stephanie whispered to Ryan, frozen to the spot.

"Come on, we gotta go." Ryan grabbed her by the wrist and started to pull her toward the back of the building when the rear entrance was.

Crackle.

"Oh hello again dear did you forget something you silly thing?" Came Roger's voice over the intercom, "I'll buzz you in sweetie."

Ryan yanked harder on Stephanie and pulled her from her daze. They started running toward the back door of the building.

There was a click and a clunk and the main front door to the building opened. The buzzing sound stopped. The door swung open further. There behind the door was the man who had been holding the gun. The guy, Gerry, who had shot Ollie.

Ryan turned as he and Stephanie made it to the back door. If it wasn't so serious Ryan would have laughed to himself on seeing the man properly. Gerry had a black thin moustache. Very pale skin. High, pronounced cheek bones. Sunken dark eyes. Drawn in cheeks. Very dark, practically black, thick eyebrows. He was wearing a black woollen hat, black jeans, a black bomber jacket zipped up to the neck and black doc martin boots. He was the stereotypical looking criminal straight out of the movies. Or lifted directly from a photofit or police sketch artists impression.

Stephanie shoved the back door open and ran outside with Ryan close behind.

"THERE THEY ARE." Shouted Gerry, "GET THEM." pointing at the pair as they ran out the back of the building.

Two other big burly thugs were stood right behind Gerry.
They all rushed forward toward the back of the building.
Outside, Ryan and Stephanie were running through the
back garden of the building. It was only a short but wide
grassy patch, in what otherwise was a concrete built up
area. They reached the back gate before the villains had
even come through the back door.

"Quick." Stephanie shouted to Ryan, "This way, maybe we
can get round the front back to the van."

They turned left on the path, heading for an alleyway that
ran along the side of her building. The path went all along
the buildings that lined the street where her flat was. You
could turn left at the corner of her building, cutting
between her building and the one next to it, or carry on
straight to the road that turned off from her street. They
heard the crash of the back door being flung open and
shouting of the thugs behind them. The leader spotted
where they were heading and shouted at one of the goons
to turn back and go out to the front of the building and
cut them off. He figured they may have had a vehicle
parked out front. The large muscly guy with a shaved head
nodded and turned back into the building. Luckily Ryan
spotted the thin man's gesture to the other man and
realised there was no way he and Stephanie would beat
that guy to the van.

"Keep running straight." He shouted to Stephanie, who
was in front of him.

She looked back quizzically.

"Just trust me." He said and gestured vigorously for her to
go straight along the path to the road instead of turning
towards the front of the building.

Stephanie put her head down and ran. Ryan was closing on

her and urged her to go faster. They passed the alleyway which would have taken them to the front of the building and their van. Ryan snatched a quick look over his shoulder, they had put some good ground between them and their pursuers. The two men had now left the grounds of the building and were heading towards them. Gerry looked quick and was pulling away from the larger, somewhat overweight but also muscly guy behind him. Ryan had a flash back to the night of the shooting, he remembered hearing Gerry call this one Sean. Ryan realised Gerry looked quick because Sean was a slow runner. Luckily Stephanie had grabbed and put on a pair of running shoes when she was in her bedroom in the flat, cursing Ollie and everything he had done to her place. Ryan had also just put on jeans and a pair of trainers, they were both ready to run. Ryan hoped this would give them an advantage and it certainly seemed to be working. Only another twenty yards and they would be at the road. Ryan saw a row of wheely bins ahead that must belong to the residents of the building at the end of the road. As Stephanie and he ran past them he stopped, grabbed all three and pulled them over, causing an obstacle for their pursuers to navigate over. They reached the end of the path and rushed out on to the pavement. They stopped for just a second and looked back at their followers. Gerry leapt on to the first bin and hurdled the other two. Sean, a good few yards behind him, tried to copy him and ended up catching his foot on the front of the first one tripping himself and catapulting him forward face first onto the other two. An almighty crash was heard and a few swore words came from the Sean's mouth. Stephanie couldn't help but laugh, mostly from nervousness but also the sight of it.

"Let's go, run." Shouted Ryan to Stephanie and they took off again turning right away from her road.

Gerry came running out from the pathway. Ryan had

started to run but stopped just out of sight from the path and was stood waiting at the corner of the building. As soon as Gerry had appeared Ryan had stuck out his right foot about shin high. Gerry ran straight into it, causing him to fall forward. His momentum carrying him headlong face first into a parked car. Smashing his face on the door panel of the car and crunching his neck. Ryan sped off after Stephanie. Gerry lay crumpled in a heap on the floor by the car. Not quite knocked out but severely dazed. A few moments later Sean appeared from the alley to find his comrade still in a heap on the floor, blood streaming from his broken nose. He looked to see where Ryan and Stephanie had gone and saw them several hundred yards down the road still running. He stopped and helped him to his feet and they hobbled after the pair. Ryan and Stephanie looked back and saw they had made good distance. They crossed the street and slowed to a jog to try and get their breaths back a little.

Stephanie patted Ryan on the shoulder, "Good move back there."

"Thanks, the guy falling over the bins gave me the idea." Ryan replied, smiling, feeling somewhat of a hero or at the very least a little braver than he ever thought he was.

Just as he was celebrating his little victory they heard the screeching of tyres from the other end of the street. The black van appeared skidding round the corner and screeching to a halt where Gerry and the Sean were. The two men, seeing the van, ran over to it and jumped in.

"Shit." Ryan and Stephanie both said at the same time and started running faster again.

There was a squeal from rubber on tarmac as the van wheel-span, before lurching forward in pursuit of the couple. Ryan looked back over his shoulder, they were still a good few hundred yards ahead of the van, but the speed it was coming it wouldn't be long before they were on top of them. He looked ahead and just another twenty feet or so in front of them on the left was an alleyway much like the one running behind the row of buildings where Stephanie's flat was situated.

"Take the left, the alley." Ryan shouted to Stephanie.

Without hesitation, as soon as she reached the alley, she turned left and continued running. Ryan turned shortly after her and they were both now running along the path, behind a row of three story buildings either side of them. The path looked very long and they couldn't tell if there were any side alleys that could take them out between the buildings. They could see that the end of the path took them out on to another street, which ran parallel to the one they had just left. Ryan checked behind them, the van had just skidded to a halt in line with the alley. It paused there, their pursuers were obviously thinking whether to chase them on foot again or make a strategic bid to get round the other end of the alley and cut them off. After a few seconds, Sean jumped out of the side of the van and started to run after them. As soon as the door of the van was slammed shut, it took off again. Ryan was hoping that there were other ways out from this alley, as he wasn't sure if they would get to the end of it before the van blocked off their escape. With Sean chasing them from the way they came, they could end up being boxed in with nowhere to run. Just fifteen yards ahead of them, Ryan thought he saw a crossroads in the path, possibly an alley cutting across this one. With any luck it would give the couple options. Which way to turn though? If the van had gone straight on in the direction it was facing it would have to turn left in order to get to the other end of the alley. It could stop and be waiting at the end of the path if they turned right. They reached the intersection.

"Turn left again." Ryan shouted to Stephanie.

Once again, without hesitation, she followed his orders and shot left down the path.

"Oh shit." Stephanie said, almost breathless.

Ryan had followed a second later.

"Shit." Ryan repeated.

On turning the corner to take the other path, only fifteen feet or so ahead of them was a fence crossing the path.

"We'll have to go over it." Ryan said to Stephanie.

"I can't climb that." She replied.

"Yes you can, I'll boost you up." He said in response.

They ran towards the fence. As they approached the fence they realised it wasn't a dead end after all. It was an optical illusion from where they were stood. As it was getting darker now they hadn't seen that the path actually turned sharply right, went a few yards then turned sharply left again. They started to run again. Ryan was confident they could out run the large man Sean, his concern though was the van. The alley had four ways in and out. Sean was following them from the way they came in, that left three exits. One to the right; the path opposite that they had taken on the left, and the exit at the end of the path that they had entered the alley. With only three guys chasing them it gave them a chance. Ryan suspected the second guy would get out of the van and start coming down the path opposite to the one they were on now. Then it just depended on what the third guy did in the van. If he made it to the end of the alleyway and looked along it to where they first entered, he'd see they are not on the path and therefore must have turned left or have been caught by his comrades. That would mean the driver of the van would assume Ryan and Stephanie would come out from the other exit onto the street that Stephanie's flat was on just another block over. Ryan was trying to think. Would the van be able to make it to the end of the alley, see they weren't there and get round to the other exit they were heading for in time to cut them off? By now, he suspected the second man, most probably Gerry, would have been dropped off at the other exit and now be running towards the intersection. There was no turning back. Sean couldn't be too far behind them either. Just then Ryan heard a shout. Luckily it didn't sound too close. It was Gerry. He had indeed gotten out of the van and started to give chase up the path towards the crossroads in the alley. The man shouted again.

"Which way'd they go?" Gerry shouted to his partner in a raspy voice, already sounding out of breath.

"Left Down here." Sean shouted.

That gave Ryan a mental image of where they both were. Stephanie and he were a little way ahead.

"Stop." He whispered to Stephanie.

"What? Are you mad?" She replied, "They're right behind us."

"No they're just near the intersection of the alleyway." Ryan said, confidently, "Here, I'll boost you up and over this fence."

"What? No that's silly, we can't be that far from the exit and the street." Stephanie protested.

"Trust me, please." He retorted.

He crouched near the fence and interlocked his fingers

making to boost her up over the fence. She took the sports bag off her shoulder and threw it over the six foot high wooden fence on the right of the path. She placed her right foot in Ryan's hands and pushed up as he lifted her as best he could. She scrambled over the top of the fence and landed safely on the other side. Ryan threw the bag he was carrying and launched himself at the top of the fence with a couple of scrambled steps and pulling himself up with his arms he was also over the fence. He landed softly on grass next to Stephanie. She was about to speak when Ryan put a finger to her lips to shush her. They had made it over the fence just in time. They heard the hurried footsteps of Sean run past just inches on the other side of the fence. Followed closely by a second set of footsteps obviously from Gerry. It was then confirmed.

"You sure they went this way?" Asked Gerry, as he passed just the other said of the fence.

"Yes I'm sure of it." Came the response from the first guy who now sounded further away as he hurried along the alley to the street.

Ryan turned and looked at where they were standing. It was a back yard of one of the buildings much the same as Stephanie's building. The high six foot fence only ran along the path of the alleyway, between the gardens of the buildings there were only short fences of maybe three feet in height.

"At last, we have a bit of luck." Ryan whispered to Stephanie. You can manage those short fences right?"

"Yeah, no problem." She whispered back, as she adjusted her bag on her right shoulder.

Ryan picked up the second bag and swung it over his shoulder, they made their way across the garden and over the first short fence. They made their way across each of the gardens and fences in turn as quickly and quietly as they could, heading towards the end of the row of buildings. As they entered the second to last garden a light came on, basking the garden in bright light.

"It's just a security light, keep going." Ryan said.

They made it over the last short fence and in to the garden on the end of the row. Ryan headed towards the back gate. Luck was certainly smiling on them, it was only held closed by a single bolt near the top of the gate. He quietly slid the bolt to the right, unlocking the gate. He opened the gate slowly, just a crack. Half expecting one of the thugs to be stood there waiting for them. He opened the gate just a little more and peaked out. No sign of anyone. He opened it a little further and peered into the alleyway. Checking both ways he could see the path was empty. He was hoping the van would've reached the end of the alley, and seeing they were not down it, the driver would have sped off round the other side to the exit they were heading for before jumping the fence. They had to risk it. He turned to Stephanie and quietly beckoned her to follow him. They were only about twenty feet from the exit of the alley and the street. They walked slowly hugging the left side of the path trying to stick to the shadows created by the high fence. Ryan reached the corner of the alley and took a quick peak out. He looked to the right and then the left. They had timed it just perfectly. He saw the black van disappearing round the corner up the road. He tugged on Stephanie's arm and pulled her out of the alley and onto the pavement. He started running and Stephanie, not needing to be told, started to run after him. They ran the opposite way that the van had gone. Ten yards down the road they crossed the street, Ryan leading the way. Ryan was hoping the parked cars would help mask them from view if the van turned around and came back down this road. Another thirty yards and they reached a junction with another road. Ryan turned them left and they continued to run a little further until they reached another road and turned right.

"Okay, we're not out of the woods yet but I think we must have a few streets and turns between us and them now. We can maybe walk a little and get our breaths back. You okay?" Ryan asked, as he slowed his pace to a walk.

"Yeah, I'm okay, nice trick again, you seem like you've done this sort of thing before." Stephanie replied, with a smile and a look of relief on her face.

Ryan chuckled, "No, not at all. My childhood friend and I used to play cops and robbers when we were young and we'd run through this housing estate near where we lived. We'd hop over garden walls and fences and run through alleys, the estate was like a maze, never got caught or told off as we tried to avoid being seen, maybe that helped. We never did any damage, we weren't bad kids we were just playing."

"Well you certainly seem to have outfoxed them." Stephanie replied.

"Let's not get too cocky. No point trying to go back for the van right now, if they think they've lost us they will probably be watching your place to see if we return for a vehicle." Ryan said, "Let's find the tube station, any idea where we are?"

"Not that far now actually. I thought that's where you were leading us." Stephanie replied.

"No, another bit of luck I guess, I don't really know this area very well." Ryan responded, "Okay miss, you lead the way."

They continued walking.

"We'll turn right at the end of this road then take the next left then one more right turn and we'll be at the tube station." Stephanie exclaimed.

"Okay cool, doesn't sound like far then." Ryan replied, "Glad you know your way around here." He smiled.

They continued until they reached the end of the road and turned right as per Stephanie's instructions. They walked in silence. Both knowing there was a lot more to be talked about, but neither feeling this was the time or place. They reached the junction where Stephanie said they'd take a left and they turned into the road. They were now moving at a decent pace, Ryan didn't feel comfortable being so close to where they were almost caught. They guys in the van were probably combing the streets looking for them and might, just might guess the couple could be heading for the tube station. When Ryan realised that, he upped his pace and told Stephanie to do the same.

"Why though? I think we lost them." Stephanie said, exasperated.

"Because if they realise how close the tube station is they must think we'd try and get there." Ryan replied, almost annoyed that he had to explain himself.

They reached the end of the road and turned right. The tube station entrance was just thirty yards away across the street. They stepped between two parked cars into the road. They checked the road was safe to cross by first looking right and then left. As they looked left they saw the black van stuck at a red traffic light not a hundred yards away. The thugs had obviously come to the same conclusion Ryan thought they would.

"So annoying being right so often." Ryan thought to himself.

The road was clear for them to cross and he pulled Stephanie by the sleeve to cross the road and start running.

"Fuck sake." Stephanie said under her breath, "Why don't they leave us alone, I thought they said they'd leave us alone."

"I guess you just can't trust criminals." Ryan said, not really trying to make a joke at all.

They ran across the road and headed for the entrance to the tube station. Ryan took a quick look back, the lights hadn't changed yet but surely must do so any second. Gerry had jumped out of the van. He had barely made it across the junction when the lights changed. The van pulled away from the lights and skidded to a stop on the corner just after the junction so Gerry could get back in. The cars behind the van had to stop abruptly and the drivers were beeping their horns. Once he had jumped back in the van, it shot forward again, narrowly missing a car that had decided to try and go round them. The car skidded to a halt across the white lines in the middle of the road and once again sounded his horn. Ryan and Stephanie ignored the commotion going on behind them and ran to the entrance of the station. They were only feet away from it now. They ran in through the entrance and down the steps into the station.

"I don't have my oyster card, or any cash or bank cards." Stephanie shouted to Ryan.

He was already ahead of her and had taken his wallet out of his back pocket. He pulled out two bank cards and passed one to her. They reached the barrier and both swiped the cards over the sensors. The lights on the sensor posts turned green and both barriers opened to let them through.

"Thank god for modern technology eh?" Ryan said, to no one in particular.

They ran through the barriers and headed for the correct platform to take them back into the West End of London.

"Wait." Said Ryan, "This way, come on."

"What, the platform for the train we need is this way." Protested Stephanie.

"I know." Replied Ryan, and grabbed her hand and lead her to the platform for trains heading north, away from the West end.

"I don't understand." She said.

They turned and headed for the other platform. They ran down the stairs and out on to the platform. There were a few people there, a group of teenagers with skateboards and a boom box playing some heavy based rap music. An elderly couple walking toward the end of the platform obviously not wishing to share a compartment with the noisy group of youths. A solitary gentleman in a black trench coat and black fedora hat sat on a bench near the end of the platform, reading a broadsheet newspaper. Ryan looked up at the sign that shows the time of the next train. Only one minute to wait. They looked across the tracks to the other platform. Ryan moved them to be standing right behind the group of teenagers just as a train pulled on the opposite platform.

"See, if we were on that platform we'd have caught that train and been out of here?" Stephanie said.

Just then Gerry and Sean appeared running down the stairs onto the opposite platform. The tube train had come to a halt just seconds before and the doors had opened. The two men looked up and down the platform then entered the tube train. From where they were stood Ryan could see them looking frantically up and the down the compartment of the train. They exited the train and ran to the next carriage. They entered that one and again through the windows of the train Ryan could see them searching frantically for their prey. Just then the train heading north pulled into the station and came to a halt at their platform. The doors clicked and slid open. The group of youths all boarded with Ryan and Stephanie close behind. The two thugs in the train next to theirs jumped back off their train before the doors shut and it started to pull away. Ryan saw Gerry shout at Sean and swing his fist angrily in front of him, showing he was frustrated that they'd lost the pair. The doors on their train also slid shut with a hiss and the train jerked forward and started to pull away from the platform. The group of teenagers had all sat down putting their feet on the seats opposite where they sat and turned the music up even louder. Ryan took hold of Stephanie's hand and led her toward the back of the train. They passed through the doors and entered the next carriage. Before taking a seat Ryan looked out the window at the platform where they had been stood and saw the man in the black trench coat still sat there, he hadn't boarded the train. Ryan saw him fold the paper, stand from the bench and start heading for the exit from the platform. It was quite dark and quite a distance from him now, the train was moving further away from the platform. But Ryan could've sworn that was the same guy he thought he'd spotted outside the Chinese restaurant that night that he had dinner with Nicole. He sat opposite Stephanie, scratched his head and then dismissed the thought.

"Something wrong?" Stephanie asked, sounding much calmer now.

"No, nothing, just thought I saw someone I'd seen before." Ryan replied.

"Other than the two arseholes who were chasing us you mean?" She said, with a rueful smile furnishing her somewhat reddened face.

"Never mind, I'm not even sure who it was I saw the first time." He replied, almost under his breath.

Stephanie didn't press him on it.

Ryan pulled his mobile phone from his inside jacket pocket.

"Shit." He said.

"What's up?" Stephanie enquired.

"Eight missed called from Nicole, she must be going out of her mind." Replied Ryan, "I'd better call her."

He tried calling but he had no signal. He sent her a text knowing it would be sent as soon as his signal returned.

The train pulled into the first station, Ryan jumped up from his seat and motioned for Stephanie to get off the train. They alighted from the train and headed for the exit. They went up the stairs and out on to the street. Ryan felt his mobile vibrate against his chest from within his inside pocket. There was a black cab rank outside the station and Ryan beckoned Stephanie to get into the first one in the queue. They both got in the cab and the cabbie asked,

"Where to?"

"What's Nicole's address?" Ryan asked Stephanie.

"You don't know it?" She replied, "How long you been seeing each other?"

"Errr, that's not important, what's her address? Tell the driver." Ryan exclaimed impatiently.

The cab pulled away from the kerbside and they headed off to Nicole's place. Ryan pulled his phone from his jacket pocket again. The display on his phone just showed;

"Message send Failed."

He called Nicole's phone and she answered in a panic.

"Ryan? You both okay? Please tell me you're both okay." Nicole's worried voice came over the ear piece.

"We're both okay, change of plans though, can we come to yours?" Ryan asked, "We're in a cab on our way now. Be about twenty minutes."

"Yes, yes, of course. Thank god you're both okay I was so worried when you weren't picking up your phone." Nicole continued, "Something happen? Or you just been ignoring my calls?"

"Not at all, sorry to make you worry, we'll fill you in when we get there." Ryan replied, "See you soon."

"Okay, see you when you get here." Nicole replied.

Chapter Eleven.

The cab was about to pull up outside Nicole's flat.

"Oh sorry, it's a little further up the street, we got the wrong number." Ryan told the cabbie, "Sorry about that."

"What are you doing?" Whispered Stephanie to Ryan.

"Just being careful." Ryan whispered back, "If we've been followed I don't want them to know Nicole's exact address. No point putting her in danger too."

"I see, yes you're right of course." Stephanie agreed.

Ryan let the cabbie drive another sixty yards or so before telling him, "That's the place." And the taxi pulled up to the kerb and opened the little window in the pane of glass that separated the driver from the passengers. Ryan paid the driver and added a tip while Stephanie was opening the door and exiting the black cab. Ryan jumped out the cab and shut the door behind him.

"Okay, let's stand here a second." Ryan said to Stephanie, "We'll let the taxi leave so even he don't know where we are going and we'll take a walk a little further up the street, then double back keeping an eye out for anyone paying us any interest."

"Wow, you're either really good at this, or really paranoid." Stephanie said in reply.

"I've watched a lot of spy movies in my time." Ryan explained, "Seriously though, I'd hate for Nicole to be mixed up in this and risk any harm to befall her but I don't see what choice we have as to where to go right now."

The cabbie pulled away and they were left standing on the pavement. Ryan held out the crook of his arm and

Stephanie slid her arm into his, looking like any normal couple that had just gotten home from somewhere. He led her up the street away from Nicole's flat as they had discussed in the cab.

"Do you see the van? Or any cars slowing to take an interest in us?" Ryan asked.

"No, nothing suspicious." Stephanie replied.

"Okay, let's cross the street and walk past her place on the other side of the road." Ryan exclaimed.

"Agreed." Stephanie responded.

It was dark now, so it was difficult to distinguish the colour and makes of vehicles from any distance. At one point during the walk both Ryan and Stephanie got spooked when a dark grey van came down the road in their direction, only to drive straight past them with the occupants bearing them no interest whatsoever. The pair had done their walk back past Nicole's residence, keeping an eye out for anyone that might be following them and had seen nothing to concern them. They had walked another thirty yards beyond Nicole's place, crossed back over the street to be on the correct side and were now heading directly for her place. They walked up the few steps to the front door to Nicole's building and just as Ryan was about to press the buzzer for her flat, the door opened.

"Hi, what were you doing walking up and down the street?" Nicole quizzed, "I was looking out of the window for you and spotted you up the road."

"Just being careful." Ryan replied, "Just making sure we weren't followed."

"Yeah, he's a regular James Bond." Stephanie added, with

a chuckle.

"Come in, come in, what do you mean followed?" Asked Nicole, "What happened? And why weren't you answering my calls?"

"Let's get in and I'll tell you everything. Stephanie, we need to talk too." Ryan replied.

They entered Nicole's place and she double locked the front door. The interior was nicely decorated, quite sparse but homely somehow, Nicole had taste. Why would Ryan think any differently, she dressed impeccably so why wouldn't she take pride in her home. The front door entered into an open living area that was spacious. Underfoot was a pale pine parquet flooring with a small door mat just inside the door. Straight ahead was a kitchen area with the oven and hob on the far wall. Cabinets and work surfaces to the right and left coming out from the wall either side of the oven and hob. The counter on the right was under the window that was at the front of the flat and looked out onto the street from where they had just came. Under the window in that counter top was a sink. An integrated fridge freezer was to the right of the oven, with a matching cabinet door hiding the appliance behind it. The work surface to the left of the oven, had cabinets attached to the ceiling and there was a gap between them. The work surface underneath acting like a dividing wall splitting the kitchen and large living area off to the left. The cabinets were a dark natural wood with dark green doors. A couple of the high cabinets had leaded glass doors in them, showing the contents stored inside. Mostly glasses of varying types from what Ryan could see. The counter tops themselves were a pale marble. It all looked very clean and organised.

"Nice kitchen." Exclaimed Ryan. "Love the colours, and so neat and tidy."

"Thanks, I'm a bit anal when it comes to my kitchen. Put off a few potential boyfriends in the past to be honest." Nicole said, then blushed slightly as she realised that probably sounded like too much information about her love life, or failed attempts at living one.

The flooring flowed through into the rest of the living area which was also spacious. There was a large flat screen television on the wall opposite the kitchen area. Below the television was a modern looking, glass fronted fire with a white marble surround and mantle. The hearth was made of the same marble and extend from the wall just over a foot in length. Laying on the floor in front of the hearth was a fake white animal fur rug. Stood either side of the fire, on the hearth, were two black and gold Egyptian statuettes, one of the bird headed god and one of the jackal headed god, both stood about eighteen inches high. There were two cream leather couches, one a three-seater, running along the wall, and at a right angle, sat a two-seater parallel to the kitchen cabinets with the leaded glass doors. There was a pale low coffee table in front of the two couches with a marble effect table top. The walls were all painted with a natural cotton looking colour and a few pictures in black frames hung on the walls. Nothing too personal in the pictures, no photographs of people, just a few paintings, acrylic or oil Ryan guessed, of yachts on water, they were modern art so they were bold splashes of colour on a bright white background, very striking. There was a narrow but tall, black bookshelf, about three or four feet wide stood in the middle of the wall opposite the three-seater couch. There were a few books and a couple of object-d'art ornaments adorning the shelves. The only other items in the room that brought a splash of colour were the five purple cushions placed equally apart on the two couches.

"I love your two Egyptian statues, Horus and Anubis right?" Ryan said, gesturing toward them as they walked into the living area.

"Wow, you know you're Egyptian gods too huh?" Nicole replied, "Not just a pretty face." And again she blushed a little. Stephanie spotted this and smiled a little smile to herself.

"I, urr, spent some time in Egypt, I SCUBA dive, I think I told you before, yes?" Ryan replied, feeling a little flattered, "I just found Egyptology fascinating, so I read up on it a little."

"So what can you tell me about Horus and Anubis?" Asked Nicole with a smile.

"Are you testing me eh?" Replied Ryan, "Well, they were brothers according to legend. Horus the bird headed one was the god of war, the sky and falcons and Anubis was the god of the dead, embalming, funerals and mourning ceremonies. The heart of the dead was weighed against the feather of truth which represented the goddess Ma'at, to see if the deceased was worthy of entering the afterlife. If the person had lived a bad life, his or her heart would weigh heavy, and he or she would be eaten by Ammit the Devourer. If a person was kind and good, the heart weighed light, and he did not have sins, he or she could continue on to the afterlife uneaten to meet Osiris. It's a little odd because even though they were brothers to each other they were of different parents. Horus being the son of Osiris and Isis, Anubis was son of Set and Memphis. That's about all I can remember to be honest."

"Oh my goodness, I'm impressed." Smiled Nicole, "I just bought them because I though they looked cool." And she laughed.

"I second that." Stephanie piped up, "There's so much more to you than meets the eye huh?"

"I guess I can be a bit geeky, to be honest I only got interested cos I thought Anubis looked cool too." Ryan replied, sheepishly and smiled gently at Nicole.

"Okay, you guys take a seat, can I get you both a drink?" Nicole asked, "Then you need to tell me everything that happened this evening."

Ryan and Stephanie both sat, Ryan went to the far end of the three-seater and Stephanie plonked herself down on the nearest end of the two-seater. Nicole returned to the kitchen and looked through the gap between the cabinets.

"You want a beer Ryan? Steph, you want a glass of wine?" She asked.

"Sure, that'll be fine, thanks." Ryan answered.

"Yes please, make it a large one, red if you have it." Stephanie replied.

Stephanie and Ryan had both placed the bags they were carrying on the floor by one end of the sofa. Nicole came back into the living area and handed each of them their drinks. She returned to the kitchen only to come back with her drink in hand and sat on the opposite end of the couch that Ryan was sat on. She took a sip of her drink and placed it on the coffee table. She pulled her feet up onto the couch so her feet were by her left bum cheek. She looked cute, Ryan thought. She was wearing black leggings and a pale blue wide necked mohair jumper. She placed her hands on her thighs and looked at both of them in turn.

"So is someone gonna tell me what the hell happened today?" Nicole said inquisitively.

"Oh my god I was so scared." Stephanie said.

Ryan went on to tell Nicole the events of the day and how they were chased by the guys in the van. Stephanie interjected here and there to mention Ryan's bravery. When he'd finished telling the story, Nicole sat there processing it for a moment.

"So that's why you were being careful when you got here? Walking up and down the street in case you were followed?" Nicole said, "Are you sure you weren't followed?"

"I think they would have tried something if they had seen us walking up and down out there to be honest." Ryan replied.

"I'm sure we gave them the slip at the tube station." Stephanie added, "If it wasn't for Ryan's quick thinking, making us board the train going in the opposite direction I think they would have caught us. If anything because they didn't see us on the other train, they're probably right off our scent now and searching in the wrong area completely."

Ryan took a swig of his beer and set it on the coffee table. He reached down by his side to grab the bag he'd been carrying.

Stephanie jumped up out of her seat and rushed to the bag.

"Wait a second." Stephanie almost shouted at Ryan.

"What?" Ryan replied, a little startled. "What's up?"

Stephanie made a grab for the bag and grasped one of the handles but Ryan had already a hold of the other and so a tug-of-war ensued.

"Steph, What are you doing?" Nicole quizzed, as she put

her feet on the floor from off the couch as if she was about to jump up and get involved.

"It's my bag." Stephanie spat out at Nicole.

"It's just the drugs, that aren't even yours." Ryan retorted, as he pulled the bag toward him, making Stephanie take another step towards him.

"Let go Ryan." Stephanie exclaimed, sounding a little desperate, "Tell him Nicole."

"What's the problem?" Nicole asked.

"It's just it's mine and I'll take care of it." Stephanie said.

"What are you hiding?" Questioned Ryan, "What's in the bag?"

"Jesus, why you gotta be so nosey?" Stephanie replied.

"I think after everything I've done for you so far I have a right to know what's going on. If it's just the drugs in the bag why are you so protective of it? We just want to help you Steph." Ryan said, in a calm but stern voice.

"Okay, I'm sorry." Stephanie finally conceded, and let go of the handle that she had a firm grip on.

The bag fell to the floor with Ryan still holding the one handle he had a hold of. Nicole moved to sit closer to Ryan and moved his beer to one side on the coffee table so he could place the bag on it.

Stephanie, deflated, slumped onto the couch next to Nicole. Ryan lifted the bag from the floor and placed it on the table in front of them and proceeded to unzip it. On opening it he could see there were no drugs. It was full of clothes, two pairs of shoes, a passport, a mobile phone, a make-up bag, a wash bag and a big wad of money.

"What the hell is this?" Ryan said, turning to Stephanie. "I, I don't understand. Is this the bag you filled at your flat? Are the drugs in that bag?" Pointing to the one over by where Stephanie was sitting.

Ryan was confused, the bag he had been carrying was definitely this one, it still had remnants of dust and cobwebs on it, just as the one that was hidden under the bath had. He stood to go get the other bag but Stephanie stood and put her hands out in front of her to gesture him to stop.

"I'm sorry. I'm sorry." Stephanie said limply, "That's my bolt bag."

Almost in unison both Nicole and Ryan looked at her and said "You're what bag?"

"My bolt bag." Stephanie repeated, she shrugged her shoulders to indicate submission and continued, "When I was with Ollie he told me I should have a bolt bag ready to take flight at a moment's notice, just in case something bad happened. Money, clothes, passport, everything you need in case you have to disappear."

"Hang on a minute." Ryan said, bemused by what he was hearing, "So you put us both in danger for some clothes, shoes, money and a make-up bag?"

"I was scared, I didn't know if I could trust you. What if you were working for them, the bad guys? What if you were just trying to make me think you were helping and all you wanted was for me to lead you to the drugs, then kill me or something?" Stephanie said, in somewhat of a whiney and defensive voice.

"Ughhhh, I can't believe you. After everything I've done

to help you, you still think I'd do that to you? I'm trying to help you for goodness sake. Do you think I want to be mixed up in this? What about Nicole? This could affect her life too." Ryan said, angrily.

"Let's all take a moment to calm down." Nicole finally said, "Stephanie, I get what you're saying but Ryan has done nothing but shown he's a genuine guy. Ryan, can you try and understand that maybe with everything that's happened to Steph, she might not be in the best place to judge things clearly?"

"I know, I'm sorry, I can see that now." Stephanie responded, as tears welled up in her eyes, "I just find it hard to trust people, especially after everything that's happened in my life since I met Ollie.

"Yeah, I get it, I'm sorry too." Ryan added, as he sat back down on the couch next to Nicole, "Question is though Steph, where are the drugs really? All I honestly want to do is deliver them back to those guys and get you, all of us, out of this mess. Without the drugs, they'll just keep looking for us."

"They're in a locker, I picked up the key when we were at my flat. I'd hidden the key in the clock on the wall." Stephanie confessed, "Paddington station, locker number 1033."

"Okay, do you trust me Stephanie?" Ryan asked.

"Yes, I guess I have no choice and Nicole's right, you don't know me and everything you've done you didn't have to. I'm sorry again, that I dragged either of you into my mess and I really, truly, want to thank you both." Replied Stephanie.

Stephanie looked like a little girl who'd been bad once too often to her parents and had finally realised the error of her ways.

"No problem, I understand. Nicole? Is it okay for her to stay here with you tonight?" Ryan said, "I'd feel better if she were here with you."

"Of course, yes, I'd feel happier if she were to stay here too but I do have to go work tomorrow. Steph? You gonna be okay here on your own tomorrow? Just until I get back from work?" Nicole replied.

"Thanks, yes I'll be fine." Stephanie answered Nicole.

Everyone sat back a little in their seats. Each of them sighing in turn. Nicole, sitting closer to Ryan put her hand on his and squeezed it. Ryan turned and looked at her. They smiled sweetly at each other. Nicole mouthed the words "Thank you." Ryan smiled a little wider, he pulled her hand to his mouth and gently planted a kiss on the back of it.

"Guys, get a room why dontcha?" Stephanie exclaimed.

And all three of them burst out laughing, Nicole and Ryan both did so to hide their embarrassment as they each in turn blushed a little.

"Anyone for another drink?" Nicole said, to break the awkward moment.

"I'm good, besides I ought to go get the rental van back then pick up those drugs." Ryan responded, thankful to having the moment broken by Nicole's question.

"Let me finish this one first girl." Stephanie said, with a smile still on her face, as she picked her glass up and downed the rest of the wine in one. "Okay, I'm ready for a top up."

"Geeze Louise." Nicole said, as she stood to go and get the bottle from the kitchen.

Ryan picked up his beer and took another sip of it. He was tired but felt he should go get these two things done and out of the way in the cover of darkness. He looked at his watch, almost ten thirty. He checked his pocket to make sure he hadn't lost the keys to the hired van, with all the running around and the chase he could easily have lost them, they were there and he let out a sigh of relief. Stephanie had kicked off her shoes and had put her feet up, almost sitting on them, much the same position as Nicole had adopted earlier. Nicole came back with the bottle of wine and topped up her and Stephanie's glasses, then sat back down between her two guests. Without making a big scene of it, she gently rested her hand on Ryan's thigh. Ryan however not expecting it almost jumped out of his chair. Which made Nicole recoil her arm and Stephanie burst out laughing.

"Sorry." Ryan said, flustered and he reached for Nicole's hand and placed it back on his thigh.

Nicole looked at him bashfully and smiled a soft smile. He took another swig of his beer which finished the contents of the glass. He set his glass back down on the table and placed his hand on hers. Nicole moved a little closer to him and put her head on his shoulder.

"Thank you." She almost whispered in Ryan's ear.

"Is it okay if I take a shower?" Stephanie interrupted, as she stood as though she assumed the answer would be a positive one.

"Yes of course. You know where it is right?" Nicole immediately answered, "There's fresh towels in the closet just outside the bathroom, help yourself."

"Thanks, yeah I remember." Stephanie replied, "I'll leave you two to have a moment to yourselves." and headed for the bathroom with a mischievous grin on her face.

"I didn't mean to make you uncomfortable." Nicole said, once Stephanie was out of the room. "I know this all started because you liked the look of her. Oh and I'm sorry, if you want to try and get to know her, I'll back right off and let you go for it."

"Oh my god no. I mean, no, not at all. What I mean is…" Ryan blustered, "What I mean is, I'm sure she's nice when you get to know her and everything but to be honest I really like you. You just took me a back a little with the hand on the thigh thing. It's been a while you see. I guess I'm just not used to someone being intimate with me. I'm sorry if I caused you any embarrassment or made you think I didn't like it."

"You are by far the sweetest, simplest yet most complicated guy I've ever met. You're smart, knowledgeable, caring and honest. Makes me find it hard to believe you're single." Nicole replied, "I guess that makes it pretty clear to you I like you too huh? I like you very much. For whatever reason, fate, life or whatever you want to call it, whatever it was that brought you into my life I'm very grateful."

"Wow, I've never had anyone say anything like that to me before." Ryan responded, feeling humbled, "I think you're wonderful."

Nicole lifted her head from his shoulder and looked up at him. She tilted her head back slightly, just raising her mouth a little towards his. He responded by turning to meet her gaze. He lowered his head and very gently brushed his lips against hers. Their mouths parted and he felt the very tip of her tongue touch his bottom lip. He slowly caressed her tongue with his and put his arms around her pulling her closer into him. She placed her hand on the nape of his neck and pulled him yet closer to her making the kiss deeper. He lowered his hands to the small of her back and squeezed her gently. She let out a gasp, her warm breath flowing over Ryan's mouth and chin. Still they kissed, deeply, slowly, passionately. He lowered his hands again to her bottom, he lifted her and slid her onto his lap. Her knees either side of his thighs. They held each other closer, she was sat on his lap now looking down at him still both in the kiss. He gently stroked her lower back just above her bottom. She was slowly and gently stroking the back of his neck. He removed his hands from her bottom and placed his hands so tenderly on the cheeks of her face and just held them there. He wanted to feel her beauty in his hands as well as kiss her deeply. He wanted her so badly now. Passion burned in the pit of his stomach. He hadn't felt like this for anyone for so long, correction, he realised he hadn't felt like this about anyone before, ever. Nicole was feeling the passion rising in herself too. She felt herself moving involuntarily on Ryan's lap. Slowly gyrating her hips and pushing down on him. She had been in relationships, even loving and quite passionate ones before but this felt different to her too. She could feel her breathing altering, her pulse increasing, a tingle shot up and down her spine. Her breath started coming in gasps as she moved with more purpose. She knew Ryan was excited, she could feel it. Ryan was a mess. His pulse all over the place, his breath also coming in ragged gasps, he felt hot, tiredness left him as this new energy flowed from within his very soul. He moved his hands from Nicole's face and placed them ever so gently on her breasts. He had an involuntary spasm caused by the excitement. He gently cupped them. They felt so good to him. Full and firm. He wanted to do so much in that instant and if not for Stephanie starting to sing, "LIKE A VIRGIN....TOUCHED FOR THE

VERY FIRST TIME..", terribly out of tune and at the top of her voice breaking the moment, he thought he would have. They were both snapped back into the room out of the almost trance like state they had gotten into and stopped kissing.

"Wow Ryan. Steph is right. There is so much more to you. You're a mild mannered Clarke Kent in everyday situations them BAM. You're Superman. Oh my god I'm talking too much right? I'll shut up, I just can't help myself. That was incredible. Oh my god. Sorry, Sorry I said I'd shut up and now I can't stop going on and on and on." Nicole blurted out.

"Wow, I've never felt like that before." Ryan admitted, "I think you're amazing, am I dreaming?"

"Really? It's not just me then that feels this is something very unique and special?" Added Nicole.

"What is?" Stephanie said, as she entered the room again with a towel wrapped round her head and sporting a white flannelling robe.

It startled both Ryan and Nicole, they thought they were still alone, totally distracted by each other.

"Oh, the situation, I was errr, just saying this is a very unique situation we're all in." Nicole said quickly, thinking on her feet, "I mean it's like something out of the movies or something, you wouldn't think this really happens in real life."

"I guess not." Stephanie replied, "They do say life can be stranger than fiction."

Nicole had slid off of Ryan's lap and was sitting next to him now. Ryan put his hand on Nicole's thigh and tapped it gently before getting up from his seat. He turned to

Nicole.

"Right, I should really make a move." Ryan said, leaning towards Nicole. "I'll text you, let you know I've done everything and I'm back at home, okay?"

He pecked her on the cheek and stood up straight.

"You have that key you mentioned? For the locker?" Ryan asked Stephanie.

"Oh yeah, one tick." Replied Stephanie, as she reached for the bag that she had been carrying.

She retrieved the key from a side pocket in the bag and handed it to Ryan.

"Go careful won't you?" Stephanie said, with genuine concern in her voice.

Nicole had stood and was standing behind Ryan with her hand on the small of his back.

"Yes, do go careful, please. Let me know you get home and you're safe. I'll be worrying about you." Nicole added.

Ryan took a step towards the door, Stephanie grabbed him and threw her arms around him. Ryan was a little surprised and looked at Nicole with a "Help me." look on his face. Stephanie had buried her face in his chest.

"Thank you, I mean it, thank you and sorry I was a bit of a jerk before." Stephanie said, a little over dramatically.

She let go of him and stepped back with a big grin on her face.

"I just wanted to see if you jumped at another woman giving you a hug." Added Stephanie and chuckled.

"Yeah very funny." Ryan retorted, as he smiled at her, "I'll message you Nicole." And with that he headed for the front door and left.

"Now which order to do this?" Ryan thought to himself, as he walked down the few steps back onto the street outside Nicole's flat.

Chapter Twelve.

"Van first I think, I don't want to be traipsing about London with a bag full of drugs. Get the van, drive to Paddington, park nearby, grab the drugs, back to the van and head for home. Sounds easy." Ryan thought to himself, as he walked toward the corner of Nicole's street and the main road that crossed at the end of it.

It was another cold night. Ryan walked briskly, not just because he wanted to get this done but to try and warm himself. He soon reached the end of the road and turned left onto the main street. Even though it was late it was still bustling with people, cars and more importantly taxis. It wasn't long before Ryan was safely in a cab on the way to Stephanie's place and the location of the abandoned rental van. He was hoping, to any god that was listening, that the drug dealers, suppliers, hired muscle men, or whatever they were, weren't still watching the place. If only he'd thought to disguise himself somehow, he thought, as the taxi took him closer to his destination.

"Hey mate?" Ryan shouted at the glass panel between him and the driver.

"Yeah guv?" Replied the gruff voice of the taxi driver, as he reached back and slid the little glass opening a little wider, "What's up mate?"

"It's bloody cold out there tonight ain' it?" Ryan said, cockneying up his accent as best as possible. "Brass Monkeys an' all that?"

"Yeah it is mate." Replied a befuddled driver, wondering what the hell this guy was barking on about.

"I could do with a nice warm 'at." Ryan continued, "Like the one you're wearin'. Ow much fer yer 'at? I'll give ya a tenner for it."

"Twenty and it's yours mate, oh and do me a favour and drop the crappy accent, that wouldn't fool a Japanese tourist mate." Said the cabbie and he chuckled to himself. He removed his black woollen hat and passed it back through the little glass window to a red faced Ryan in the back holding out a crisp twenty pound note.

The rest of the journey Ryan sat in silence, arms folded across his chest but sporting a black woolly hat that could serve at least as a partial disguise. When he gets out of the cab he'll pull it down further so it sits just above his eyes. With the collars of his jacket pulled up he'd be hard to spot for the guy seen earlier. At least that's what he was hoping.

His thoughts turned to Nicole and what happened just a short while ago at her flat. Even though they hadn't known each other long or knew that much about each other he was really taken with her now. He leant his forehead against the window but stared at nothing. He was completely lost to his imagination. Images of Nicole appeared in his mind's eye, her smiling, her coming back from the kitchen area with a beer for him, her sat on his lap and looking down at him, deep into his eyes, he felt she'd seen his very soul. The outside passed by a blur, he'd forgotten all about the events of the last week or so. The death of Ollie didn't even enter his head. Nothing was affecting where his mind was right at that moment. His eyes focussed on nothing through the window. Flashing amber lights, red lights getting brighter as cars broke in the lane next to his. The darkness of the night, the bright white light of headlamps of cars coming the other direction, all of it faded into one blurry abstract that he paid no attention to. The cab pulled up outside Stephanie's place and Ryan held out the cab fare which the driver took with a flash of his hand through the small window, like a

Moray eel darting out of its hidey hole to grab an unsuspecting passing fish.

"Keep the change." Ryan said, in his normal accent, snapping back to the reality of the moment.

"Thanks guv, stay warm." Replied the taxi driver.

"Cheers." Ryan replied as he stepped out of the cab into the street.

He pushed the cab door shut and reached into his jacket pocket for the keys to the van. The van was only parked a few feet away from where the cab had let him out. He took the keys out of his pocket ready to unlock the van and get in. Just as he was about to put the key in the door lock he heard a shout. He turned and looked behind him, looking for the source of the shout. Forty yards behind him on the opposite side of the street was the black van. The passenger side door open and one of the large men of the three who had chased them earlier was in the road running towards him. He fumbled to get the key in the lock of the door. The headlights of the van had turned on. Another occupant of the van had reached over and pulled the door closed. The large man, Sean, was still running toward him in the middle of the road. Luckily he was not the fastest of pursuers. Ryan looked down at the lock that he was still struggling to get the key into.

"Duh." Ryan let out in anguish at how stupid he was being.

He clicked the "unlock" button on the remote key fob and saw the door lock ping up on the driver's side door. He yanked the van door open and jumped in, he slammed the key into the ignition and started the engine. He stuck the gear stick into reverse and pushed down on the accelerator. He looked in the passenger side wing mirror and saw Sean running still but was a good twenty yards or so away. Ryan reversed the van back far enough to be able to drive forward around the parked car that was in front of him. He grabbed the gear stick, slammed his foot down on the clutch and shoved the gear lever in to first gear. Lifted his foot off the clutch pedal and stamped on the accelerator. The van lurched forward just as he heard the Sean bang on the back of the van. He was soon moving into second gear accelerating up the road. He checked the driver's side wing mirror and saw the large man had stopped running and was leaning forward, hands on his knees obviously trying to catch his breath from the little exertion he'd just undergone. The black van pulled up behind him and the passenger door flew open. Sean turned and jumped into the cab of the black van. By this time, Ryan had reached the end of the road, he'd slammed on the brakes as he approached the junction and with a quick look left and right, floored it again and shot round the corner to the left. He needed to lose these guys.

"How the fucking hell did they know I'd be back here?" Ryan shouted to the roof of the van, "I've gotta focus, I'm an idiot, if I'd had my mind together I'd have seen them and I could've had the cabbie drive on instead of stopping. Ughhhh Idiot."

Ryan accelerated, he wasn't sure about this area and needed to get his bearings, checking for street signs for anything he was familiar with. He looked again in the wing mirror and saw the black van turning from Stephanie's road to give chase. His rental van was newer than the beaten up old black van his predators were driving and the driver of the black van had the additional weight of the two passengers. Ryan hoped this would give him an advantage, it would in a straight road race but the streets of London, other cars, traffic lights, pedestrians and no real knowledge of the area hampered any escape he hoped to make. He'd have to keep his wits about him and get to somewhere he knew well. He had to shake them. He had to get away. He had the key to the locker housing the drugs on him. They'd probably kill him and take the key. It wouldn't be too hard to work out what the key belonged to. Or worse, they'd torture him first for the location of the drugs and then kill him. A few hundred yards ahead Ryan saw something that pleased him greatly. A Road sign. Cricklewood, straight ahead, and the sign showed the A5. He knew roughly where Cricklewood was and that the A5 would take him straight into the centre of London. It was late and the traffic had thinned. He pushed the pedal further and sped up as he drove toward the crossroads and the A5. He was getting closer and could see the traffic lights ahead at the junction, at the moment they were red, he prayed they would change just as he reached them. He checked the wing mirror again, the van was quite a way behind him. If he could make it to the junction and was lucky with the lights, he could well lose them at this junction. His mind was racing now, thinking several steps ahead like a game of chess. If he could make it on to the A5 and leave them at the lights, he could take several turns off the main road and lose them in the smaller streets. With any luck they'd sail past him thinking he was heading for central London as fast as he could. He could then double back and head for Paddington another way. Up ahead about another hundred yards he saw the lights change to green.

"No, no, no, not yet." He said, and pushed the accelerator even further to the floor, "Shit, gotta be careful, if a cop sees me and pulls me over I dread to think what these guys would do. Would they go as far as to kill cops to get to me and their drugs?"

Even though the lights were green Ryan eased off the pedal slightly and the van decreased speed. He checked the dial, he was still doing sixty miles an hour. He reached the lights as they turned amber. He booted it and took the turn anyway with the light turning red just as he went through. He straightened up the van and headed down the A5 towards the centre of the city. The black van would have to stop at the lights, Ryan dropped his shoulders a little and slowed his speed to stick to the speed limit. In the mirror he saw the other lights had turned green and the traffic that was waiting, started pulling away from the line. This was good, it meant he'd have a few cars between him and his assailants. He did think about his plan of turning off the main road into a side street, but as of yet he hadn't seen one that didn't look like a dead end. Nor did he want to risk the black van's occupants seeing him make the turn if he timed it wrong. He heard a few cars honking on their horns and checked the mirror again. A few hundred yards behind him, back at the junction with the lights he saw the black van come skidding around the corner. They obviously jumped the red light not caring about breaking the law, or the other road users they'd caused to slam on their brakes to avoid smashing into the van. There was about six or seven vehicles and approximately three hundred yards between Ryan and the black van. Ryan looked ahead and seeing the next car in front of him was a good quarter of a mile away, he put his foot down and sped up again. He increased the distance between him and his followers. He could see in the mirror the black van was swerving behind the other vehicles, looking for a chance to overtake them in order to close the gap between them and Ryan. Luckily there was traffic on the other side of the road preventing their manoeuvre. Ryan had caught up to the car ahead of him and it caused him to have to slow down. The car up ahead put his right indicator on, slowed then took the turn. This made Ryan have to brake hard and narrowly missed hitting the rear quarter of the car as it turned. Once clear he dropped a gear and again accelerated, pulling away from the vehicles that were already quite away behind him and his pursuers. For the moment, there was no other vehicles he could see ahead of him, he increased his speed to what he thought wouldn't bring him any unwanted attention from the police if they saw him. He continued scanning the roads for police cars as well as checking the mirrors to see if the van had made any progress on reducing the gap between them. The A5 turned from being named Maida vale road into Edgware road and he knew he was getting closer to the centre of London. He'd have to be careful now, which way to go? If he got on to Marylebone road, it would give him the chance to go faster and hopefully lose his trackers, but it had multiple lanes, that might give them a chance to catch up to him. He had already witnessed they didn't give two hoots about the law. He had to risk it. As he came down to the junction the lights turned red. Several cars that were waiting at what were the red lights to his right started to pull away across the junction to get onto Marylebone road. He checked his mirrors. The vehicles that were some distance behind him were getting closer. He wasn't sure, but he thought he caught a glimpse of the black van and it seemed like there were fewer cars between them and him now. Ryan checked the junction, there were going to be a few sets of lights that had to change before his would turn green again. Taking note from seeing the black van doing the same Ryan saw a gap in the traffic crossing the junction and floored it. He jumped the red light, a car coming from his right that he hadn't noticed, slammed on its brakes and beeped his horn long and hard at Ryan, as it had to slide over into the other lane to avoid colliding with Ryan's van.

"Fuck. Sorry." Ryan said, knowing the other driver wouldn't hear him anyway, as he made an apologetic motion with his right hand.

His adrenalin was coursing through his body now, as if it wasn't enough to be being chased by killers he was just in a near smash. He accelerated away onto Marylebone road and changed up through the gears rapidly. Hopefully even if the black van wanted to jump the lights, there would still be other cars in their way blocking them from being able to do so. He checked his mirrors again, still no sign and the other traffic had started to flow through the lights that were now green. More traffic behind him, more obstacles for his chasers to get around. There were more cars on this road of course, London never slept, people always going somewhere no matter what the time, day or night. Ryan eased off driving so fast and erratically to meld in with the other traffic. This was London, there were white vans everywhere even at this time of night. Unless they got close it would, in itself make it difficult for them to know which white van was his. He passed Madame Tussauds and continued to follow the road. Matching the speed of the other cars around him now. Several minutes had gone by and the lights must have changed, enabling the black van and its occupants to turn onto the street and continue the chase. Ryan had made good progress though and felt fairly certain they'd struggle to spot him now let alone catch him. He continued to follow the main road through the city. He passed King's cross and St Pancras street stations and headed for Shoreditch passing through the area of Pentonville. He kept checking his mirrors but still had seen no sign of the black van. Maybe they thought he had turned off onto another street and they had actually given up the chase. He relaxed a little and breathed a sigh of relief. Even though it wouldn't have been possible, it felt to Ryan like he'd been holding his breath since he first got in the van. Ryan turned left at Old Street station round-about and headed for Whitechapel. He had caught up with some traffic now and his pace had slowed. Traffic lights also slowed him. He felt pretty confident now that he'd done enough to lose his tail. As he sat at the junction of Commercial Street and Whitechapel high street waiting for the lights to turn green he checked his mirrors again.

"No bloody way." Ryan exclaimed, seeing the black van

only five cars behind him, "How is that even possible."

His heart started racing again, he checked again, maybe it was another black van. Just then the passenger side door opened, he was sure it was them. The lights changed though and Ryan shot forward. Looking in his wing mirror, he saw the door of the black van close again as they pulled away from the lights.

"Come on." Shouted Ryan, to no one, "That's not possible." Then a flood of thoughts entered his mind. "Could they have put a tracker on the van or something? No that's not plausible, how would they even know this was his hired van?"

The thoughts coming thick and fast as he tried to reason out how they could possibly have known which way he went. Sheer luck? No that didn't stand to reason either. He couldn't understand it. He shook his head trying to clear it so he could focus on his escape. He sped down Leman Street and turned right on to Prescot street. Several of the cars between him and his stalkers had turned off leaving only two cars blocking them now, they were closing the gap. He turned left and headed for the Tower of London. In front of him was a pedestrian crossing with people stood at the side of the road waiting for the lights to change to halt the traffic in order for them to cross. He pushed the pedal to the floor as the lights changed amber and zipped across the crossing just before they turned red. He'd gotten a break. The cars behind him and the black van were forced to stop as the people crossed the road. Ryan headed for Tower Bridge. As he pulled onto the bridge he could see it was fairly clear of traffic, another couple of vehicles had turned onto the same road and were now behind him. He accelerated along the road heading for the bridge. As he was about to pass under the first tower he saw the traffic light change from green to amber. He couldn't believe his luck. The bridge was about to open. He looked to his left and could see a fairly tall ship, the old fashioned kind with masts and sails heading slowly towards the bridge. It was too tall to fit under the bridge when it was down but with the bridge lifted it would fit easily under the higher part of it. Ryan burst out laughing with relief.

"Thank you God, or whoever." Ryan said to the ceiling of the van.

The car directly behind him had come to a stop, not wanting to risk being caught on the bridge as it opened. Ryan was laughing with relief all the way across the bridge, as he passed the middle section and under the second tower. All the cars on the other side of the road coming towards him had also stopped at the light on the other side of the bridge, confirming the lights were definitely red now. His pursuers in the black van had no chance of following him now. They would have no idea which direction he would go, so even if they drove along the embankment to the closest bridge they'd have completely lost him. Ryan stayed on Tower Bridge road and headed for elephant and castle, then on to Waterloo station and crossed over Westminster Bridge.

"What a night." Ryan thought to himself. "Still got to pick up the drugs yet from Paddington."

He now felt calmer though, he had most definitely lost them now and they had no idea where he was heading. It wasn't long before he pulled up in a side street not far from Paddington station, he was lucky and had found a road that had parking meters with a few empty spaces. Given the time of night he didn't need to put money in the meter and exited the van and headed to the station on foot. He pulled the black woollen hat down a little, it was a cold night. He turned the collars up on his jacket and thrust his hands in to his jacket pockets and headed for the station entrance. From his inside jacket pocket he felt his mobile phone vibrate. He pulled it from the pocket and looked at the screen. It was Nicole. He swiped a finger across the screen to answer it.

"Hello babe." Said Ryan, then wondered if that was too soon to call her that but it just felt natural to do so. "Sorry I haven't called or messaged you yet."

"That's okay, I was getting worried, you left ages ago and I thought you might have forgotten or something had happened to you." Nicole replied, sounding concerned yet relieved at the same time.

"Well, yes, they were there, waiting outside Steph's place." Ryan reported, "I have no idea why they were there, why would they think we'd go back there for anything? It just doesn't make any sense."

"Oh my god, you okay?" Came her immediate response, "How did you get away? What happened? Where are you now?"

"Yeah, I'm okay, was a bit touch and go here and there but I got lucky." Ryan responded, hoping to calm her down, "I gave them the slip on Tower Bridge. I'm heading to Paddington now, to pick up the stuff."

"Wow, okay, please be careful. Steph has gone to bed and is sleeping now. I am pretty tired and it's late, so I was gonna hit the sack myself soon but just wanted to check on you, make sure you were ok, I was really quite worried." Nicole said, "I keep thinking about earlier on the couch."

Ryan chuckled, "Me too sweetheart, me too."

"If I hadn't been maybe the whole chase and almost getting caught would've been avoided." Ryan thought to

191

himself but at the same time he wasn't angry. There really was something about this girl he really liked and to hear her say she'd been thinking about him made him smile.

"So, get some sleep. You have work tomorrow, I'll message you when I get home but if you're asleep I hope it doesn't wake you and at least if you wake in the night you'll see it, you won't be wondering." Ryan said calmly.

"Okay, thanks, please do. Speak in the morning." Nicole said softly and hung up the call.

He placed the phone back from where he'd taken it and stuck his hands back into his pockets. He should have felt tired too, but with the rush of the chase and almost getting caught, he felt wide awake and realised he'd probably feel wired for some time yet. He entered the station and looked around. It was almost deserted but for a few staff and the odd sleeping passenger awaiting their next train that was probably not for another hour or two. He looked at the clock on the big board that showed the departure times. 1.35 AM.

"Geeze." Thought Ryan, and a sudden tiredness swamped over him like the crash from a sugar rush, "Wow, so tired now. So much for thinking I'd be on a buzz all night."

He looked around the station at all the signs and eventually caught sight of the one that pointed to the lockers. He squeezed his eyes shut, opened them and headed off in that direction. Before long he was at the lockers, he found the correct one, inserted the key and opened the locker. Inside was a blue sports bag. He reached in and carefully unzipped it. He looked around to make sure no one was watching and took a peek inside. There were lots of drugs, pill packets, polythene bags with what he assumed to be grass, or weed. Red pills, blue pills, yellow pills and under those, small bricks of white powder, wrapped in what looked like clingfilm and then taped up with silver tape.

"Got ya." He said, under his breath.

He zipped the bag back up, took a hold of it by the handles and pulled it from the locker. He closed the door and locked it again. Placing the key in his trouser pocket, he slung the bag over his right shoulder and headed for the exit. Moments later he was back outside and heading for the van. On reaching it he looked around to make sure there was no one around and unlocked the van, threw the bag inside onto the passenger seat and got in. He locked the van doors from inside by pressing a button on the dashboard and lent his head back on the headrest and sighed. He closed his eyes and just took a moment to himself. He put the key in the ignition and started the engine. It was just a short drive home to the safety and security of his flat. Minutes later he arrived at the parking area behind his place. He switched the engine off, pressed the button to unlock the doors and got out of the van. He reached in, grabbed the bag and locked the van using the remote key fob. He entered the building at the rear and was soon back in his flat. He dumped the bag on the floor just as he entered his flat and kicked his shoes off. He was home, he'd made it. He needed a drink though, more than ever that he could remember, he needed a drink. He took his jacket off and hung it on the hook by the front door and walked further into his flat. He poured himself a shot of whiskey and downed it in one. He put the glass in the sink and headed upstairs to his bed. He walked into the bedroom and fell face first on to the bed. It was just after ten AM. When Ryan woke. He was still dressed in the clothes he had on yesterday. He got up off the bed and removed them, then pulled on a robe. He checked his phone. There was a text message from Nicole just hoping he'd had a good night's sleep and stating she'd text or call him during the day. He smiled and sent her a reply saying he hoped she'd slept well and to have a good day at work.

He ambled down to the kitchen and put the kettle on, made himself a tea and took it into the lounge. He looked over to the front door and the bag containing the drugs. He figured the best place to hide it would be with his laptop and other hacking equipment. He sat down on the couch and turned the T.V. on with the remote. It was on the news channel. More doom and gloom. Flooding in South East Asia, another flight had gone missing, storms in the Gulf of Mexico, and the FSTE index down to an all-time low. The stories were endless. An outbreak of the Zika virus in South Florida, the NASDAQ and NYSE both showing losses and financial experts reporting this is going to be a trend for a while. There was also a report of an upcoming trip by some American official. There were to be discussions surrounding the exchange of technologies used in the military between America and Britain. He flicked through several channels and eventually turned the T.V off. He finished his tea and went and showered. After his shower and a shave he dressed in fresh clothes. He went back downstairs, grabbed the bag containing the drugs and stowed it with his hacking kit. Just then his mobile rang, it was on silent but he could hear it buzzing as it vibrated on the coffee table where he'd left it.

"Hey Ryan, how are you? It's Justin." Came the voice of Justin through the earpiece.

"Hey Justin, yeah not bad thanks, how's you?" Ryan replied.

"My mate's band is playing a new place this weekend coming, the Saturday night if you're up for getting out for a few drinks again mate." Explained Justin.

"Hey that's cool to hear, I'll have to let you know though to be honest mate, it has been a crazy couple of weeks since I saw you." Ryan replied, "I met a girl, long story but

I think we might be doing something this weekend. I'll check with her and let you know mate for sure. It was good seeing you the other week."

"Ohhh cool mate, yeah no worries. Well you could bring her along. No pressure, was good to see you too. Let me know, just call or text any time mate." Justin said in return. "Ciao for now dude."

"See ya, thanks, speak soon. Bye." Ryan said and hung up the call.

As soon as he'd hung up the call and was about to put the phone back down on the coffee table it buzzed in his hand. It was Nicole.

"Hey honey." Ryan said in to the phone, "How's your morning going?"

"Hey handsome." Nicole said and chuckled a little, "Yeah not too bad thanks sweetheart. How's you? Did you sleep okay?"

"Yeah, I didn't think I would but I certainly did, guess it was coming down from the adrenaline rush." Ryan explained, "I actually fell asleep in my clothes, that's how tired I was."

"Awww, bless you my sweet. I'm not surprised to be honest, everything you've been through recently." Nicole said, in her soft, genuine voice. "Maybe you should take this opportunity to get some rest."

"You're probably right, I thought I might chase that company up I had an interview for, I've not heard anything back from them as of yet." Ryan went on to say. "Companies these days, it's like no one's lives matter, I could be desperate for money for all they know."

"I hear you, maybe you should give it until early next week though, you don't want to come across like you need them right? If they want you it might give you a better stand on demanding more money if that makes sense." Nicole said wisely, "Besides one way or another if you chase them it won't necessarily speed them up to a decision eh?"

"I guess you're right, on all points, thanks." Ryan conceded, "Well I ought to get out and at least do a bit of shopping today, cupboards are looking a bit bare."

It felt so nice to have someone to run things by, share his thoughts and get an unbiased opinion Ryan thought to himself. He had missed that, with his best friend being away and not having had a relationship for some time you get used to depending on yourself. It's hard sometimes to be subjective when giving yourself advice.

"Okay my sweet, go careful, those guys could still be looking for you remember, even if you are just carrying groceries." Nicole exclaimed.

"I hear you baby, I'll let you get back to work, text or call any time you wish. It'll break my day up." Ryan chuckled, trying to make light of it.

They said their goodbyes and dropped the call.

Ryan went to the kitchen, opened the fridge, freezer, a few kitchen cabinets and made himself a short list of things he needed. He would just go to a local store, nothing on his list was that extravagant. Nothing on it the local Tesco Metro shouldn't have readily available. He'd be in and out in no time. He put his shoes on, grabbed his keys, wallet and the list and left the flat. The shopping excursion was done and he was back home within a couple of hours. There had been no sign of the black van and it felt like a normal trip out, no incidents and nothing out of the ordinary. He put the shopping away, made himself a drink and did a little tidying up of his flat. He was really just passing the time. He was sat at the kitchen table and started wondering how he was going to make contact with the owners of the drugs. How could he go about returning their stuff and get out of this without any reprisals for Stephanie or himself? What could he do to guarantee their safety? He didn't want to live a life looking over his shoulder. A plan started to formulate in his mind. He retrieved his every day laptop from his bedroom and powered it up on the kitchen table. He started the internet browser and went to Google. After a bit of searching online, his plan was coming together. He had an idea. Ryan just hoped it would work.

Chapter Thirteen.

Time had flown past and it was already almost six PM. Ryan's phone that was beside his laptop on the table, started buzzing. It was Nicole.

"Hey, I didn't realise the time. How was your day?" He asked, as he answered the call.

"She's gone Ryan." Nicole's frantic voice came over the phone, "She's gone, Stephanie's gone."

"What? How do you mean gone? Did she leave a note? Any sign of a break-in?" Quizzed Ryan, "Have you heard from her at all today?"

"No, I've not heard from her, no sign of a break-in or a struggle, and I haven't seen a note." Nicole replied rapidly, "I'll look around my place see if she did leave a note but I would've thought if she had it would have been in an obvious place."

"Okay, do that. What about her so called bolt bag?" Ryan asked, "Maybe she's decided to skip town."

"Ahh good thinking I'll go check the spare room." Nicole said, her voice sounding a little calmer, "No sign of a note in the kitchen, nothing on the table, work tops or stuck on the fridge."

"What's she playing at?" Ryan said, a little annoyed she'd be stupid enough as to just go out, but where would she have gone? "I don't get it. If somehow those men had found her at your place we'd have heard from them making demands about the drugs. Maybe she just wanted to get out for a bit."

"I don't know, do you think maybe there's more stuff that she didn't tell us about?" Nicole quizzed in return, "Those guys seem terribly persistent for one bag of stuff?"

"But you should see the contents of that one bag, there's a ton of stuff in there, goodness knows what the street value of it is, I'm guessing quite considerable." Ryan replied, "You could be right though I guess, who knows what she hasn't told us."

"Okay I'm in the spare room, her bag is still here." Nicole said, sounding a little surprised.

"Is the money and phone that was in it still in there?" Ryan asked.

"No, well the phone has gone and some of the money by the looks of it. I mean the money was wrapped in a plastic bag and that has been opened." Nicole's reply came, "But there is still a quite a thick pile of notes in the bag, I'm guessing she hasn't done a runner or she'd have taken the whole bag, right?"

"I agree." Ryan said, then was silent, pondering what Stephanie could be up to and why, if she was okay, hadn't she contacted Nicole; she had a phone now,

"She could be anywhere, I can only imagine she might have just wanted to get out. You have to remember she was tied up, confined and since we found her she's been virtually locked up at mine, or your place since."

"You could be right but why hasn't she called or texted?" Nicole argued, "It makes no sense."

"Who knows, maybe she thinks we'd be angry and have a go at her. Alright, you stay there by your phone in case she either calls you or comes back." Ryan suggested, "I'll go take a look for her, I contacted the rental company for the van earlier and extended the length of time I have it for."

"Okay Ryan, go careful, if I hear from her I'll let you know. Keep in touch." Nicole responded, then hung up.

His plan would have to wait for now. "What is Stephanie thinking, what is she up to? She is not making this any easier." He thought to himself as he grabbed his keys and headed for the front door. He left the flat, got in the van and was soon leaving the parking area and heading towards Nicole's place. They had no idea how long Stephanie had been gone, if it was five minutes before Nicole got home she could still be local to Nicole's place. It could account for why she hadn't left a note or been in touch, maybe she was just popping out to feel a bit of freedom, figured she wouldn't be long so didn't need to worry them. The drive to the area around Nicole's place was an easy one and didn't take that long, it made sense to Ryan to start there and extend his search further afield. He drove slowly around the streets keeping an eye out for Stephanie. On some of the roads, which had shops on, he drove up and down twice. After about thirty minutes of doing this, he had covered quite a bit of the surrounding area and decided she wasn't here. There were only two other places that Ryan knew of that she could possibly have gone to. Her place, or Ollie's. He decided, as dangerous as it was, he'd have to go see if she'd gone home again. He was hoping the guys in the black van would think no one would return there now, so hopefully that would work in his favour. Besides, he was in the van and had his head on straight this time. He could be careful and scope out the street before parking and getting out of the van. He drove to Stephanie's flat and in no time at all, was at the corner of her road. He pulled up on to the side of the road and texted Nicole.

"Have you heard from her? I searched around near you but no sign. I've come to her place. Only other place I think she'd come to. X"

Within a few seconds his phone buzzed to indicate he'd received a text back. He opened the message.

"No. Nothing. Be careful. I hate that you're there on your own doing this. N x"

Ryan looked up the street, from where he was sat, he had a pretty good view of most of it. The only vehicles parked up were all cars, no big vans and certainly no sign of his chasers. He turned into the road and drove slowly along it. His eyes darting from left to right, half expecting, if not to see the van, then one or two of the men that had been in it. There was no sign of any of them. He looked over to Stephanie's place as he passed it but couldn't see any lights on. He drove to the end of the road and circled back around just double checking there really was no sign of the criminals. He parked up right outside Stephanie's flat and exited the van. He looked up and down the street again before hopping up the few steps to the front of the building. He pushed the buzzer for Stephanie's flat. Nothing. He pressed the buzzer for Michael and Roger's flat upstairs. After a short exchange over the intercom with Roger explaining that Stephanie had sent him over to get a few things but had neglected to give him the main entrance door key, Roger buzzed him in. He entered the hall and walked towards Stephanie's front door. As he approached he could see the door was slightly ajar. This didn't bode well. It was at this point, he wished he'd thought to bring a weapon of some kind, even if it was a baseball bat, tyre iron or crow bar, something at least. He approached the gap in the door. There was no light on, from what he could see. He listened and heard nothing. He slowly pushed the door open, just a bit and it creaked a little. He froze on the spot. Nothing stirred from within and he opened it a little further. He leant his head in through the opening. The room was in darkness, but coming from under the door at the far end of the room, was a light. Someone was there. He entered the room cautiously, he was now standing in the living room, watching the door at the other end intently. He approached it slowly and quietly. Seconds later he was at the door and he tilted his head so his ear was almost pressed up against it. He listened. He could hear muffled sounds like someone was looking for something. Things beings moved. Then he heard Stephanie's voice.

"Where the fuck is it?" She said, sounding exasperated.

"Steph?" Ryan called out.

"Jesus." He heard her cry out, "You scared the shit out of me."

He opened the door into the kitchen. She was in the middle of the room on the floor. She'd pulled all the plinths off from the bottom of the cabinets and was looking underneath them for something.

"Steph? What the hell are you doing?" Ryan said, angrily looking down at her on the floor, "What are you looking for that is so important or so secretive that you couldn't tell Nicole or me?"

"I'm sorry, I couldn't." Stephanie replied, all defensively as she thrust her arm under another cabinet.

"What if those guys were here waiting for you to show up?" Ryan continued his tirade of questions, "They were here yesterday. They nearly caught me. I only just managed to get away by sheer luck."

"YEAH." Came a raspy, angry voice from behind him.

Ryan span, he'd been so angry with Stephanie and so intent on getting answers from her he hadn't heard the three men from the black van sneak in and they were now stood right behind him.

"You were extremely lucky." Said the thin man of the three, "Looks like you're luck has run out though mate."

Ryan looked around in the kitchen there was nothing close enough for him to grab to put up a fight. His eyes came back to Gerry. Now close up he could see the shifty, dark little eyes of the man above his high, pronounced cheek bones, the man's thin lips were closed tight. Gerry's skin was pock marked and scarred from acne. He had a thin black moustache, he really did look like a stereo-typical criminal if there were such a thing. Ryan wondered why they hadn't jumped him from behind or bashed him over the head. It was then that he looked down. Gerry was holding a gun in his right hand pointed directly at Ryan's chest.

"Don't do anything stupid mate." Said Gerry, "Back away, stand over there in the corner, we're gonna have a little chat with your girlfriend here."

He waved the gun, gesturing for Ryan to move away towards the far corner of the room.

"Turn around shithead. Face the wall." Said Gerry to Ryan.

Ryan had no choice. Millions of thoughts ravaged his mind. There was nothing he could do this time to get him and Stephanie out of this. He turned and faced the wall. He closed his eyes waiting for the clap of thunder as the gun went off, then the immediate darkness would follow and it would all be over. Ryan's thoughts turned to his parents, his sister, Matt and Nicole. He'd never see them again. Never know how things would have been with Nicole. He'd just be a headline of a news story in tomorrow's papers, probably not even a front page story. Then a memory for those who loved him.

"Tie him up." Came Gerry's voice.

One of the two large men, Sean, stepped around Stephanie and was now stood behind Ryan.

"Put ya hands behind your back." Barked the large, tattooed man, "I fucking hate running, you made me run you bastard."

Ryan was confused, why would they tie him up if they were just going to shoot him. He obeyed the command and placed his hands behind his back, crossing his wrists over one another. A glimmer of hope entered his mind. Maybe they had other plans for him. Perhaps he shouldn't get too optimistic and this was possibly only delaying the inevitable, for the moment though it didn't seem like he was going to be shot.

"Where is it then you bitch?"

Ryan heard Gerry question Stephanie.

"I don't know, that's why I'm here looking for it." Stephanie lied.

"Don't lie to me you stupid little girl." He said.

Ryan heard the sound of a slap and Stephanie cried out in pain.

"I don't know honest. I don't, I'd tell you if I did, I swear." Stephanie said, sobbing loudly now.

"She doesn't know." Ryan said, without thinking, "I do though. You told us we had three days to return your stuff and no harm would come to us."

"You've had your three days you shit bag." Gerry spat at Ryan.

"No, no we haven't. You've been chasing us around threatening us. Acting like you're gonna kill us." Ryan was talking rapidly now. Even though he figured he couldn't reason with these people he had to try, the more he spoke the more there was a chance they would live.

"You promise no harm will come to either of us or anyone we care about and I'll get you your stuff." Ryan continued.

"You think you're in a position to make demands you fucking twat?" Replied Gerry, "Who's holding the gun you stupid bastard?"

"Look, I'm not making demands, but the way I see it is this. Your boss, bosses or whoever you are answerable to, have sent you to retrieve the drugs right? So far you haven't done that. Your boss can't be too pleased with you right now yeah?" Ryan went on, not really knowing how his speech was going to end but he'd continue winging it, "I know where the stuff is, I will give it to you, it's all we've wanted to do since that night you shot Oliver. We don't want to be involved. It was just a string of unfortunate events that dragged us into this in the first place. We don't want any trouble, we won't go to the police or anything. You get the stuff back to give to whoever and we go back to getting on with our lives. Neither of us having anything to do with each other ever again. You can see that makes sense right?"

"He's got a point mate." Sean said.

"You think you're in charge now do you?" Gerry almost shouted at him in response.

"No, no, but he's got a point is all I'm saying." Sean replied, sounding submissive.

"Come on." Ryan continued, "What ya gonna have if you kill us both? Two dead bodies and nothing to go back to your boss with."

"We could beat it out of you as to where you've hidden the stash." Grinned Gerry.

"What if I don't tell you before you accidently kill me?" Replied Ryan, who didn't like the way this was going.

"I could torture the girl until you tell us." Gerry retorted.

"I hardly know her, I was just helping a friend out, she means nothing to me." Ryan parried, hoping the thin man and his cronies wouldn't call his bluff.

"Ryan?" Screamed Stephanie, "Don't let them hurt me."

"They won't, if they really want the stash." Ryan gambled.

"Okay, you win, the stash in exchange for your lives." Said Gerry, sounding like he was losing his patience yet conceded this wasn't going anywhere fast, "Now where is it?"

"I don't have it with me." Ryan replied, "Besides if I did and gave it up now what's to stop you killing us and leaving us here?"

"What's to stop us doing that later?" Replied Gerry.

"I swear to you, neither of us are interested in the stuff, we just want to return it and go back to our lives, we don't want to be looking over our shoulders forever." Ryan continued, "We'll stay out of your way and business goings on and you let us get back to our normal way of life? Do we have a deal?"

"Okay we'll take the girl." Snapped Gerry, "Mack, grab her, she's coming with us."

"No." Stephanie protested, "Ryan, say something, do

something."

The other large man that was stood by the thin man grabbed Stephanie by the arm and hauled her to her feet.

"Come on love, the less you struggle the less it'll hurt." The second large man called Mack said.

"Don't hurt her." Ryan said, "We have a deal."

"I'll leave you a number to call. What's your name? Ryan?" Said Gerry, sounding nastier than ever, "When you have the stuff you call me on that number and we'll set up a meet to do the exchange, the stash for the girl."

He searched around the kitchen and found a scrap of paper and a pen in one of the drawers and proceeded to write a number down on it.

"Now, you think about doing anything stupid like involving the cops we'll know. We'll slit her throat and dump her in the river." He said, in a most chilling voice, "You got that? Then we'll come looking for you and anyone you care about, got it?"

"I got it, just don't hurt her, we all stick to our words and we'll all be better off, agreed?" Ryan asked, trying, though it probably didn't mean anything, to get this lunatic to stick to the deal. He hoped the thin man would at least be an honest criminal, or at least have some honour in him.

"I already said it didn't I?" Gerry replied sharply, "You trying to piss me off?"

"No, just making sure we understand each other and we stick to the deal." Ryan replied, he himself trying to sound submissive.

"You keep your end and we'll keep ours. Simple." Gerry

replied, "Okay lads, let's go."

"Hey, you gonna untie me?" Ryan called out as the men dragging Stephanie headed for the door.

"We'll let you get yourself out of that bind." Laughed Gerry, "Get it lads? Get yourself out of that bind."

Both men laughed, both sounded like very fake laughs and said "Yeah, good one."

Ryan heard the front door shut. He waited a moment. No sound, they had definitely left. His hands had a zip tie round each wrist, and in turn were tied together by a third. There was no breaking them, if he tried all he'd do is cause himself injury. He moved to the kitchen door and turning his back to it, managed to get a few fingers on the handle and he opened the door into the lounge. He walked in to the middle of the room, sat on the floor and rolled backwards so he was balancing on his head and shoulder blades. He curled his legs up and pushed his bound hands past his buttocks. He rolled forward so he was sat with his legs bent, feet on the floor and his tied hands behind his knees. He pushed forward with his hands and in turn moved his feet over the zip ties. He got to his feet, walked back into the kitchen and searched around. He soon found a bread knife that looked sharp enough. He clamped it, blade pointing up at the ceiling, in one of the few, in place drawers. Using his hip he applied pressure to the drawer front to hold the knife steady while he moved his hands up and down on one of the zip ties. Within moments it had cut through and he was now free of his tethers. Now with his hands free, he took hold of the knife and cut the zip tie from his other wrist. They had been tight, red marks and slight indentations had appeared in the skin. Ryan rubbed his wrists. Glad to be free of his bonds. He felt around his pockets to find his phone. He called Nicole.

"Hi Ryan, you found her?" Nicole said, dispensing with any pleasantries, "Was she at her place?"

"Yes, yes I found her, but so did the guys in the black van." He replied, "They've taken her."

"What? Why? What are they going to do to her Ryan?" Nicole asked, "Couldn't you have stopped them?"

"No, they had a gun Nicole. We're lucky we're still alive." Ryan replied solemnly, "We made a deal. I hope they stick to it for all our sakes."

"A deal, Ryan what are you talking about? You can't trust these men, they're criminals, killers even." Nicole's voice came over the phone sounding despondent, "What makes you think they'll stick to any sort of deal?"

"I didn't have a choice." Ryan explained, "Luckily they didn't hurt either of us. I told them Stephanie doesn't know where the stash is and only I did. If they killed us they'd have nothing to return to their boss, except the news they created two more bodies. I'm sure they don't want that, bringing more interest from the police if they go around killing more people. I'm hoping they'll see the sense of doing an exchange and leaving us the hell alone. Besides, I have a plan."

"Where are you now?" Nicole enquired, "You still at Stephanie's place?"

"Yes, they tied me up with those plastic cable tie things like the cops use. I just got free. I thought I'd call you before I did anything else." Ryan replied, "I'm gonna head home and pick up the drugs. Can you meet me there?"

"Yes, yes of course, I'll leave now. See you when you get there." Nicole responded, "Ryan? Be careful please?"

"Of course Nicole, see you at my place very soon." He replied.

Ryan took a quick look under the cabinets where Stephanie had been looking. "What were you looking for Steph?" He thought to himself. The gap under the cabinets was not that big. It certainly wouldn't have hidden another stash like the one he already had hidden at his place. It was something important enough for Steph to risk coming here alone though. He did a quick search but didn't find anything.

Ryan got to his feet and headed for the lounge. He turned the light off as he left the kitchen and carefully navigated his way through the lounge to the front door of the flat. As he left he pulled the door closed behind him. He headed outside to the van. He was on edge. He nervously left the main entrance and walked down the few steps to the pavement checking either side for any sign of the black van or the three men. He was half expecting to be jumped again but that wouldn't make any sense. He unlocked the van and got in. He put the key in the ignition and started the engine. As he pulled away from the kerb he instinctively checked his mirrors, there was no sign of them. They must have gone. He took a detour and double backed several times, to make sure he wasn't being followed. Of course he wasn't a professional at this, all his manoeuvres were from spy films or T.V. shows he'd seen over the years. He went round several round-a-bouts a few times to he could see if anyone was following him. By the time he arrived at his place Nicole was already there waiting outside.

"Hi Nicole." He said, as he reached to her with open arms, "I'm sorry."

Nicole hugged him as he put his arms around her.

"You couldn't have done anything." Nicole replied, "I can't believe she was stupid enough to run off like that, what on earth was she thinking?"

"She was looking for something." Ryan explained, "I had a look where she was searching but I couldn't find anything. I suspect there must be something else she hasn't told us."

"Let's get inside." Ryan continued, he opened the main door to the building and they entered. "I have a plan that I hope will work."

They entered his flat and walked into the kitchen.

"Would you like a coffee or tea or anything?" Asked Ryan.

"Coffee, please." Replied Nicole.

Ryan made them both a coffee, they took them into the lounge and sat on the couch together. Ryan leaned back into the sofa and closed his eyes. He rubbed his face and breathed out deeply.

"Who knew all this would happen just from finding that I.D. badge?" Ryan said, more of a rhetorical question than actually wanting an answer.

"I know, it's crazy how we came into each other's lives." Nicole replied softly, "Ryan?"

"Yes?" Ryan replied.

"I just want to say something to you. I don't want you to take it the wrong way so please hear me out." Nicole began.

"Oh no, is this where you tell me you don't want to see me anymore and it's not me, I'm a great guy and all that but it's you etcetera, etcetera?" Ryan interrupted.

Nicole chuckled a little.

"No, not at all, quite the opposite actually, that's why I asked you to let me explain everything before you jump the gun." Nicole replied solemnly, "I know we haven't known each other long at all so we barely know each other. In fact there is a lot we don't know about each other. There's things I really want to tell you but at the moment I can't."

"Okay, I understand." Ryan interjected, "I won't put any pressure on you but I will say you can talk to me about anything. I won't judge you or hold anything against you. We have both had lives before we met and our past is our past."

"Thank you. I hope this doesn't scare you off and I'm not telling you this to put any pressure on you whatsoever but I feel I have to tell you this, just so you know where I am. I think communication between two people is so important, I've made mistakes in the past in relationships where I allowed that communication to dwindle. Both parties pretending to themselves and the other that everything is okay and you just carry on. Then one day out of the blue one of you turns round and says this isn't working and you break up. I'm done with doing that." Nicole said, "What I'm trying to say is, it has taken me by surprise how I feel about you. There is just something about you, from the first moment we met I've felt it."

"Oh wow." Exclaimed Ryan, "I certainly wasn't expecting that. Truth is I feel the same about you."

"Ryan, you don't have to say that just because I did." Nicole replied, "I just think it's important that you know how I feel. I'll be honest, I have thoughts and feelings about you that I've never had about anyone before, it is, I have to admit a little scary."

"Wow again." Ryan exclaimed, "Thank you for sharing, I agree, I feel there is something really special about you and not wishing to be premature but I too have made mistakes in relationships so I totally understand where you're coming from. It's so refreshing to find someone that thinks the same way I do."

"Okay, my turn to say wow." Nicole said, with a big smile on her face, "I can tell you are a really genuine guy, I think that's what it is about you I find so attractive."

"I see the same in you." Ryan replied, "I'm not just repeating everything you are saying although it probably sounds like it. I guess we do just think and feel the same things and I think that's rare between two people."

Nicole looked down into her lap. Ryan felt there was more she wanted to say but was holding back. The moment and discussion felt rather intense. The both of them, sitting there baring their souls to each other, sharing their inner most feelings and thoughts. It should have felt strange given that just a few weeks ago they never knew the other existed. Somehow though it didn't feel odd. It felt the most natural thing in the world to be doing.

"What do we do about this?" Nicole said, looking up at him, "Where do we go?"

"Well, I think we keep going, keep being who we are. It's such a shame about the circumstances in which we met but maybe it's how we were supposed to meet." Ryan replied, "Fate or kismet or whatever you wish to call it."

"I totally agree, more than you know." Nicole smiled as she spoke, "There's so much I want to tell you, so much more I want to say but I think now is not the right time. I hope we get this mess sorted out with Steph and can get back to a more normal life, that's when I think I can tell you everything I want to."

"That's cool, like I said, you won't ever get any pressure from me." Ryan replied, with a smile of his own.

"Thanks for listening." Nicole said, "That's another thing I like about you, you're a good listener." And she smiled.

"I try, I think how can you possibly understand someone if you don't actually hear what they have to say?" Ryan said.

"Good answer." Nicole replied and smiled, more to herself than to Ryan.

They both reached for each other's hand at the same time and both smiled at each other. They seemed to have a real synergy between them. They held hands and looked into each other's eyes. Ryan felt something stirring inside him. Not in a sexual way, this feeling came deep from the pit of his stomach, almost a nervous or anxious feeling but not. He was trying to understand it, it was more of an excited feeling or a rush of adrenaline. He felt his pulse quicken. They leant toward each other and they kissed. A soft sensual kiss. Their lips just gently brushing together. They were taking their time. Feeling the other's lips with their own. Both wanting to take in the feel of the others. Slowly but surely the kiss became more passionate. Ryan started it by slowly touching Nicole's lips with a gentle motion of his tongue. Nicole responded, her tongue slowly caressing his lips and tongue. They kissed for a few minutes. Ryan had placed his hand gently on Nicole's cheek. He felt the smoothness of her skin. She in turn had placed her hand on the back of his neck, pulling him closer to her, making the kiss feel deeper. They slowly stopped kissing and removed their hands from each other.

"That was amazing." Nicole exclaimed, "That felt so good."

Ryan sat back in the sofa with a big grin on his face.

"I've never kissed like that before, you bring something new out in me." Ryan said, "That felt incredible."

"Really?" Nicole questioned, "You're not a player are you?" and she laughed.

"No, if only." Ryan shot back.

Nicole playfully punched him on the arm.

"Oh really?" Nicole laughed.

"No, I'm not good looking enough to be a player." Ryan replied and laughed.

"I think you're very handsome, and sexy." Nicole said bashfully.

"Well, thank you very much. I think you're gorgeous and very, very sexy." Came Ryan's response.

"You are such a copycat." Nicole bleated out and smiled.

"I'm just not getting the chance to say any of these things first." Exclaimed Ryan and laughed as he dodged her next playful punch.

He stood from the couch and picked up their empty cups from the coffee table. He started to walk to the kitchen.

"Would you like anything? Another coffee or something else?" Ryan asked, as he turned to look over at her.

"There is something else I would love right now but we should wait." Nicole replied, with a cheeky, devilish twinkle in her eye.

Ryan laughed and walked into the kitchen to place the

cups in the sink. He returned to the lounge.

"I think I need to get on with the plan of how to get Stephanie back." Ryan exclaimed.

"Yes, tell me, what's your plan?" Nicole asked.

"To be honest, I'd rather not tell you for your own safety." Replied Ryan.

"What do you mean?" Quizzed Nicole.

"Well, god forbid you're taken, the less you know the better. I want to keep you as distant from all of this as possible." Ryan answered, "I hope you understand."

"Yeah I get it. Okay well I'd better leave and let you get on with what you need to do. I worry about you Ryan, your safety I mean. Please be safe, don't do anything silly." Nicole said.

"Of course not." Ryan smiled a reassuring smile to her.

Nicole stood from the couch and walked over to him and hugged him, she squeezed him tightly. They kissed again.

"I'd better go or we'll end up doing something and I want that to be at the right time." Nicole said, shyly as she looked into his eyes.

The pair said their goodbyes and Nicole left after Ryan made her promise she would text him, to let him know she'd gotten home safely.

"Wow." Ryan thought to himself, this girl is amazing, "I wonder what it is she's not telling me."

Chapter Fourteen.

Ryan retrieved the bag of drugs from its hiding place and placed the bag on the coffee table in the lounge. He grabbed his phone and the piece of paper Gerry had given to him with the phone number on it. Ryan looked at the time on his phone. It was now 9.34 PM. It was a little over an hour and a half ago since the men took Stephanie. He hoped she was okay. He put the piece of paper on the table and punched the number in to his phone. After a second or two there was a click then a ringing tone. After three rings the phone was answered.

"Hello?" Came a raspy voice that Ryan recognised as Gerry's.

"It's me, I have the stuff." Ryan replied, trying to sound menacing but realised he probably didn't to this maniac on the other end of the line.

"There's a good boy." Came Gerry's reply, "Take it to.."

"No." Ryan interrupted the thin man mid-sentence, "We're going to do the exchange my way."

"Who the fuck do you think you are?" Immediately came Gerry's response, "We have the girl, for the moment she's still alive and unharmed. Don't push us to do something to make that any different."

"Listen, like I said, we don't want any part of this, we just want to go back to our normal lives and let you get on with whatever business you do. It's none of our business, we're not interested and we won't go to the police. You have my word on that." Ryan continued.

"Your word?" Replied Gerry, "What do you think this is the fucking eighteenth century?"

"Some men still have some honour you know?" Ryan exclaimed, "Are you saying you are not a man of your word?"

There was a silent pause like the man on the other end of the call was working out which would be the best way to answer this question. If he said no Ryan wouldn't trust him to return the stuff in order to get Stephanie back, if he said yes, Ryan might think he was lying anyway.

"As it happens yes I am." Came the answer.

"Then you'll trust me and understand this is nothing to do with our ordinary lives. We just want to be left alone, return your stuff and have nothing more to do with you." Ryan continued.

"Okay, how do you want to play this then?" Questioned Gerry.

Ryan got the feeling Gerry mellowed, there was just a hint of something different in his voice. He so hoped this man was getting fed up with this situation, truth be told he'd probably been getting a hard time from his boss. Even though he was a criminal, living and working in a criminal world, there were still bosses to answer to. Still a job to do, whatever that might be, at this moment in time his goal was to return the stolen drugs to his boss and he'd been failing miserably. Of course that meant the repercussions would probably be more than a poor year-end review and no bonus or pay rise. Ryan smiled to himself at that thought.

"Okay, I'm going to place the drugs somewhere safe, we'll meet and you'll give me the girl. Once you have let us go and we are safe I'll call you with the location of the drugs."

"Do you think I'm a fucking idiot?" Replied Gerry angrily, "What's to stop you having a bunch of coppers waiting for us?"

"Look I don't know how many times or how many different ways I can say this, we want nothing to do with your world. We just want to return your shit and be left the fuck alone." Said Ryan, he himself getting annoyed now, "Besides firstly you'd see the cops from a mile away, secondly you'd always be able to track us down, we just want to forget this whole horrible situation, we only ended up involved because of that twat ex of hers."

"Alright, alright, you've made your point. We will do it your way only 'cos I gotta get this shit done and dusted. You and the girl have caused me a lot of grief." Conceded Gerry.

"Ok, good. Can I talk to the girl?" Ryan asked.

"You taking the piss?" Came the reply.

"I want to know she's okay." Ryan said, "I'm not going to do a thing unless I know she's okay."

"You've got balls, I'll give you that." Exclaimed Gerry, "Alright, one second."

Ryan heard a couple of muffled words through the earpiece of his phone, he presumed it was the thin man giving orders to one of his sidekicks to bring the girl or remove her gag.

"Ryan?" Came Stephanie's voice, "Is that you?"

"Yes, it's me, you okay? They haven't hurt you have they?" Ryan questioned.

"No, I'm okay. I'm scared though." Stephanie responded in a shaky voice, "Are you coming to get me?"

"Yes, I am, we're working out a deal." Said Ryan, "We'll be out of this mess…"

"That's enough." Gerry cut their conversation short, "So, where do you want to do the exchange?"

Ryan looked at the time on his phone. 9.43. He did a quick calculation as to how long it would take him to get to where he really wanted to meet for the exchange and do what he wanted to with regards the drugs.

"Somewhere public so you can't do anything we don't like. Be at the Imperial War museum in Mary Geraldine Harmsworth Park at ten thirty, I'll call you again then." Ryan replied.

"That's not going to be very busy with people at that time of night. I was starting to get a bit of respect for you but that just undermines your reasoning of meeting somewhere public." Gerry scoffed, "We're not running round London playing some fucking game.", his voice came back almost immediately, starting to sound angry again.

"It's not a game, I just need time to put the drugs in the location and it's getting late. I'm not telling you where until I've put them there. There'd be nothing to stop you getting there before me, taking the drugs and killing us both." Ryan replied, in his sternest voice he could muster.

"Where's your trust Ryan?" Asked Gerry, in a mocking voice.

"I'm trying, I'm also sensible though." Ryan fired back.

"You're hurting my feelings." Came the reply.

"I'll call you at ten thirty. Don't hurt the girl otherwise you'll never get the drugs back." Ryan said nervously, trying to take the upper hand.

"Don't get cocky Ryan and don't try and fuck us over or you'll be very sorry." Replied Gerry.

"I won't, we just want out of this." Ryan spat back, then cut the call.

He hoped he hadn't tried too hard to play the hard man but this really was getting on his last nerve now. He just wanted to be out of this situation. He wanted Stephanie to be safe, he wanted to not have to look over his shoulder. Of course even if the exchange went down smoothly and he got Stephanie back and they got their drugs it didn't mean that would be the case. He just had to hope though that his thoughts about them not wanting more unwanted attention from the police would keep them away. As far as the criminal underworld was concerned, Ollie paid the price for not taking care of business as he should've. He had paid with his life. That would send a strong enough signal that this group of criminals were not to be messed with. They had no need to hurt or kill Ryan, Stephanie or Nicole if they were even aware of her. Ryan grabbed his keys, wallet and the sports bag full of drugs and left his flat. He ran down to the van and got in, throwing the sports bag onto the passenger seat, started the engine and took off toward his destination. The drive was quicker than he had accounted for. He parked up on a side street and ran into a building with the sports bag. It was a public place and though it was late it was still fairly busy with people.

"Great, just how I hoped it would be." Ryan thought to himself.

He looked around for something specific, the thing he had searched for online earlier in the day. After a few moments of walking around he spotted what he was looking for. He did what he had to do with the sports bag and looked around the place. He had a pink slip in his hand. He went over to the information desk in the centre of the building and asked if he could possibly leave a written message for a friend. He made up some cock and bull story about how he was supposed to meet the friend here, but he had to leave as he was a doctor on call and had been called for an emergency. The young girl had given him a piece of paper, an envelope and a pen to borrow, asking him to promise to return the pen as it was the only one she had that worked. Ryan had given her his best smile and said,

"Of course, I have to leave the message anyway."

She had smiled and nodded an acknowledgement back at him. Ryan stood and leant on the counter off to one side so as not to get in the way but also to not be scrutinised by the young woman. He wrote a very short note and placed it in the envelope along with the pink slip of paper and sealed it. On the front he wrote;

Mr T. Hinman.

Ryan was nervous about this, he was taking a risk, not just with Stephanie's life but his own. If his plan failed there was no way out of this. He couldn't think of another way to do this though. It was like the riddle of the chicken, the fox, the grain and the farmer who had to cross a river with all three. He could not let Gerry and his cronies be in possession of the drugs and both he and Stephanie at the same time. He had to take this chance and hope it paid off. Ryan looked around one more time and spotted C.C.T.V. cameras everywhere in this place. This would be useful later on he thought. An idea came to him about a form of insurance so these guys would leave him, Stephanie and Nicole alone. He went back to the young woman behind the counter and handed her the pen. He smiled and asked how long before her shift ended. She replied that she only had just over two hours of her shift left to go and couldn't wait to go home.

"Perfect." Thought Ryan.

He handed the young woman the sealed envelope.

"Please be sure to pass this only to Mr Hinman." Ryan said, as he smiled at her, "It's very important he gets this."

"Of course sir." Came the reply from the young woman, as she smiled back at him.

Ryan looked at the big clock not far from the information desk. The clock showed it was 10.25. His timing had worked out perfectly in the end. Ryan pulled his phone out of his pocket as he walked towards the entrance he had entered through. The entrance he had used was not far from the side street he had parked his van on. The time on his phone turned 10.29. He dialled Gerry's number. After a short silence the phone rang.

"Ryan." Came the thin man's voice, "Where is the meet?"

"Waterloo station." Replied Ryan, trying to keep any hint of nervousness out of his voice, "Use the main entrance just you and the girl, you don't need your colleagues with you."

"You ever thought about working in a life of crime Ryan?" Asked Gerry sarcastically, "You're quite demanding seeing as you really haven't much to bargain with."

"I couldn't deal with the hours." Ryan joked, "Or the stress of getting caught or killed."

Ryan had no idea why he tried joking with this killer, he wasn't trying to build a rapport with the guy. He put it down to nerves.

"We'll be there in ten." Gerry said, sounding slightly amused as he cut the call.

Now all Ryan could do was wait and hope this would go without a hitch. He walked back towards the centre of the station. There were more people there, they were looking up at the screens showing the train times. He positioned himself in such a way that he wasn't going to be easy to spot when they walked into the station but he could see the main entrance clearly. He figured it would only be a few moments before Gerry and Stephanie would enter the station. Sure enough, almost as soon as he'd mingled with the crowd, he saw them enter the station. He was trying to determine if Gerry was holding a gun in Stephanie's side. Gerry was flitting his eyes from left to right. Probably to determine if he'd been set up and was half expecting that any second a load of armed police would appear from nowhere and arrest him. It could of course just been because he was looking for Ryan, hoping he'd spot him before being spotted. Gerry had Stephanie by the arm and was escorting her into the station. To anyone else they probably just looked like a couple in a bit of a rush to get to a train. The pair walked further into the station and for some reason was drawn to the large clock. Ryan watched from the obscurity of his position within the small crowd of people, making sure it was just the two of them and the goons were not following in behind. Once he felt safe he stepped out of the small group of people and was immediately spotted by Gerry. He walked towards them, ever mindful the two other thugs could enter the station any second. It looked on the surface of it at least that he had kept his word. Ryan didn't want to allow himself the thought that his plan was working and everything would be okay. Gerry and Stephanie had reached the clock and were now standing still underneath it waiting for Ryan to approach them. When Ryan got close he saw the thin man's grip on her arm tighten. Stephanie's face showed it was a little painful for her. Ryan got closer.

"You're hurting her." Ryan said between gritted teeth, "You said you wouldn't hurt her.

"Just making sure you're alone before I let her go Ryan." Gerry replied, "Don't be so squeamish. As you can see we haven't touched her.

"You okay Stephanie?" Ryan asked, "They haven't hurt you have they?"

"No, they haven't." Stephanie answered, "I'm okay."

"Okay, let her go, please." Ryan whispered to the thin man, "You stay here, once we are a safe distance I'll call you with instructions on how to get your drugs back."

"You'd better not screw us over Ryan or next time I see you it'll be from the other end of a gun." Replied Gerry, in a lowered but menacing voice.

"You have my word." Ryan replied, "Do we have yours this is the end of it? I mean you'll leave us alone?"

"As long as we get what we want and you keep your mouths shut then yes, sure, we have nothing to gain by killing either of you." Replied Gerry, "Bear in mind it doesn't mean we wouldn't, just like that, if we felt we had cause."

That to Ryan felt more chilling for some reason than any of the other threats made by this man.

"We won't give you cause, like I've said numerous times, we just want to be left to walk away from all this." Responded Ryan.

"Then neither of us should cross paths again." Said Gerry,

as he released Stephanie's arm and slightly nudged her forward, "We'll give you fifteen minutes to call us Ryan, then we'll come looking for you, and don't think for one moment there's anywhere you'll be able to hide."

Ryan looked at the clock above them and made a mental note of the time.

"Come on Steph, let's go." Ryan said, as he held out his hand for Stephanie to take hold of.

Stephanie reached for Ryan's hand and grabbed hold of it hard. They turned and started walking towards the entrance Ryan had used earlier. Heading for the van.

"Oh my god thank you Ryan, I'm so sorry I've caused all this shit for you and Nicole." Stephanie whispered toward Ryan.

"Don't talk, let's just get out of here." Ryan replied, increasing their pace as he pulled Stephanie along by the hand.

Ryan's eyes scanning in front of them, he was half expecting the other two henchmen of the thin man to be waiting for them. So far so good. They were getting closer to the entrance and the street outside. Ryan took a quick look back to where Gerry was standing. The thin man hadn't moved. There he was still standing under the clock. Staring after the pair of them. The couple left the station and walked out in to the street.

"This way." Ryan said, and pulled her gently in the direction of the side street and the awaiting rental van.

"Where are we going?" Stephanie quizzed, "You sure they're not following us?"

"I parked not far from here." Ryan answered, "I can't be

sure but they couldn't cover all the exits unless they brought more men. How many were with you when they brought you here?"

"Just the three of them, the same one's that chased us before." Stephanie replied.

"Well, like I said, that would mean one in the black van as a driver, Gerry in the station, only one other to cover the exits and they weren't to know which exit we would use." Ryan said, to try and calm her, not really confident himself that he was right.

It wasn't long before they reached the van, Ryan unlocked it and they got in. He pressed the button that operated the central locking and turned the key in the ignition. They put their seat belts on and Ryan pulled away from the parking spot. He check the time on his phone, he had only eight more minutes before he had to make the call. He got back onto a main street and headed for the river. He wanted to get as far away as possible in the short time he had. He headed over Westminster Bridge, passed Big Ben, round Parliament Square and onto Whitehall. He headed for Trafalgar Square, he drove round the round-about three times just to check if he was being followed. There was no sign of the black van. Ryan headed for Pall Mall. He checked the time. One minute before he had to make the call. He pulled into a side street and pressed redial on his phone. Within seconds Gerry answered the call.

"Ryan." He said, sounding back to his menacing and impatient self.

"Yes. There is an envelope at the information desk. Go to the young woman there and ask if there are any messages for a MR Hinman." Ryan exclaimed.

"Mr Hinman?" Gerry quizzed.

"Yes, I don't know your real surname and I don't wish to." Ryan snapped back, "Just get the envelope, there's a message in there with instructions."

"You'd better be on the level Ryan." Replied Gerry, "If you're setting me up I'll be in touch."

With that he cut the call.

"Is that it? Is it over?" Stephanie asked. "Will they leave us alone?"

Ryan thought about it. Gerry will get the drugs and if he stuck to his word that should be it. He didn't say anything about calling back to say everything was fine and Ryan wasn't expecting a courtesy call. All he could do was hope this was the end of it.

"I'm sure once he has followed my instructions and they have the drugs in their hands that'll be it." Ryan replied, trying to sound as convincing as possible even though he himself was not so sure.

Ryan pulled out of the side street and continued on his journey towards his flat. Meanwhile back at Waterloo Station, Gerry had approached the young woman at the information desk and asked if there were any messages left for Mr Hinman. The young lady had smiled at him, told him there was and his friend who had left the message had to rush off for an emergency. Gerry smiled at her in return, took the envelope and turned away from the desk. He took a few paces to make sure he was away from prying eyes and opened the envelope hurriedly. Inside was a pink slip of paper with a number on it, like a receipt from a dry cleaners. There was also a small piece of white paper folded in half. He carefully placed the pink slip in his inside pocket and unfolded the white piece of paper. On it was scribbled a short note in Ryan's hand writing:

"Take the pink slip to the left luggage desk, give them the pink slip and you'll be given the bag of stuff."

Gerry folded the paper again and placed it back in the envelope. He looked around the station, his two colleagues had entered the station now and he caught their eyes and nodded to them. They nodded back they're acknowledgement that they had seen him and he nodded in the direction of the left luggage place. He turned and started walking toward it. The two other men followed along the side wall of the station keeping their distance from him and watching out for anything out of the ordinary. It wasn't long before he had reached the desk for the left luggage. No one was at the desk at the time when he got to it and no sign of any staff. He looked down at the desk there was a small white doorbell fitted to the top of the desk and an A4 piece of paper crudely cello-taped next to it stating:

"Please press bell for attention."

Gerry extended a finger and pressed the button down firmly. He looked past the desk, just a few feet behind the desk was a wall. At the right end of the wall was a door. He heard a bell ring somewhere off behind the door. The storage area he presumed correctly. After just a moment an old man came through the door.

"Good evening sir, how can I help?" asked the old man.

He pulled the pink slip from his pocket and handed it over to the old man.

"A friend left a bag for me to collect." Gerry replied, slightly louder than his normal voice as he had spotted the old man had a hearing aid in each of his ears.

"Okay let me see." Replied the old man, as he took the pink slip and looked at it through his small gold wire framed reading spectacles, which were sat half way down his nose, "Won't be a moment."

The old man turned and went back through the door into the storage area to go hunt out the bag. Gerry looked back around at his colleagues who were now propped up against the far wall in line with him. He rolled his eyes at them and they both smirked back. The thin man stood there, resting one hand on the counter top tapping his fingers while he waited. About five minutes had passed before the door opened again and the old man came ambling through carrying a black sports bag. From the look of it and the way he was seemingly struggling with it, it must have been quite heavy. He heaved it up onto the counter and pulled at the pink tag that was attached to one of the handles of the bag. He checked the number on the tag matched the one on the pink slip once more to be sure he'd gotten the right bag.

"There you go sir." The old man said, as he looked up at Gerry, "That's the one."

"Yes I believe so." Gerry replied, "Thanks very much."

He grabbed the bag and pulled it off the desk so it swung down by his knee. He turned to walk away to go and join his colleagues.

"Did you want the docket sir?" The old man asked.

"No, that's fine thanks. I'm sure this is the correct one." Replied Gerry, speaking back at the old man over his shoulder.

He placed the bag on the floor between his feet and opened the zip just a little. He pulled the bag open just a small crack and looked inside. Sure enough it was the right bag. Inside were the packets of all the different coloured pills, he pushed one of his hands in to the bag and felt around a little. It wasn't long before he felt the cellophane wrapped bricks of white powder. He did this as a terrible thought had crossed his mind. Even though Ryan did as he had said he would about leaving instructions and making the call, what if he had filled a bag full of old newspapers or something and then made a run for it. He zipped the bag back up and hoisted it on to his shoulder. He headed over to join his colleagues who now had stepped away from the wall and were walking slowly toward the main exit, waiting for him to catch up to them. Within a few moments he was walking alongside them both. One of the other two men moved to the other side of him so he was walking between them.

"Is it in there?" One of the men asked him.

"Yeah, looks and feels like it's all of it too." Replied Gerry, "He kept his word."

The three of them left the station at the main entrance and walked round to the parked van, got in and drove off into the night.

Back in the van with Ryan and Stephanie, the drive after the call had been a quiet one. Ryan pulled the van in to the parking area out the back of his flat and switched off the engine and lights. They exited the van and walked quietly up to Ryan's flat. He let Stephanie in to the flat and shut the door behind him. Stephanie headed straight for the couch. She kicked her shoes off as she had entered and sat on the couch, pulling her feet up in her usual position. She leant her head back on the couch and closed her eyes. It was late now and the time and stress of everything she'd been through had caught up with her. She was tired. Ryan had taken his shoes off at the door and placed them neatly next to each other under the row of coat hooks. He headed for the kitchen area. As he walked from the door to the kitchen he looked over at Stephanie on the couch.

"Do you want a drink or anything?" He asked, "I'm going to have a tea."

"No, I'm good I think, I just need some sleep." Stephanie replied sounding exhausted, "Actually, you wouldn't have hot drinking chocolate would you?"

"I think I might have some." Ryan responded, "I'll take a look, not sure if it'll still be in date. Does it go out of date?"

"I think so, but I doubt it makes much difference." Stephanie shouted back from the couch thinking Ryan had already entered the kitchen.

There was a few banging of cupboard doors and clinking of jars or bottles coming from the kitchen.

"You're in luck." Ryan said, between the kitchen work top and over counter cabinets, "I do have some and it is still in date."

"Can I be awkward and ask if I can have it made with milk?" Stephanie asked.

"That's the only way I make it, I think it's disgusting if it's made with water." Ryan replied.

"Ahhh, man after my own heart." Stephanie said, leaning her head back further on the couch and angling her face toward the kitchen.

Ryan finished making the drinks and brought them into the lounge, he placed them on the coffee table and plopped himself down on the couch next to Stephanie.

"There you go young lady." He said, as he offered her a weak, tired smile.

"Thank you Ryan." She replied, her head was still leant back into the back of the couch and her eyes were closed. "You've been so good to me and I'm sorry I got you and Nicole messed up in this."

"Don't worry about that now." Ryan smiled to himself, "If it wasn't for you and that I.D. badge I'd have never met Nicole."

"You really like her huh?" Stephanie asked.

"Yes, yes I do." Ryan replied coyly, "I'll be honest I've never met anyone like her before. She's something kinda wonderful. I don't know what it is about her but she's different.

"That's sweet." Said Stephanie.

Just then Ryan's phone started buzzing and vibrating. Ryan pulled the phone from his jeans pocket. Without even looking to see the screen to determine the caller he answered the call.

"Hello?" Ryan said in to the phone.

"Where's the fucking money Ryan?" Came the angry voice of Gerry.

"What? What money?" Replied Ryan, a little perplexed.

"The money Ollie owed us for the last lot of merchandise we supplied to him and he sold." The thin man said sounding serious.

Then it clicked for Ryan. That's the other thing Stephanie must have been looking for. She must have found the money probably with the drugs but hid it separately. This girl was a real piece of work.

"Look, I don't know what you're talking about." Ryan said into the mouthpiece.

"Okay, let's say for one moment I believe you. I bet you're new girlfriend knows about it. She been holding out on you Ryan?" Gerry exclaimed.

"Maybe you're right or maybe she never had it?" Ryan responded thinking on his feet, "I'd have to ask her, she's not with me right now."

"Where is she Ryan?" quizzed Gerry.

"I don't know, after I left the station she freaked out and told me to stop the car and let her out." Ryan replied.

Ryan looked over at Stephanie with a look of contempt on his face. Stephanie looked back at him with a worried look on her face. She had obviously figured out who it was on the phone and what this was about.

"So if I turn up at your place I wouldn't find her there with you?" Questioned Gerry, "Yes, I know where you live Ryan."

Ryan couldn't tell if he was bluffing or not. Surely Gerry and his goons would have crashed in to his place by now if they had followed them home and knew Stephanie was really with him. There were many times previous to tonight they could have followed him and found out his address. Question is did this man really know where he lived? Ryan had to gamble.

"That's right, she's not here." Ryan said, in as confident a voice that he could muster. He had to sound believable.

"Whatever Ryan, thirty grand. That's what he was holding for us and we are expecting that back." Said Gerry menacingly, "Twenty four hours Ryan, that's what I'm giving you to get the money back and hand it over. No more games. You fail to deliver and you're a dead man and we'll do horrible things to the girl before we're done with her and hand her over to the Russian's as a sex slave."

With that the thin man cut the call.

Ryan's hand that was holding the phone dropped to his side. He looked at Stephanie.

"What the fuck Stephanie?" Ryan said, that was all he could think of to say.

"I'm sorry." Stephanie began.

"Do you want to get out of this mess or do you want to get us killed?" Ryan cut her off.

"I'm sorry, yes of course I want out, I didn't know it was their money." Stephanie pleaded, "I just thought it was Ollie's and no one would miss it."

"So where is it?" Ryan asked, "That's what you were back at your flat looking for wasn't it?"

"Yes, and to be honest I don't know." Stephanie said shakily, "I couldn't find it where I am sure I had hidden it. Do you think they found it and took it already and are making out they didn't?"

"I have no idea, all I know is they have given us twenty four hours to return thirty grand to them or they'll kill me and do worse things to you." Ryan replied, he'd lost his patience with it all now, "How much money do you have in your so called bolt bag?"

"Maybe fifteen thousand give or take a couple of hundred, why?" Stephanie asked.

"I just want this to be over, I'm done with this. I think we just pay them and be done." Ryan responded, "I might be able to put up the rest."

"I couldn't expect or even let you do that Ryan, it's not right." Came Stephanie's response.

"What choice do we have?" Ryan quizzed, "Do you have another fifteen or so thousand just laying around?"

"We could go back to my flat and have another look." Stephanie suggested.

"I think they'd be looking for us and if they find us without the money on us it could get horribly bad very quickly. I'd rather not risk it." Ryan immediately replied.

Ryan had over thirty five thousand from his redundancy package left in the bank, obviously it wasn't what he had wanted to use the money for but if it meant staying alive he'd gladly use it. It'd just mean he'd have to start looking for a job sooner than he wanted and who knows, maybe that interview he went for with Mr Edwards would come good and he'd be earning money again very soon.

"I don't know Ryan, I'd feel terrible letting you put up the cash for my problem." Stephanie said.

"Let's sleep on it. I think for your safety though to be honest you should stay at a hotel tonight." Ryan practically ignoring her last comment. "Drink your drink and let's get you to a hotel."

"Why? Why can't I stay here?" Stephanie protested.

"The thin man suggested he knew where I live, if they do come here in the middle of the night I don't want them finding you here." Ryan said honestly, "What he said they'd do to you doesn't bear thinking about."

Stephanie fell silent. She didn't want to think about what Ryan could have meant by that. She drank her hot chocolate, got her few bits together and put her shoes on while Ryan finished his drink and took the cups back out to the kitchen. He put his shoes back on, grabbed his phone, wallet and keys and they left the flat. He looked around carefully to make sure no one was outside before beckoning Stephanie to follow him out to the parking area where the hire van was. They entered the van and headed off to find a hotel.

Chapter Fifteen.

Ryan returned to his flat and parked the van in his usual spot. He entered the building and he found Nicole, waiting at his front door.

"Hi honey, Surprise." Nicole said, before Ryan could even open his mouth.

"Wha… Hi, what are you doing here? It's almost two in the morning. I thought you'd be home fast asleep." Ryan replied, a little taken aback that she was here.

"I couldn't sleep, I was worried about you and I just wanted to see you." Replied Nicole, "I was going to call you but thought I'd surprise you."

"It's certainly a surprise." Ryan responded smiling, "A nice one, I mean."

They entered Ryan's flat.

"Is Stephanie not here?" Nicole asked.

"No, I took her to a hotel, I thought it'd be safer." Ryan answered.

He went on to tell her all that had happened and how the thin man was demanding the money that Ollie owed them from sales of their product.

"Stephanie sounds really messed up." Nicole interjected.

"Yeah, I guess when she found that money, for all the good intentions she had with regards Oliver and getting him out of the business it's difficult to turn away from that amount of money. Especially if you thought the owner was no longer alive." Ryan reasoned, "I'm hoping she's not lying to me about her not being able to find it now though."

"It's missing?" Nicole questioned.

"So she says." Ryan said, not sounding too convinced, "Though she did seem to be looking for something the last time I found her at her flat."

They had walked into Ryan's kitchen on entering the flat.

"Would you like a drink or anything?" Ryan asked.

"Would you have any wine?" Nicole replied, "I know it's late but I just feel I could use a drink, not a large one, just a small glass if you have a bottle open."

Ryan looked in the wine rack and found a bottle of red, it hadn't been opened but he figured it would probably get drunk over the next few days anyway. He poured them both a glass and pushed the cork back into the bottle as far as it would go. He handed Nicole a glass and they clinked their glasses together.

"Would you like to go sit in the lounge with these?" Ryan asked, lifting his glass slightly.

"Sure, let's go get more comfortable." Nicole replied, in her soft voice.

Ryan wondered if she was getting flirty but he was never very good at reading women's signals. He knew she liked him of course, she'd told him so but he always had an air of self-doubt. He figured he'd not try and think too much or analyse everything and just go with the flow. They walked over to the couch, placed their drinks on the coffee table and sat down into the comfortable sofa. Ryan had sat at one end and rested against the arm. He stretched and leaned back, kicking off his shoes at the same time. Nicole had sat right next to him, she leaned forward, took her shoes off then pulled her feet up on the couch and leant against Ryan. As she placed a hand on his chest he instinctively put his left arm around her shoulders and pulled her closer to him. Her perfume, soft and subtle, smelled amazing. She rested her head on his shoulder and snuggled in closer. He planted a kiss on the top her head. Her hair felt soft and silky. His mouth lingered there and the clean fresh scent of coconut filled his nostrils.

"Hmmm, love the smell of your hair." Ryan said, almost in a whisper, "Coconut, I love coconut."

"Are you calling me a coconut?" Nicole said, slowly also just above a whisper.

"God no, I mean your shampoo must be coconut something or other." Ryan said, a little panicked that he had offended her. Feeling a slight hot flush.

He felt Nicole jiggle as she chuckled to herself.

"I was just teasing you." Nicole said quietly, "And thank you."

She tapped his chest gently as if to calm him down. Ryan realised with her head on his shoulder and hand on his chest, she most likely felt his panic. He admonished himself mentally for being so bad at this kind of thing. What must she think of him? He decided he was going to come out of his shell a little. He liked her a lot. She was, so far at least, seeming to be everything he wanted in a woman. Intelligent, funny, tactile, caring and thoughtful. The fact she was beautiful and had a stunning figure was a massive bonus. He didn't want to mess this up. He had to let her know, show her he was really keen on her. He started to gently stroke her upper arm and shoulder with his left hand. Her breathing was soft and with each breath of hers he became acutely aware of her right breast rising and pushing into his rib cage. The feel of it, the firmness of it started a flood of thoughts in his mind. He tried to imagine what she looked like undressed. He pictured a perfectly statuesque figure. He started to imagine her stood in front of him naked, a beautiful sight of perfect curves. Given her complexion, a soft caramel colour, she would certainly be a wonder for the eye to behold. Her dark brown hair with its gentle, soft bouncy curls cascading over her shoulders, half covering her perfectly formed pert breasts. He wondered if the reality would be as good as the image swirling around in his mind.

"What are you thinking?" Nicole asked him, out of the silence.

He was snapped back to the reality of the moment. The images in his mind exploding into a cloud of mist, dispersing as quickly as they had manifested.

"Just about you." He replied, not sure on how honest he should be with the details of his thoughts.

"I hope you're thinking nice things about me." She replied.

Ryan smiled and thought, "If only you knew."

"Yes, definitely good things." He answered.

Ryan placed his right hand on her cheek and gently lifted her head so she was looking up at him.

"Always nice things." He said softly, and leant his head forward to kiss her.

"In for a penny in for a pound." He thought.

Nicole responded, her left hand reaching round the back of his neck. The kiss started gently. Ryan felt his pulse quicken. He heard Nicole's breathing change, shorter but deeper. With his hand on her cheek he felt her face flush, a gentle warming of the skin. They both moved a little awkwardly in their positions to make kissing easier and more comfortable. He continued to gently rub her upper arm and shoulder and she in turn was now stroking his chest. The kiss had turned into a more passionate kiss, both trying it seemed to devour each other. Neither of them could get enough of the other. If they could've, they'd have swallowed each other whole, such was their desire for the other. Ryan's right hand moved slowly and gently down her cheek to her neck. He felt the warmth of her neck against the palm of his hand. He dared to move his hand gently further down her neck, slowly easing his hand under the soft material of her blouse. His hand now on her collarbone, he slowly moved it further down. He was waiting for Nicole to stop him any second as his hand was getting closer to her chest. Instead she took her hand from the back of his neck and undid a few of the top buttons of her blouse. Ryan felt himself getting more excited. He had to restrain himself from moving too fast. If this was going to progress to being more than a bit of smooching he wanted to enjoy it but more importantly he wanted Nicole to enjoy it. His hand slowly moved down to her left breast. He carefully slid his fingers into the cup of her bra. He felt Nicole tense for just a split second then relax. He gently cupped her breast with his hand and squeezed softly. It was better than he imagined. Firm with smooth skin. His fingers found the nipple, it was stiff. Nicole was obviously as aroused as he was. She let out a little gasp as he closed two of his fingers over it gently pinching it between the two knuckles of his index and middle finger. They continued to kiss deeply. Both of their breaths coming in shorter, shallower rasps. He continued to massage her breast with his right hand. He moved his left hand that was around her shoulders lower down her back towards her bottom. Her left hand that was on his neck was back on his chest. She'd moved her right hand to hold his neck now. She pulled back from the kiss and leaned back in pleasure. Ryan leaned forward and kissed her on the neck. Gentle long, slow kisses, taking in her perfume, she quivered a little. Her neck was obviously sensitive to this kind of attention. He slowly moved his attention down from her neck to her chest. Soon he was planting soft kisses on the soft but firm flesh of her left breast. Hungrily and almost greedily he was pulling at her bra trying to release its contents. She helped by sitting forward and with one hand behind her back unfastened the clip. He felt the release of tension on the bra and he lifted it above her boobs. He wanted to see them, it was not enough just to feel them. He sat back for a moment to take them in. Nicole lifted her head and opened her eyes.

"Something wrong?" She said, looking at Ryan right in the eyes.

"No." Came Ryan's immediate response, "Nothing wrong at all, I just wanted to see them. They are..... Wow. I can't think straight, can't think of a word to describe them that would do them justice, there just isn't a word with enough scope to cover how amazing they are."

Nicole laughed, grabbed Ryan by the back of the head and pulled his face into her chest. Ryan planted kisses all over her chest. He'd slid from the couch now and was kneeling on the floor in front of Nicole. He undid the few remaining unbuttoned buttons on her blouse and pushed it aside. She removed her blouse over her shoulders and let her bra slide down her arms until that was also completely off. Ryan had his hands on both of her breasts as he kissed each of them in turn.

"Take me upstairs Ryan." Nicole asked, in as sexy a voice as you could imagine.

Ryan jumped to his feet, most probably the quickest he'd

ever moved in his life. In doing so though he kicked the coffee table quite hard knocking over one of their wine glasses, luckily it was Nicole's glass and she had managed to drink most of it, so only a little was spilt.

"Ohh Ryan, quick get a cloth or something to soak it up with." Nicole said.

"Never mind that." Ryan replied, and he held out his hand to pull her up from her seating position on the couch.

"It might stain." Nicole protested.

"I honestly don't really care right now." Ryan said, grinning from ear to ear as he pulled her up from the sofa.

"No, don't be silly." Nicole replied, as she moved past him to go to the kitchen and grab a cloth or anything to soak up the little spillage.

Ryan followed very close behind putting his hands on her waist. He started kissing the back of her neck as they walked.

"Ryan, this'll only take a second." Nicole laughed, and paused in her walking to stop and enjoy the attention her neck was receiving.

She leant back into Ryan and placed her hands on his hands. She pulled his hands from her waist to her belly so he was hugging her as he gently kissed her neck and shoulders. This went on for a moment then Nicole pushed her bottom back pushing Ryan away from her as she giggled.

"Come on, let's clean that wine up and get upstairs." Nicole said, over her shoulder as she broke free of his hug.

"Okay, miss, as you command." Ryan replied, as he

chuckled and let her go.

In no time at all Nicole had grabbed a cloth, ran it under the tap to dampen it, walked back to the lounge, wiped the spilt wine up, picked up the glass and returned to the kitchen. She rinsed her hands under the tap and dried them on a tea towel. All of that with Ryan planted on the same spot watching her.

"You okay?" Nicole asked, "Sorry, did I kill the moment."

"No, I could watch you doing things topless all day. You look incredible." Ryan answered, with a massive smile on his face.

"You're so sweet." Nicole replied.

She walked over to him, kissed him on the cheek then on the mouth. He put his arms around her and grabbed hold of her bottom. Even with his eyes closed he rolled them upwards to the heavens as he kissed her. Her bum was so firm also, cute, perfectly sized for his hands. Nicole broke the kiss and leaned back a little.

"You getting fresh with me mister?" She asked, with a cute, jokey, quizzical look on her adorable face.

"I certainly am miss." Ryan replied, attempting to sound like they were in Victorian times, "Do you take umbrage to that?"

"Not at all young man, but please, take me upstairs now good sir, as you had earlier intended." Nicole continued on with the mocking of a time gone by.

This made Ryan smile, not just to her but to himself on the inside. He really liked this girl.

"But of course young miss, it would be my pleasure." Ryan

said, as he took a slight step back, bowed, held out his hand for Nicole to take it and stood again.

"Not just your pleasure kind sir, one does hope you are not a selfish lover." Nicole said, instantly with a humorous tone.

Ryan burst out laughing.

"Oh you are a naughty girl huh? All prim and proper on the outside but get you alone and the real bad girl comes out eh?" Ryan said, teasing her.

"You'll just have to find out won't you?" Nicole replied, and skipped past him heading for the stairs to the bedroom.

Chapter Sixteen.

A blade of sunshine pierced the room through the slight gap in the curtains of Ryan's bedroom window. Ryan was sleeping on his bed, a very restful, deep sleep. He woke slowly, without opening his eyes he reached across the bed instinctively. Searching for Nicole who he knew was there just a short while ago. His hand found nothing but empty bed. He opened his eyes to see that she wasn't there beside him. He propped himself up on his elbow, rubbed his eyes and half expected to see her out of bed getting dressed. The shaft of sunlight illuminated the room enough for him to see she wasn't there. Maybe she was in the bathroom. He looked over at the bedside cabinet, on it he saw a note. He reached across the bed and grabbed it. He rubbed his eyes again and held the piece of paper to his face. Although there was the shaft of brilliant sunshine coming from the window, the rest of the room was still quite dim and he struggled to see the writing clearly. His eyes adjusted a moment later and he read the note.

"My Darling Ryan,

I hope you are sleeping well my lover. I have to leave for work, I hope I don't wake you as I leave. I have to go, though I really don't want to. I wish things in this world were different and I could spend all day in bed with you. Maybe one day we will. Hope this doesn't inflate your ego too much but that was the best, you are the best. Meet me for lunch, please, 12:30 Kangaroo Café just round the corner from work. I'm sure you'll find it if you don't know of it, I know how resourceful you are.

Love N

XXX"

"Wow" Was all Ryan could think after reading that.

He too had enjoyed that night's activities with Nicole, she was in fact the best he'd ever had too. Whether her note was genuine or not, and Ryan scolded himself for doubting it, it was incredible and it just felt so natural. Not rushed and certainly not boring. It was as if the pair could read each other's minds as to how to move or what to do next, where to touch and how. They had actually made love twice in the course of just over two hours. There was plenty of passion, emotion, kissing, cuddling and even a little talking. Ryan had taken the time to explore every inch of Nicole's body, not just with his eyes. She had responded to every little kiss, each of the gentlest of his touches. She in turn at one point had also explored his body, an interest in wanting to really get to know it. Everything she did felt amazing to him, she did things in some ways that gave him feelings he'd never felt before. He'd said to Stephanie that he felt there was something special about Nicole and he was right. The thing he felt, an overwhelming urge to do today had nothing at all to do with the physical, he literally just had this desire to be in her presence, her company, if he could spend some time, any amount of time today with her, it would be a great day. It made him reflect on his past relationships. He couldn't recall ever feeling like this before. Sure he'd been in a few relationships and at the time would have told you he loved each of those girls. This was different though, he couldn't recall having such a longing just to be in any of those other girls company as much as he yearned to with Nicole. As per usual Ryan was trying to fathom this out. His analytical brain working overtime. Was it that he was more mature now? Was it for the fact that he'd been single for some time since his last relationship went south? Or was it simply because of the person Nicole was? It just felt so right. Ryan could actually be his real self. He hadn't once put on any front or pretence to try and impress her. From the second they had met he'd just been his truest self and it seemed so far that Nicole was as taken with him as he was with her. Ryan grabbed his phone from the bedside cabinet that was on his side of the bed. He swiped the screen to unlock the display. The clock on the phone showed just after nine thirty. There were no texts or missed calls from Nicole but he assumed this was just her being considerate and not wishing to wake him. Nothing from Stephanie either but he figured that was most likely because she was safe and probably still sound asleep in the hotel he left her at late last night. He thought he should probably check on her though. Last thing he needed right now, was for her to do her independent routine and go running off back to her flat to try and find the stash of cash. He had made her promise him that she wouldn't do anything so rash and put herself in danger again. She had at least made it appear to him that she wouldn't. He'd also told her if she had any such daft ideas to contact him first and he would go with her. She then replied stating that she really thought the guys in the black van had probably found it and taken it already and they were just trying to be clever with them. Ryan wasn't so sure and felt he couldn't necessarily trust Stephanie any more than he could the thin man and his goons. He decided to text Stephanie to check on her. If she was asleep he hoped his text wouldn't wake her. He just sent a simple text asking if she was okay. He then sent a quick text to Nicole. He thanked her for her note and being so considerate to not wake him. He went on to say he really wouldn't have minded if she had though, as he would have liked to have seen her before she left for work. He finished the text by saying he thought their night together was wonderful, she was the best and he was really looking forward to their lunch date. Within a few seconds his phone buzzed. It was a text from Nicole, calling Ryan a copycat for saying she was the best, followed by a smiley face and that she was also looking forward to seeing him for lunch. He smiled to himself at the text. He placed his phone back on the bedside cabinet and stretched. He stood from the bed and was about to head for the bathroom when his phone vibrated. He picked it up, it was a text from Stephanie stating she was fine and had only just woken following the best night's sleep she'd had in a long while. Ryan texted her back saying he was happy she'd slept well and to keep in touch. He added that in the afternoon he would visit her at the hotel and they could talk about how to sort out the issue of the missing money with the thin man. He immediately received a message back thanking him again and that she promised to stay put until she heard from him. This at least reassured him a little that for once she might actually stick to her word. He fired a quick text off to Nicole to let her know he'd heard from Stephanie and that she was alright. His phone buzzed once more with a simple text with just the one word, "Thanks."

He dropped his phone on to the bed and headed for the bathroom. Above the basin was a mirror. He turned on the hot tap and placed his hand in the stream of water checking the temperature, waiting for it to turn from cold to warm. Once he felt the temperature rising he placed the plug in the sink and watched as the level of hot water started to rise. He sighed. He looked at himself in the mirror, he looked tired. Stubble adorned his face. He rubbed it and felt its coarseness on his fingertips. He rubbed his eyes and on opening them, smiled at his reflection staring back at him. Thoughts from the passionate activities just a few hours ago filled his mind.

"You old rascal." He said, out loud to no one but his reflection, "You've still got it."

He chuckled at that. He wasn't bragging, there was no one there to boast to. He was happy for himself, excited at this, this what? He knew not where this was going, what to even call it now for all that it was. After all, what would you call it? It certainly hadn't started in any orthodox manner, boy meets girl, boy and girl go out, boy and girl both like each other and a relationship blossoms. This, their situation had started because he was interested in meeting another girl. Then a dark, intriguing, malevolent set of circumstance brought these two together. He saw Nicole as a shining light in all of what had come to pass. A security, a safeness, a sanctity. For when he was in her arms the world disappeared and it was just the two of them. The darkness, the violence, the madness of everything that had happened, might as well have happened to someone else. She, Nicole, was the very reason, the force that had unbeknownst to himself on a conscious level had driven him in his actions. He felt compelled to be that chivalrous, brave, determined man he'd shown he could be over the last few weeks. And then, just a few hours ago, she brought out in him such passion, he made love like he'd never made love before. Exploring her body like it was something mystical, a gift from the gods. He found that the more she seemed to be enjoying it the more he enjoyed it himself. He felt like a different man this morning. He had turned off the hot tap and added some cold water so as not to burn himself. He looked back at himself in the mirror.

"I like this me, this is the truest me, the real me." He simply said to himself.

Ryan shaved then showered. Flashes of images entering his mind of Nicole, not just from their night together but other times that they had spent together also. Back in his room he dried and dressed. His mind turned to the thin man and the money. Thirty grand. Not a small sum by any means. Ryan was trying to reason why, if Stephanie was indeed correct and they had already taken the money, would they really be bothered chasing them down for another thirty grand. No matter which way he looked at it, it just didn't add up. Yet when he found Stephanie back at her flat she was definitely looking for something and if it was not the money what on earth could it have been. Then thinking about it some more, the bolt bag seemed to have a fair amount of cash in it. Could that have been some or all of that money or was that from somewhere else? He wished he could read Stephanie's mind or at least be able to determine if she was being honest or not. For now though, he felt the priority was giving the thin man and his gang the money they said they were owed, even if it meant using some of his own money and then once they were out of the picture try and resolve it with Stephanie. Ryan shook his head and tried to put it all out of his mind for now at least. He headed down to the kitchen and made himself a tea. He went and sat on the couch in the lounge and turned the television on. The news channel was on. The current story they were covering was another upcoming tube strike. A reporter was stood in one of the stations doing her report. Then a thought hit Ryan like a balloon being popped behind his back. Everything Stephanie had told him from the start about how Ollie had abducted her, how Ryan had found her I.D. badge and lipstick under that bench on the station platform. How did Oliver manage to abduct her in such a public place? He stood from the couch and turned the television off. He moved his mug of tea to the kitchen table and retrieved his hacking equipment from its hiding place. Thought after thought now bowling over one another as his mind raced. The more he thought about it, the more none of what Stephanie had told him made any sense. If she'd gotten out of the relationship with Oliver, wanting no part of his life as it was, why go back and involve yourself? Were Stephanie's intentions not in fact to help her ex to a better life but for purely selfish financial gain? Then Ryan's mind started wandering on to the path of an even bigger conspiracy, had perhaps Oliver and Stephanie colluded to make it look like he had been robbed? The amount of cash and saleable drugs he had in that stash would probably have a street value of several hundreds of thousands of pounds, maybe more. Enough at least for a simple couple to make a new life for themselves somewhere away from London, away from the gangs and the violence. Maybe there was some truth in Stephanie's story, perhaps she had gotten to Ollie and suggested a way out? Before they could implement their plan though something went wrong. Perhaps Gerry and his cronies had come looking for payment. Maybe they had gotten the truth out of Ollie. Ryan stopped himself. Caught himself before his mind ran further away with itself. He did however want to investigate at least part of Stephanie's story. The kidnapping from the underground station where he had found her I.D badge. He removed all the equipment from the case in which it was stowed and connected it all together. He powered up the laptop and entered his login name and password. It wasn't long before he was connected to the London underground's servers. It was a few years ago that the underground stations had their C.C.T.V systems overhauled and updated. Each station had several servers of their own all connecting to a central data hall just outside the M25 London orbital road. An unmarked, brown bricked building in the middle of an ordinary looking business park. High fences with razor wire atop of them and tremble sensors that would detect anyone or anything trying to climb them. The sensors connected to the system in the security office, any alarm triggered by any of the sensors connected to the fences demanded instant investigation. Since 9/11 2001 in America and the bombings in London on the underground on 7/7 2005 more importance was placed on C.C.T.V footage in the fight against terrorism. Security services urged companies that ran public transport systems of any kind, to make it a priority to get good coverage of public areas. More importantly they were requested to store many months of hours upon hours of recordings, so that they could prove useful if any other such atrocities were to threaten or indeed take lives. Unknown to Ryan or the general public, another such day of planned carnage was thwarted by the United Kingdom's secret service in 2009. Intelligence officers had received a tip from a good source that there was a plan for four men to carry out similar bombings on the underground. When officers scoured many hours of video footage it was believed the four men in question were indeed rehearsing their routes and were promptly arrested. Their homes were searched and the damning evidence of homemade explosives were discovered. Ryan was soon searching for footage from the station on and around the date approximately two weeks prior to the night he discovered Stephanie's badge. From his recollection of the conversation he had first had with Nicole about Stephanie's disappearance he had deduced it was any time from the Friday that she was last seen at work and the Monday when she had not returned for work following the weekend. When Ryan first met Nicole she had told him Stephanie had been missing for two weeks. Ryan tried hard to remember the date. He checked his calendar on his phone. It was around the time of his interview with Mr Edwards. That same week he had gone out to that pub with Justin to watch his friend's band perform. That was the night he'd found the I.D. badge and it was only a couple of days after that he met Nicole. He found, in his calendar the date that he had gone out with Justin. He now had a date from which to work. Each day was divided into two twelve hour halves and each twelve hour period had its own video file. Each file was named by using four characters from the station's name, the date and start time of the twelve hour period. In no time at all Ryan had created a search query to only list the file names for the three days in question and the station from where she was supposedly abducted. He stared at the screen waiting for the results of his search to be returned to the display. He picked up his mug of tea and took a swig of it. The tea had long since turned cold and he spat his mouthful back into the mug and voiced his disgust. While the search ran its course, he made himself a fresh cup and returned to the laptop to see the list had now been sent to his waiting screen. In the list of the files, as well as the file name it also showed creation date and size of the file in megabytes. Five of the six files listed were identical in size but the sixth, the evening of the Friday was smaller by a considerable amount. This made that file stand out like a sore thumb to Ryan. He promptly started to download all six files from the server to his laptop so he could view the videos for himself. They were quite large in size and so each one would take a decent amount of time. He checked the time on his phone. He mustn't forget his date with Nicole. He had already spent a considerable amount of time on this task and the morning had skipped along quickly. He checked the time again as another of the six files completed its download. At this rate, he would not have the time to view the videos before he had to leave to go and meet Nicole. He finished his fresh cup of tea as the last file completed. He checked the time again. He didn't have long. He opened the smallest file and watched as the view flitted and looped between five cameras that covered the station, each view would stay on that camera for five seconds at a time then flip to the next one. Camera three showed the platform where Ryan had found the I.D badge and indeed the bench under which he found it was in clear view of the camera. He watched the time in the corner of the video that showed the real time as the footage was filmed. The video showed the usual throng of activity that you would expect in a busy London underground station on a Friday night. The clock in the corner of the display showed 10.30 PM, then the next second it had changed to 11 PM. Ryan rewound the video a little and indeed saw it happen again. That would suggest thirty minutes of footage was missing. Ryan checked it again to find it was as he had seen the two previous times. His brain burst into activity. Was that the time Stephanie was taken? The missing footage would explain the file size being smaller but had that been erased? Ollie nor the thin man and his gang would have the ability to do that would they? No, perhaps before he drove himself silly with conspiracy theories, there must be a plausible explanation to this. Perhaps there was maintenance to the system at that time. Perhaps a power cut to the cameras. There could be any number of reasons as to why it seemed there were thirty minutes missing on that date. He would have to check the video files from another station for the same time and date; maybe it was maintenance across the entire system. For now though that would have to wait. He checked the time on his phone, if he didn't leave in the next five minutes he would surely be late. He hurriedly disconnected his hacking equipment and stowed it all back in the case. Instead of returning it to its usual hiding place he placed it in the cupboard under the stairs. He grabbed his keys, wallet and jacket, threw a pair of shoes on and left his flat. He jogged to the tube station. It would be quicker to cross London at this time of day on the underground as opposed to driving.

Chapter Seventeen.

Ryan was lucky with the tube and arrived at the Kangaroo Café five minutes early. He hadn't known of it but as Nicole had rightly suggested, it had not taken him long to search for the place on his smart phone. There were only three in London, and only this one was close to her place of work. The establishment was by the river. A wide promenade stretched alongside the Thames. The sun was shining and there was a slight breeze making for a comfortable temperature when walking, but not for sitting outside a café for too long. There were several aluminium tables and chairs arranged outside on the pavement in front of the café. There was just one man who had decided to sit at one such table and he had a coat on with the collars pulled up almost around his ears. He sipped on a coffee and looked out across the water. Around the perimeter of the tables and chairs ran a red rope that was connected to brass poles which had huge weighted bases. Each section of rope had a brass end on it and a quick release sprung loaded clamp that was used to affix it to the pole. Just outside the roped off perimeter to the left of the entrance stood a sandwich board. It would have been the usual wooden rectangle affair; save for the fact that someone had made a Kangaroo shape cut out of plywood and had secured it to the board somehow. The kangaroo was painted like a cartoon kangaroo and on its front paws were red boxing gloves. In a speech bubble coming from the kangaroo's mouth, the words "Try our knock out lunches.", were painted in black on the white background of the speech bubble. Below the kangaroo's gloved paws, were the menu items written in different colour chalks. Ryan checked the time on his phone, it was exactly twelve thirty. He looked up and down the promenade, no sign of Nicole. He guessed she had probably been just held up at work with some last minute thing she had to complete. He checked his phone to make sure he hadn't missed a text from her, or a call. He hadn't, he slipped his phone back into his coat pocket. Kangaroo café was one of several eateries and bars that did their trade on this section of the Thames. He looked at the others, a coffee shop, a burger joint, an Italian restaurant and some sort of bistro, they all looked nice with each having seating area outside the front of them too. Running behind the parade of buildings and elevated a good fifteen feet or so was a road, Ryan wasn't sure which road it was but he could see the tops of the buildings that were across it, facing the river. To the right of the Kangaroo café, which was the last in the row of establishments, was a set of stone steps that first went right, dog-legged and turned left up to the road. The wall around the steps matched the long wall that ran the entire length of the promenade. It was a dark slate grey that almost looked like it was made of flint stone. The wall that followed the steps up had sand stone coloured flat capping bricks that stood out in a stark contrast to the dark grey bricks. Along the top of the capping bricks a metal hand rail was fixed, it was a weathered, dark, almost rusty iron colour. Ryan turned back to look out across the river. He was amazed at how much river traffic there still was in this day and age. In history of course the, Thames was teaming with boats, traders of all sorts ferrying their goods into London, the thriving capital of commerce. But it still played an important part even though road systems and rail networks were heavily used for the transport of goods, the river still showed signs that it too was a massive part of that infrastructure. There were not that many people out and about on the promenade today so when he heard the click, click, clickety, click of a woman's stiletto heels coming from behind him, he turned around. Coming down the last few steps to the right of the café, was Nicole. She was wearing a dark grey, wool blend, three quarter length coat, black trousers, black high heeled shoes, cream coloured felt gloves, a white woollen scarf and a white woolly hat that Ryan thought looked like a scotch bonnet chilli. He smiled as he realised the irony of his thought. A hat that looked like a chilli that got its name from the fact that it looked like a particular type of hat. Nicole looked beautiful as she stepped off the last step. Her long dark hair, which she had straightened, flowed out from under the white hat and cascaded over her shoulders. Her smooth, flawless, caramel coloured skin looked radiant in the cool yet bright sunny day's air. Her complexion looked a shade lighter today Ryan thought, most likely due to the cool air. He had started walking toward her and as they came closer he smiled. The tip of her cute little nose and her soft cheeks were slightly flushed red.

"Hey beautiful, you look so cute all wrapped up like that and with your red nose and rosy cheeks." Ryan said, as they approached each other yet closer.

Nicole giggled and smiled a bright, wide, beaming smile back at him.

"And you look very handsome my dear sir." She said, "Have you been waiting long?"

"Only about an hour or so." Ryan answered, with a big smile, "I was so eager to see you."

"No, really?" Nicole questioned, as she reached him and gave him a hug, "I told you twelve thirty, why would you get here so early?"

Ryan hugged her tightly.

"I didn't, I'm just messing, I got here about ten minutes ago." He explained.

Nicole playfully tapped him on his upper arm while still embracing.

"Silly, I thought you were being serious." She said, then kissed him on the cheek, "Too cold to be stood about waiting for anyone today."

They broke from their embrace, Ryan placed his hand on the small of Nicole's back and gently steered her toward the café.

"Oh I think you'd be worth waiting around in the cold for young lady." Ryan said, "Especially seeing the way you look today. Gorgeous."

Ryan removed his hand from her back and bent his arm, offering her his elbow. Nicole placed her arm through the crook of his and placed her other hand on his arm. They walked together, heading for Kangaroo café's entrance. On reaching the door she let go, as Ryan held it open for her to enter first.

"After you my lady." He exclaimed.

"Why thank you kind sir." Nicole replied, with a smile.

Ryan followed her in. The place was clean and smart looking on the inside. The same tables and chairs that were laid out in the front of the place also furnished the interior. The floor was covered with black, polished, granite tiles so the aluminium tables and chairs gave the place a real modern look. The walls were cream but were covered in so many curios and memorabilia from Australia that there was not much of the painted wall left to see. White ceiling fans hung from above but were sat dormant, given the cooler temperatures of this time of year. To the right was an L-shaped bar, the part that faced the door had a Perspex cover and shelves, where assorted sandwiches and pastries laid on display. Atop the long straight part of the bar that was parallel to the right hand wall, sat a cash register and several wicker bowls that contained an assortment of different flavoured bags of crisps. On the counter behind the bar sat two large black coffee machines, the proper barista type coffee machines, used to make all sorts of wonderful coffees. Between them sat a large, wide sandwich press used to make grilled sandwiches and panino. At the far end of the bar, in the back wall was a door that lead out into the kitchen where burgers and the like were made fresh to order. A tall, young man came from the kitchen just after the couple had entered.

"G'day guys." The young man said, in an authentic Australian accent, "How are ya?"

"We're good thanks." Ryan replied, "How's you?"

"I'm great mate thanks." Replied the young man, "What can I get for ya, or d'ya need a minute to think about it?"

"I'm good to go." Nicole said, "I'll have one of your Australian sunrise sandwiches and a mocha please. What about you Ryan?"

"Been here before huh?" Ryan asked Nicole with a smile, "What's the sunrise sandwich?"

"It's the best, it's a large soft white bap, slightly toasted, crispy bacon and a fried egg." Nicole replied.

"You could work here." The young man said. "You want mushrooms in yours?"

"Oh go on then." Nicole replied, and smiled at him.

"That sounds great, I'll have the same please?" Ryan said to the guy behind the counter, "Could I get a tea though please?"

"Sure mate. You want mushrooms too?" The guy asked.

"Yeah go on, sounds good." Ryan replied.

"Do you want anything else?" The young guy asked, "Oh how d'ya both want your eggs done?"

"That's all for me." Ryan replied, "Can I have the egg done so that the yolk is still runny but the white is all cooked? You want anything else?"

"I'll have my egg the same and no, I'm good thanks very much." Nicole added.

"Okay guys, take a seat. I'll bring it over when it's ready." Replied the Australian.

"Where do you want to sit?" Nicole asked of Ryan, "By the window?"

Ryan looked over to where Nicole had suggested. There was one man sat alone on one of the tables near the window and a young couple sat at another. The rest of the place was empty.

"No, let's sit over there." Ryan responded, as he pointed to a table near the back of the café in the far corner away from the bar, "I have something I want to talk to you about."

"Oh?" Nicole replied, "That sounds ominous."

The pair walked over to the table in the corner and Ryan pulled out a chair for Nicole. She sat, and Ryan pushed the chair in slightly for her.

"Thank you sweetheart." She said, as she looked up at him.

"You're very welcome." He replied, as he stepped around the table to sit on the chair opposite her.

"So, what's up Ryan?" Nicole asked, once Ryan had sat

and pulled himself closer to the table, "Should I be worried? Are you going to tell me you don't want us to see each other anymore or something?"

"Oh good lord no, nothing like that." Ryan rushed to reassure her, as he reached out to hold her hand, "How well do you know Stephanie?"

Nicole hesitated for a second then took hold of his hand.

"Why?" She quizzed, "Pretty well, I'd like to think. Why do you ask?"

"I, I don't know her that well and this could be a little awkward, what I'm about to say, seeing as you're friends and all." Ryan stuttered to say, "I don't want to offend you with my thoughts about her but I'd like you to hear me out. Maybe you'll see it's possible or maybe you'll tell me I'm barking up the wrong tree entirely."

"Okay, well you don't have to worry about me getting upset with you, as you said, you don't know her that well and you are entitled to your opinion." Nicole explained, "The whole situation she has been in since you met is not typical and so perhaps her actions haven't shown you the real her under normal circumstances."

"That is true enough." Ryan admitted, "I didn't think of that."

"Go on though." Nicole suggested, "Tell me what you were going to say. Don't let that influence you in what you were going to say, I'm curious now."

"Okay, thanks sweetheart." Ryan said and smiled a coy smile, "If you really thought about it, do you think she could be the type to be influenced by money? I mean do you think perhaps, that she could have possibly had some plan with Ollie to run off with him, the money and the drugs?"

Nicole burst out laughing.

"That unbelievable huh?" Ryan asked, feeling a little stupid by her reaction, perhaps he really had gotten Stephanie's actions wrong and his thoughts of some big conspiracy were wildly off track.

"No, sorry, it just sounds so unbelievable, not because I know Stephanie but just everything she's been through. Would anyone have risked putting themselves through that?" Nicole started to explain, "You saw how she looked when you found her, bound and gagged in Ollie's flat. If they were in it together would he have tied her up?"

"Hmmm, you're right, I'd forgotten about that." Ryan replied, such an obvious argument to everything he'd been thinking about.

Yet still questions begged for answers as to why she got involved with Oliver again. Perhaps she really was just a kind soul and wanted to help him. Maybe she had been honest about that. What was she looking for? If not the thirty grand that she had taken from Ollie and now supposedly missing. What about the missing footage? The C.C.T.V camera footage, was that just a coincidence? To be honest and fair about it, Ryan realised he hadn't even begun to look at the videos from the station. It could well turn out that it is missing due to any number of reasons and that her abduction could still be in one of the other video files from another night. Ryan sat there momentarily contemplating his whole reasoning on Stephanie and the questions his mind had created.

"You okay Ryan?" Nicole asked, as she squeezed his hand.

"Yes, yes, sorry, I'm good, just got me thinking about everything, I guess I need to re-evaluate it all. I guess I've been trying to understand everything that's happened recently and I'm trying to make it all fit by conveniently forgetting certain aspects." Ryan replied, and smiled a gentle smile, "Thanks honey."

"Thanks?" Nicole replied, "For what?"

"Being a sounding board." Ryan responded, "I've been so used to trying to figure things out on my own, I'd forgotten the importance of sharing one's thoughts with another and getting their opinion. It's so easy to miss things that give a reasonable explanation. Then the other person points them out or reminds you of them and it becomes as clear as day."

"Well you're welcome, but do go ahead and share your thoughts that you did have if you wish." Nicole prompted.

"Okay, though they may seem a little silly now." Ryan started but was interrupted.

"Here you go guys." The Australian guy had come to the table carrying a tray with their food and drinks on. "Can I get you anything else?"

"No, that's great thanks." Both Nicole and Ryan answered.

"Enjoy." He said, as he placed their things in front of them and walked back to the kitchen holding the empty tray.

"You were saying." Nicole reminded Ryan.

"Oh, yes, there's just a few things that have been niggling at me about Stephanie's story." Ryan continued, "It still bothers me that after they're break up why she would go back to getting involved with him? Why has she still got a bolt bag? She must have realised it was a dangerous thing to do, to steal the drugs and money so why do that, why not, if she was so bent on helping him, didn't she just try talking to him again? Being kidnapped from an underground station seems a little far-fetched, I mean wasn't there anyone around? Everyone knows the stations have cameras everywhere these days, would Ollie have risked taking her from there? How did he get her out of there? Why didn't she put up a fight? Why didn't she tell us about the money and only admitted to taking the drugs to start with? She told me that she felt the thin man and his gang may have taken the money already but it wouldn't make sense that they would still be asking us for it? They have no idea if we could raise that sort of money if we didn't have it. Finally what was she looking for when she left your place if it wasn't the money when I found her at her flat?"

Ryan leaned forward to get a little closer to Nicole and she naturally leaned in closer too.

"I hacked into the London underground's video surveillance vault this morning and downloaded some videos from around the time we suspect she went missing." Ryan whispered over the table.

Nicole's eyes widened a little.

"You did what?" Nicole asked back in a whisper.

"I hacked into London under…" Ryan began but was cut off by Nicole.

"I heard you, why on earth would you do that?" She questioned.

"Looking for answers, if she was taken by Ollie where I found her I.D. badge it will almost definitely be caught on camera." Ryan replied, "I'm just trying to make sense of everything and also protecting us, I had got to thinking, that maybe Stephanie's role in all this was more than she would have us believe. Anyway, after everything I've just told you why are you only bothered by me hacking into the London underground servers?"

Nicole shifted slightly uneasily in her chair.

"Because I care about you Ryan, you could get in a lot of trouble, even go to prison if you get caught." Nicole replied just above a whisper, "I can see how you think all of your other questions are valid, but who knows? Maybe bumping into Ollie really got her thinking about him and she just wanted to honestly try and help him. Maybe she's a little emotionally screwed up still and hasn't been thinking or acting rationally?"

"You could be right I guess." Ryan conceded, "After all as you said she was in a bit of a state when I found her tied up at Ollie's flat."

"We'll go see her together later at the hotel and ask her, we'll get answers to all your questions okay?" Nicole added, "For now though eat up, it's better when still hot."

"Sure thing." Ryan replied, picked up his roll and took a big bite.

"Have you looked at the video files yet?" Nicole asked.

Ryan finished chewing and swallowed the mouthful he had.

"No, not yet, I looked at one briefly, 'cos it was smaller than the others in size." He replied, "That was odd too, there was about thirty minutes of footage missing from it."

"What do you mean missing?" Nicole quizzed.

"Well the clock in the corner of the screen jumped from ten thirty to eleven." Ryan answered, "It could just be because there was an outage or maintenance on the cameras going on, it just seemed a little weird. I'll go over them all when I get back."

"Okay, well let me know what you find." Nicole said, in a normal voice, "Gee look at the time, I'd better get back to work."

Nicole had finished her food and drank her coffee while Ryan had been telling her of his suspicions. Ryan hadn't yet finished his.

"I'll walk you back." Ryan suggested, as he prepared to stand.

"No, no, no, it's ok, you haven't finished your lunch. My treat by the way." Nicole said, as she stood getting her purse out of her handbag.

Nicole walked over to the counter, exchanged a few pleasantries with the young man and handed over some money telling him to keep the change. Ryan had finished his coffee and grabbed the rest of the roll off the plate, stood and walked after her.

"I'll bring this with me." Ryan said to Nicole.

"Thanks guys." The Australian said to the pair as they headed for the door.

"Thank you." They both replied.

Ryan grabbed a napkin from the counter and placed it around his half eaten sunrise sandwich. He made it to the door first and held it open for her to exit then followed her out. They headed for the stone steps.

"Ryan, honestly you should've stayed in there and finished your food. I'm running late and honestly can't take my time getting back." Nicole said, walking quickly towards the steps.

"It's okay Nicole, I can eat and walk." Ryan replied, "Are you trying to get rid of me? Did I say something that upset you?"

"No, don't be silly, I just didn't realise the time. You'll get indigestion." Nicole responded.

"Alright, I'll just walk you up to the top of the steps and let you get on your way, is that okay with you?" Ryan asked.

"Of course, I'm sorry, I'm just in a rush." Nicole replied, seeing that Ryan probably felt a little rejected.

They reached the top of the steps and walked out on to the pavement. The road was quite quiet and Nicole took hold of Ryan's free hand and pulled him across the road in a slight jog. Once across the road she turned and faced him.

"Everything will be alright Ryan." Nicole said, looking straight into his eyes. "Don't be scared and don't worry, everything will be fine, I promise."

"Who said anything about being scared?" Ryan said, a little befuddled with her choice of words.

Before he could say any more, she kissed him full on the mouth. They hugged and once they had let go she turned and walked off hurriedly.

"What was all that about?" Ryan thought to himself.

He stood there for a moment watching her. He took a bite of his roll and smiled. It really was very good. He looked up from his food just in time to see Nicole disappear around the corner at the end of the row of buildings he was stood in front of. From just behind him, came a loud, piercing, squeal of rubber on tarmac. It made him jump. He turned just in time to see the black van had skidded to a halt right alongside where he was standing. The side door of the van was already open. Before he could do anything someone behind him put a black hood over his head. Ryan dropped the roll and tried to struggle. Whoever had put the hood on him had now grabbed both his arms and held them tightly behind his back. He felt a second pair of hands grab hold of one of his arms. Before he could make a sound or try to call out, he felt a hand grab the top of his head and he was bent forward and bundled in to the back of the van. He heard the door slam and the van wheel spin away from the kerb.

Chapter Eighteen.

Ryan was laying on his side in the van. As soon as he had been thrown into the back of it he had been held down. One of his assailants had bound his ankles together with what Ryan guessed was duct tape from the sounds he'd heard when it was being done. Another of his captors had put a plastic zip tie over his hands and pulled it tight at his wrists, he felt it cutting into the skin. He couldn't see anything due to the black hood that had been placed over his head. Someone lifted the hood slowly, Ryan thought they were going to remove it but they didn't. They pulled the bottom of the hood up just far enough to expose his mouth then stuck a piece of duct tape over it to stop him from making any noise. The hood was then pulled back down over his chin. The shock of it all happening so quickly was slowly subsiding, but was now being replaced by an ever growing fear. A dread forming from deep within. He knew these men were killers, what was to become of him? The boldness of them, snatching him off the street in the way they had, in broad daylight. They must have a total disregard of the law and no fear of retribution. From the sounds around him and a sense of others being close, he figured there were two men in the back of the van with him. Given their strength, he guessed they were the two larger men of the three and that the thin man was most likely the driver. Where were they taking him? How did they know where he was? Had they followed him? Had they waited for Nicole to disappear round that corner so she wouldn't be a witness or was it just plain luck that she'd gone? Ryan felt a sense of relief that she had gone before they took him, only for the fact he thought she was safe and hadn't been taken with him. The men in the van with him stayed silent, he got the sense they were sat most likely on the internal wheel arches, a more comfortable prospect than his position. He felt like he was laying on some sort of sheet, perhaps the kind used by decorators. A distinct smell of white spirit or turps was permeating through the cloth of the hood and assaulting his nostrils making him feel a little light headed. He tried to shuffle backwards away from the smell, only to be kicked in the ribs by a booted foot from behind and told to stay still. It was more of a stamp than a kick and though it shocked Ryan into remaining motionless, the initial sting of it soon subsided. Though he was laying on some sort of sheet it offered very little cushioning from the hard metallic floor of the van. Every pot hole and bump Ryan felt. At one point the van hit such a bump, he felt he was almost lifted clear off the floor and came back down hard, hitting his head and making him wince. Thoughts of movies or television programs started to fill his mind. Where someone had been bound and gagged and tossed in the back of a truck much like he had been. In the movies, the captive, when released is asked, "Did you hear anything? Any peculiar smells? Bumps in the road?" and so on. They would somehow be able to tell police where they had been taken and by which route. All bullshit, Ryan thought to himself. He had no clue as to where they were, where they started or even how long they had been in the van. Sense of time had completely gone. Right now he couldn't tell up nor down or left from right. For all he knew, they could have been driving at seventy miles an hour or twenty. Only thing he could tell for certain, was that they were not driving on cobbled streets, fat lot of use that was. To Ryan it felt like they had been driving for an eternity, truth of the matter was, in reality only fifteen minutes or so had passed. The journey continued. The smell was making Ryan start to feel queasy. He felt sure he was going to vomit. He wretched once or twice and the man behind him pulled him up so he was sat upright against the wall of the van. That at least offered some relief from the overwhelming stench. Ryan breathed heavily through his nose, he wanted to rip the tape from his mouth so he could take in huge gasps of air to clear his lungs of the horrid smell that filled them. Slowly the sickly feeling left him and his breathing returned to somewhat normal. Morbid thoughts started to fill his mind, he wouldn't see Nicole again, would never know what kind of life they might have had. He felt this was to be his end. He imagined news stories of his body being found dumped in some waste land by some dog walker. Gang crime style execution with no leads, the headline would read. How long would it be before his corpse was found? Would Nicole ever know what happened to him? Would he ever be found? Would his family be informed?

"NO." He thought, "I'm not going out without a fight."

Ryan pushed the thoughts from his mind, a grim determination, a survival instinct, an overwhelming desire to live, filled his heart and mind. He will see Nicole again, he will fight tooth and nail to be free of his captors. His fear breaking down and giving way to an anger, a rage like he'd never felt before. Who were these bastards to be doing this to him? Threaten his very existence and the life he hoped to live? He would kill every one of them in order to be free if that's what it was going to take. He didn't have a plan, not an idea on how he was going to get free, but if he got the chance that's what he was going to do. He'd punch, kick, claw and even bite, tear their throats out to be able to walk free and see where his life took him with Nicole. A sense of clarity washed over him, a calmness, having just one clear purpose, one single goal, to survive and god damn it he will. He tried prizing his wrists apart, testing the strength of the zip tie keeping him bound. The plastic cut into his flesh, he didn't care, he didn't really feel it such was his anger. It wouldn't give, no matter, the position he was in didn't afford him much leverage. He felt confident he could break free of it if he wasn't sat in the van up against a wall. If he was standing or left alone, he would slip his hands over his bottom and get them in front of him, then he'd find a way to break his bonds. After what felt like another eternity to Ryan, the van stopped, he heard the side door open followed by a metallic rattling and scraping sound. Concentrating on the sound now, he guessed it was one of those large sliding concertina doors that were found on the front of warehouses goods in and goods out bays. The sound lasted for a few seconds, the van started moving again and then stopped soon after. He heard the same metallic sound again and guessed that was the door being shut behind them. He heard the person who had gotten out of the van, get back in and seconds later two pairs of hands had grabbed him by the arms and he was man-handled out of the van. He was standing now, his ankles still bound with the tape and his hands held behind his back with the zip tie. He stretched as best as he could within the confines of his restraints. Wherever they were felt cold. Even through the hood, a faint smell of damp dust and concrete found its way to Ryan's nose. It reminded him of when he was a teenager and during the school summer holidays one year, he'd gotten a job with one of his friends helping the friend's father clear out an old warehouse. He felt one of his captors to his right, stoop and then felt the tape around his ankles being cut so as to free his legs.

"That's better." Thought Ryan.

His anger was still boiling away inside of him, they had done half a job of freeing him. Just his hands needed to be free and he could remove the hood himself. The two men either side of him had hold of him by his arms, and they started walking him forward. One of them pulled the hood from Ryan's head. He instinctively blinked, expecting bright light to sting his eyes. Instead where they were was also really quite dark. His eyes adjusted quickly. He was indeed in a large empty warehouse looking place. It was empty except for a small table and two chairs that he could see, the men were walking him towards them. A large, solitary light hung over the table casting a cone of light to bathe the table and chairs. This light, so bright, caused the rest of the warehouse to appear darker than it probably was. Ryan peaked about to see if he could see anything. Nothing could be seen through the velvet blanket of darkness. Behind him he heard another of the van's doors open and shut, the thin man, Gerry, he guessed, getting out of the cab of the van. The table and chairs were still a good twenty feet ahead of them as they continued to walk him towards them. They reached the table and chairs and one of the men let go of him and pulled a chair back from the table.

"Sit." One of the men said.

Ryan did as he was told. The thin man had caught up to them and walked around the far side of the table and sat in the chair opposite him. The two other men stood either side of Ryan. Gerry placed a claw hammer, a pair of pliers and a knife in a deliberately slow and careful manner, neatly on the table in front of him.

"You and I are gonna have a little chat Ryan, as to the whereabouts of that bitch and our money." Said Gerry, in a menacing tone.

Ryan remained silent. He looked at the implements laying neatly in line with each other. These tools, the three tools laying just across the table could be his way to freedom. He imagined himself breaking the zip tie, grabbing the hammer first and bringing it down with all his might on the top of the thin man's head, smashing his skull. Then in a fury, swinging and hitting one of the other two men that were stood behind him, knocking him to the floor before the third one could move. Ryan would swing the hammer in a wild rage at the other. He'd then grab the knife and stab each one through the heart if any of them still had any sign of life left in them. His feeling of rage did not however show on his face. The stoic look about Ryan made Gerry think he was just petrified of the upcoming inevitable, brutal acts he was about to perform on Ryan, if he didn't give up the location of the girl and or the money.

"Are you going to say anything?" Gerry said, in a louder voice, "Where's the girl Ryan?"

"Honestly?" Replied Ryan, "I don't know. The last time I saw her was when I collected her from you. I stopped at a red traffic light and before I could do anything she opened the passenger door and bolted."

The thin man slammed his palms down on the table so hard it made the tools jump.

"You fucking expect me to believe that?" He shouted at Ryan, "Why on earth would she run from you?"

Ryan sat there, unmoved, his thoughts were only focussing on how he was to break the binds on his wrists. He tried again to break the plastic by pushing his wrists apart. It was no good, all that happened was he could feel the zip tie dig deeper into the skin.

"That I don't know either." Ryan said calmly, "You have to know I barely know her, she owes me no allegiance. I did hear from her once more since she ran though. She suggested that you had already taken the money from her flat and you were asking for money we don't have. Maybe that's why she fled."

The thin man stood abruptly, pushing the chair away with the back of his knees. He was angry with the accusation.

"We didn't find any fucking money. Why would we be chasing you around if we'd already gotten the money?" Gerry shouted angrily, spittle flying from his mouth with almost every syllable.

"So you haven't got it then?" Ryan asked, almost mocking the thin man.

"No, we fucking don't." He shouted back, "Do you know Ryan, how many bones are in the human hand?"

The thin man turned and pulled the chair back towards the table and sat on it. He ran his fingers down the handle of the hammer, then looked at Ryan with a smirk.

"No, I honestly can't say that I do." Ryan replied, still unnervingly calm.

"I shall tell you. Twenty seven Ryan. Three in each finger, except the thumb which has only two, they're called the proximal, intermediate and distal bones. Eight carpal bones and five metacarpal bones that connect the fingers to the wrist and make up the palm of the hand." Gerry said, in an authoritative tone. "Can you imagine the damage that can be done to them with a single blow of a hammer? Such as this one."

Gerry played with the hammer, picking it up by the end of the handle allowing the weight of the hammer's head to keep it on the table so it pirouetted on the spot.

"You seem quite educated." Stated Ryan, "Did you train to be a doctor?"

The thin man grasped the hammer firmly, lifted it and smashed it down on the table making an incredibly loud bang that echoed around the empty warehouse.

"Are you fucking mental? Have you lost your mind Ryan? Do you not see the gravity of the situation you now find yourself in?" Raged Gerry.

Ryan had flinched at the action and the noise.

"Yes, I do, but I cannot tell you what I do not know can I?" Ryan replied.

"Boys?" Gerry said, as he nodded to the two men stood either side and slightly behind Ryan.

The two men, following orders like obedient dogs, stepped forward. The thin man passed one of them the knife from the table. Ryan tensed, half expecting to be stabbed in the back. The large man to his left, Sean, stooped behind him and cut free the plastic zip tie that had bound his hands at the wrists. Ryan looked at Gerry, he was still grasping the hammer. He had to be patient. His hands were now free but he couldn't make a move yet. The two large men, Sean and Mack, were too close. Gerry had the hammer, all that was left on the table was the pair of pliers. Not much use against a man with a hammer and another with a knife. He had to stay focussed. Already they had freed him from his binds and removed the hood. He had to be ready, if Gerry put the hammer down and the two other men had stepped back away from him, that would be his chance and he had to be ready to take it. Just as he imagined he would. The anger far surpassing any fear he may have felt. He will get out of here, he will survive this and he will see Nicole again. Ryan rubbed his wrists, there was dried blood and fresh blood intermingled. Red welts rose from the surface of the skin where the zip tie had been.

"Give me his left hand." The thin man said to the man on Ryan's left.

The man put the knife back on the table and grabbed Ryan's left wrist.

"Be a good boy now and hold your hand out flat, palm down sonny." Sean said, in a gravelly voice.

Ryan struggled against the man's strength but he was no match, Ryan was right handed so this was his weaker hand. Ryan tried using his right hand to pull the man's hands from his wrist. The second large man on Ryan's right, Mack, grabbed his other arm and pulled it away and held it on the table too. Ryan was sat there now, unable to move either hand as they were both held down on the table by the two large men. Ryan looked down, both his hands with fingers spread, palms down being pinned to the table by the two large men holding them down by his forearms to keep them still.

"I'm going to give you one last chance Ryan, my patience has worn so very thin." The thin man said, in a slow and deliberate fashion, "Where is the girl? And where is the money?"

Ryan realised his thoughts of emerging from this unscathed as he had imagined were stuff day dreams were made of. His heart sank, the anger was still there but the fear was coming back strong now.

"I really don't know." Ryan said, in a shaky voice, "I would tell you if I did, do you think I want to suffer whatever it is you are going to do, for a girl I hardly know?"

Gerry pinched his lips together. He took a good, firm hold of the hammer by its handle and raised it above his head.

"Last chance Ryan." He shouted at Ryan.

Ryan squeezed his eyes shut tight and braced himself. His heart racing now, he could almost hear each beat of it in his inner ears. A deathly silence consumed the warehouse.

"Alright, that's enough Gerry." Came a voice from out of the darkness that shattered the silence.

Ryan felt the grip of the two men on his arms loosen and

let go. He recognized that voice, it was familiar to him. Ryan opened his eyes. From the darkness, behind the thin man, a dark shadowy figure appeared. As he came closer, Ryan could see he was wearing a hat, a fedora and a long dark trench coat. The thin man, Gerry, put the hammer down on the table.

"As you say Mr Edwards." Gerry replied, in a softer voice Ryan hadn't heard come from him until now.

"Do you agree he'll do?" Asked Mr Edwards.

"That's not for me to decide Mr Edwards but I've known worse that have been trained to be honest." Gerry answered.

"I think he will." Piped in one of the two large men that had now backed up a few paces behind Ryan.

Ryan shook his head. Confusion took over every sense and feeling he had been having.

"What the fuck is going on." Ryan thought.

The man, Mr Edwards, had continued to walk closer, he was now in the light. Gerry stood and offered him his chair. Mr Edwards nodded a thank you to him as he took the seat. He took his hat off and placed it over the hammer and other tools.

"Hello Ryan." He said, in a soft, calm, familiar voice that Ryan remembered from his interview for that job a few weeks back.

"What? What's going on?" Ryan asked through a befuddled haze.

"Firstly I want to apologise for everything you've been through over the past few weeks." Said Mr Edwards.

"What?" Was all Ryan was able to say at first, "How do you know what I've been through over the last few weeks?"

"We belong to an organisation, all of us Ryan, Gerry, Mack and Sean there" As he pointed to the large man on Ryan's left, "and myself."

"What are you talking about?" Ryan exclaimed, "Organisation, what organisation?"

"It's a government organisation Ryan, MI5, do you know what that is Ryan?" Asked Mr Edwards.

"Err yes." Ryan stuttered, still bewildered about it all, "Yes, it's the ministry of intelligence, domestic I believe, England's equivalent to America's FBI isn't it?"

"That's right. We are sworn to protect the nation from both external and internal threats to our way of life here in Britain Ryan." Mr Edwards replied.

"What does that have to do with any of what I've been through?" Enquired Ryan, still utterly confused, "Why were you interested in a drug dealer?"

"I'm sure you have many questions Ryan and I will be happy to answer them all for you in time." Mr Edwards responded, "For now though, rest assured you are safe, no harm will come to you. Nicole and Stephanie are okay and will remain so also. It's all over now."

"What is all over? How do you know about Nicole? How do you know Stephanie is safe?" Ryan started, blurting out question after question, "Why did you kill Oliver?"

"We didn't kill Oliver, he's one of us too." Mr Edwards said calmly.

"I saw that man.", Ryan pointing his finger at Gerry, "Shoot him in cold blood not twenty yards in front of me."

"Can we get some proper light in here now?" Mr Edwards barked, "Feels like I'm in a damn gangster movie."

There were a few heavy clunking noises as large industrial switches were thrown and lights started rapidly coming on, one after another like a Mexican wave above their heads. A warm yellow light illuminated the whole of the warehouse, Ryan's eyes soon adjusted, off to his left, about fifty feet away was a small office with large windows that looked out in to the warehouse. Through the window he could discern there were three figures stood there. Two females and a male. One of the females looked pensive from her body language. She looked like she was biting her nails as if nervous about something. Ryan tried to focus his eyes, he squinted a little. It was Nicole, Stephanie and Oliver, all stood there, plain as day staring back out from the office at him. Ryan shook his head. Was he dreaming, had they given him some hallucinogenic drug without his knowing?

"What the fuck?" Ryan eventually spat out. "I saw him die. He was dead, he's dead."

"No, Oliver, as you can clearly see, is alive and well." Replied Mr Edwards, "Blanks. The gun shot you heard was a blank, like they use in the movies. Oliver is a bit of an actor you know, he wanted to be a stunt man or an actor. To be honest with you, we were worried he'd over done his acting when he was supposedly shot."

"It looked real enough to me." Ryan admitted, "So what is this all about?"

A sense of calm had now come over Ryan. He realised now that he was safe and having had a few seconds to process all that Mr Edwards was telling him, he'd realised the danger had passed. Now he wanted answers though. So much was still unexplained.

"You're a gifted individual Ryan." Mr Edwards started to explain, "You have certain talents we need, your country needs, to safeguard us against acts from those that wish to see our way of life destroyed."

"Oh? What are those?" Ryan questioned, completely perplexed.

"You're ability to hack into computer systems Ryan. Your knowledge surrounding cyber security. We've been interested in you for quite some time." Mr Edwards began, "We felt you were too young before, but now you have matured a little and other matters have accelerated our need for you. We've done our homework on you, you are considered one of the top five people in the western world when it comes to computer security."

"Top five huh?" Ryan was astonished, "What other matters? What do you mean, your need for me has been accelerated?"

"Well firstly let's just say an opening has come up and we'd like to offer you the job. Before I can say any more we need to know whether you'll be joining us." Mr Edwards answered.

"So what about all that has been happening over the last few weeks? You said all of you are in MI5, so Oliver is not a drug dealer? Gerry and the other two aren't in an organised crime gang?" Ryan quizzed, still trying to grasp the meaning of it all.

"That's right. Oliver is no more a drug dealer than you are, and those three are not part of any gang, organised crime or any other kind." Mr Edwards responded, "Again, I want to apologise for everything we have put you through but it has been a test Ryan."

"A test? What sort of fucking test?" Ryan asked, he was getting angry now. "Are you saying this has all been some sort of interview to see if I cut the mustard? Why didn't you just approach me and ask me if I wanted the bloody job?"

"Ryan, this is a little difficult, but I hope in time you'll get to understand why I put you through what I have. I'm old school, I still like to recruit people in my team, the old fashioned way. There are many in our organisation that like people to apply as if it were a normal job, fill out forms, supply certificates for this that and the other. They put them through an interview process and run a series of aptitude tests. This is far from any normal job Ryan. I believe people only show their true selves when put in abnormal situations, stressful, life threatening situations. You get to see how a person thinks on their feet, how they act when given only a split second to react to something. How they overcome obstacles, find solutions to problems when it's in not in the safety of a classroom, where the only punishment for failure is a mark against your name or a negative score." Mr Edwards began to explain, "We can teach people trade craft, counter espionage, hand to hand combat, demolition, bomb disposal, advance driving skills, we even send people on fire arms courses. What we can't teach Ryan, is courage, instinct, determination, lateral thinking, morals, and the desire to do what's right. You have shown you have all of that in abundance. That along with your computer skills, make you a very desirable and valued asset to our organisation Ryan, we really hope you'll join us."

"You're not kidding are you?" Ryan said, unable to hold back the anger in his voice, "I don't know whether to be flattered or tell you all to go to hell, you actually had me thinking I was going to die."

"I understand Ryan, you don't need to give me your answer right now. You are free to go, take some time to think about it, then when you've decided whether you want to join us or not, give me a call on this number." Mr Edwards said, as he handed Ryan a card. "If you are still undecided or have any questions, just call me and we can talk more."

Mr Edwards stood from the chair. "I really hope you join us Ryan, you are a remarkable man."

Ryan stood and looked Mr Edwards in the eye. "It was you. I just realised. It was you wasn't it? Outside the restaurant, when Nicole and I first went out for dinner and again at the train station when we were being chased."

"Yes, you are correct. I wanted to see for myself the kind of man you are." Mr Edwards said, through a soft smile, "I was impressed and I thought you saw me each time, I had to up my craft so you wouldn't keep spotting me after that."

Mr Edwards extended his right hand looking to shake Ryan's. Ryan just stood motionless, staring back at him. Mr Edwards dropped his hand to his side.

"No hard feelings Ryan, you were never in any real danger." Mr Edwards said, then turned and headed for door in the back wall of the warehouse.

Stephanie and Nicole came out of the office and walked over to Ryan.

"We're sorry." Stephanie said first, "We hope you'll join us."

"Ryan?" Nicole said hesitantly. "Can we talk?"

"I'll leave you two alone." Stephanie said, and turned and walked back to the office.

Gerry and the other two followed her, to leave Nicole and Ryan alone. When the last of the others had entered the office Ryan spoke up.

"It was all a lie. You'd make a fantastic actress, you really had me believing everything there." Ryan said, sounding deflated.

"Not all of it." Nicole replied, almost sounding desperate.

"Don't worry about it, you wouldn't be the first woman to pull the wool over my eyes." Ryan said bitterly, as he turned and headed for the large metal concertina door through which they had entered the building.

Nicole walked after him.

"Ryan wait." She called after him, "Please, let me explain."

Ryan stopped and turned to face her before he reached the door.

"What is there to explain Nicole? Nicole, is that even your real name?" Ryan said, through tight lips.

"Yes it's my real name." Nicole replied, "Please, you have to let me talk to you. There are certain parts of this job I don't like."

"Oh, and what would they be?" Ryan interjected, "The having to sleep with men you don't know? Or the lying?"

"Lying is part of the job yes, I hated lying to you. As for sleeping with men I don't know, that isn't part of the job and if I didn't want to sleep with you I didn't have to." Nicole explained, "I wanted to, and for the record I believe I do know you."

"So what were you? The honey trap? Is that what you people call it in your line of work? Send in the beautiful girl to get the guy on side and do your bidding?" Ryan said angrily, "Am I supposed to believe anything you say is the truth now? Trust doesn't work like that lady."

Nicole stamped her right foot and clenched her fists by her thighs. Ryan could see her eyes were welling up with tears.

"Ryan, I know, I want to put this right. I really care about you. Stephanie was actually supposed to be the beautiful damsel in distress to get your attention, your involvement." Nicole said, desperate to be understood, "But the moment we met I took a liking to you, I couldn't help it."

"I don't know why I feel the need to apologise but I'm sorry Nicole, you might say or think you know me but I don't know you." Ryan replied, turned, pulled the door open and stepped out into the daylight.

"Ryan, please?" Nicole called tearfully after him.

Ryan looked over his shoulder back at Nicole.

"Leave me alone Nicole. You fooled me right from the start. I feel like a complete idiot thanks to you." Ryan sad sadly, shaking his head.

Nicole didn't know what else to say so she just stood there and watched him walk away.

Chapter Nineteen.

Ryan walked. He didn't really know where he was going, he just walked. His mind filling with questions which he tried to find answers to. Everything he'd been through since finding that I.D. badge was not real. The last, however many weeks it had been, he had been living in a make believe world. How could anyone come to terms with that? All those people, Nicole, Stephanie, Oliver, Mack, Gerry, the other one, all playing characters, each with a part in an elaborate fabrication. A fiction, a play, where he was the leading man without knowing it and all for what? Mr Edwards' entertainment? Ryan felt lost, feeling like he didn't know what was real and what was not anymore. He'd been lied to, been completely suckered in to believing the whole thing. He felt betrayed, betrayed by someone he had grown very strong feelings for. Someone he thought he could fall in love with, if in fact he hadn't already started to do so. But then how could those feelings be real, was that person actually the real person or was she pretending to be someone he would fall for? Had she read some kind of profile on him to know what he'd like in a woman? How far did the acting go? How far was Nicole willing to go to get him involved? How much of the woman had he grown so fond of was the real Nicole? So many questions. So many thoughts to get straight in his head. Then, on top of all of that, there was Mr Edwards' offer of a job. Ryan, except for the fact they wanted him for his computer and hacking skills, had no idea what the job would entail. How could someone make a decision about a job if they didn't even know what the job was? Should he expect to be sat behind a desk tapping away at a keyboard? Hacking into other government's computer systems? Breaking codes? Or running around streets trying to get away from people trying to kill him? All questions he'd need answers to in order to be able to decide whether he'd want the job, then he would have to decide if he even wanted to work with these people that had done nothing but lie to him. Ryan had walked far. His mind so full of thoughts he wasn't aware of how far he'd walked or in which direction. Somehow he had found himself at the river. He continued to walk along the embankment. He felt his phone vibrate in his coat pocket. He pulled the phone out, it was a text from Nicole.

"Ryan, please, we need to talk. You have to hear me out. N. X"

He shook his head, pressed the button to blank the screen and placed the phone back in his jacket pocket. What was it that Nicole was going to say? Was there going to be anything she could possibly say that would make him believe her? He stopped walking, he turned and leant with his forearms on the wall that ran along by the side of the river. He looked out across the water. There were a few boats bobbing along on their merry course. He breathed a long, drawn out sigh. He looked down at the water, it was a murky brown colour. "Just like life." He thought, "You think you know what you see when you look at it. It's a river. It's water. Quite simple. But what is underneath the surface? What is hidden? What can't be seen? What sort of activity is going on that we have no idea about in the obscure?"

He scoffed at his thoughts and snorted a half cynical laugh.

"Maybe I'm thinking too hard about all this. So I was played. Isn't everyone at some time in their lives? Normally by a boyfriend or girlfriend and we end up getting hurt or by some scam artist that robs us for being so easily taken in. I'm not physically hurt, disappointed in Nicole yes, but am I really that hurt?"

His thoughts drifted off to previous relationships. He decided he'd just stop thinking about everything that had happened, at least try to and just go home. He followed the embankment until he recognised where he was and from there walked to the nearest tube station. It wasn't long before he was back home and drinking a cup of tea on his couch. He had put the television on but had no mind for it, he was distracted. One thought kept going over and over in his mind.

"What could have been?"

It had been quite some time since his last relationship, and that had died a slow, horrible, lingering death. One of those kind of relationships where both parties weren't really happy but were going through the motions. The prospect of being alone or not knowing what it was going to be like without the other person, was a daunting one. Giving up on something you had known for some time, a way of life that would be no more. The family get-togethers that would never happen again, the shared friends would all be disseminated and scattered to the four winds. Which side would the friends fall on? Ryan's last relationship had lasted seven years, they had been living together for four of those. Who would take what? Should we sell the property and split the proceeds, should one of us take it on alone? So many factors to consider, each the next more dramatic than the last, at least that's how you feel at the time. In Ryan's case, they had rented a flat together, it was a little easier. One night they finally had a talk about the relationship and both felt it wasn't working. The talk had been mostly prompted by the fact the lease was due for renewal in less than six weeks. Each of them, it turned out, had been thinking the same thing. They had both taken stock and asked themselves the question as to whether they wanted to sign up for another twelve months and had both come to the same conclusion. Since then, Ryan had bought a flat, which is where he now lived. He'd been on a few dates but no one girl ever captured him. Caught his attention. Made him feel the desire to spend more time with them. None had made him laugh so hard that his face ached. None had made him have her as his last thought at night and his first on waking in the morning. To him they were all signs, that none of them were right for him. Then out of nowhere comes Nicole. She woke in him, something that lay dormant, forgotten, in fact something that perhaps he never knew existed. His feelings for her had grown so quickly. She was funny, intelligent, beautiful and sexy as hell. She brought him back to life, for until he met her he has just been existing. Doing the necessary to survive. Getting up in the morning and going to work. It was probably the relief from all the stress that the last few weeks had placed him under, but he had fallen asleep on the couch. He woke and it was gone ten thirty at night. His cup of tea sat in front of him on the table, cold. He got up off the couch and took the cup to the kitchen, poured the contents down the sink, rinsed the cup and placed it upside down on the draining board. He returned to the lounge and picked up his phone. He checked it, he had six missed calls and three texts from Nicole. He didn't even read the texts and shoved his phone in his pocket and headed up to bed. His phone started buzzing in his pocket when he was halfway up the stairs. He took the phone from his pocket, it was Nicole calling. He switched the phone off and on reaching his bedroom, put it on the bedside cabinet. He took a quick shower and after drying, got into bed and fell back to sleep.

Chapter Twenty.

Ryan woke early. His eyelids fluttering before he squinted through his eyelashes at the digital clock that sat on the bedside cabinet. 7.16 AM displayed in bright red numbers glared back at him. He closed his eyes and rubbed them with the heels of his palms. He interlocked his fingers behind his head and stretched. Arching his back and then straightening his legs. He spread his legs, almost trying to reach each corner of the other end of the bed. But something stopped his left foot from reaching the corner. Something was on the bed. He pulled his foot back and sat up sharply opening his eyes. Sat, on the end of the bed, on the left corner was Nicole.

"Jesus, you scared the hell out of me." Ryan said startled, "Have you come to assassinate me?"

Nicole laughed.

"No, but perhaps I should kill you for making me worry. I tried texting and calling a dozen times, why didn't you answer?" Nicole said, half smiling and half sounding a little angry or hurt.

"You were worried were you?" Ryan replied, a little sarcasm in his voice. "I just wanted to be left alone with my thoughts to try and figure a few things out."

"Okay, I get that." Nicole responded, "But you could've at least texted me back and said you were okay and that you wanted some time alone."

"How did you get in here anyway?" Ryan quizzed, ignoring her last comment.

"You're not the only one adept at lock picking you know?" Nicole said, smiling at him, "I had to know you were okay, you didn't answer my texts or calls, what else is left for a girl to do?"

"Nicole? Why are you here?" Ryan asked, after letting out a sigh.

"I just told you, I was worried about you." She replied, "You've been through a lot over the last few weeks. After finding out none of it was real, that could make you do some weird stuff."

"Weird stuff? How do you mean? You thought I'd go top myself or something?" Ryan replied, almost scoffing at the thought.

"No, of course not. You know, I was put through a similar recruitment process?" Nicole replied, "I went on a three day drinking spree. My scenario lasted almost three months. Three months. Then to find you'd been caught up in a lie, you do feel foolish, you see some of the signs that just didn't add up when you look back and think why didn't I realise it at the time?"

"So did some guy make you fall for them in your scenario?" Ryan questioned, with yet more sarcasm in his voice.

Nicole looked down at her hands that were folded on her lap.

"No, mine was a seven year old girl that had supposedly been kidnapped." She replied, painfully remembering the scenario that, at the time was as real to her as Ryan's had just been to him, "I had found her and had to keep her safe. I grew very fond of her, she played the part very well indeed. She was Mr Edwards' niece. Turned out she was actually eleven years old but very small for her age. She was told it was part of a game, a long, drawn out prank and that if she played the part well she'd go to Disney world as her treat for her part in it."

"Is there nothing that man wouldn't do? His own niece?" Ryan remarked, annoyed at the thought of it all. "He just uses people, fuck the consequences or their feelings."

"She was never in any danger and I have spoken to her since on occasion and she still believes it was one big joke." Nicole responded, "I don't necessarily condone it, his way of doing things, but you have to understand Ryan, it's a scary world we live in. Threats daily of types you couldn't imagine Ryan, coming from people and places you wouldn't even think of. It's all a means to an end. It's us Ryan, us that provide the security and safety of our country and our people. Mr Edwards' looks for the best."

Ryan sat there listening intently.

"Are these more lies?" He thought, "Had she been sent to try and close the deal? To get him to join the team?"

Nicole continued on her rhetoric.

"He looks for the best people and the way he does it perhaps is not the right way, but he really does get to see the person you really are. Personally, knowing how you acted and the things you did, tell me a lot about you as a person Ryan."

"So are you here to talk me into joining the team?" Ryan asked.

"No, they don't know I'm here. I'm here because I want to be. Personal reasons. I hope you join us I really do, you are just the kind of person we need. You'd make our team stronger, our fight a little easier against those that would destroy what we know. But no, whether you join us or not, I'm here for purely selfish reasons, I think I love you Ryan." Nicole said, a little nervously. "In this line of work it's very difficult to find someone. Very hard to meet a person that could even begin to understand the kind of life it would mean, being involved with someone in this job. Even outside of this job, it is so hard to find someone special, someone that just understands you and you get them. Don't you agree?"

Ryan smiled to himself. Nicole, in her words, if she was being genuine of course, just defined what he thought was so special about her. It wasn't her words exactly, it was the fact she echoed his own very thoughts. Ryan rubbed his face with both hands.

"Ugggghhhh." He exclaimed, "Why you? Why now? Why do you have to be doing this stupid job? Why did we have to meet in such a way? Why couldn't you actually really work in a law firm and we met at a bar or a party like normal people?"

Ryan grabbed his hair and pulled at it, showing his frustration.

"You care about me too don't you Ryan?" Nicole asked.

"To be honest, that's a little hard to answer." Ryan said slowly, "I mean, yes my feelings for who I thought you were, were definitely growing. But how much of the person you let me believe you were was actually you? How do I know you are actually being genuine and sincere now?"

"Ryan, everything you saw of what kind of person I am was all me. Only the situation and job at the law firm was not real. If I was not sincere I wouldn't be here Ryan. If I didn't truly and honestly care about you I wouldn't be talking to you now. I would walk away and think of you as just another part of my real job. I don't know what I can say to make you believe me." Nicole replied sincerely.

"I don't know either." Ryan said quietly.

Ryan looked at Nicole. He stared at her, deep into her eyes, hoping he could see something, anything that would make him believe her. Because he so wanted to. The way his feelings had grown for her, the way she looked now, beautiful, sexy in an understated way. He so wanted for what she was telling him to be the truth and for them to get past this and be together.

Nicole sat there, just looking back at him, looking like she was trying to telepathically reach out to him. Wishing he could read her mind so he'd know that she was indeed telling the truth. Her eyes welled up a little as she realised that perhaps there was nothing she could say to make him believe.

"I hated lying to you Ryan, I hated the fact that I had to. It upset me enormously." Nicole began, sounding a little tearful, "Oh, do you remember when you thought I was crying and I blamed it on allergies?"

Ryan cast his mind back and remembered it vividly as he thought it was strange at the time.

"Yes." Ryan eventually answered.

"I was crying. Because I was hurting. I was stood in front of you thinking what a wonderful man you are, and if this led to something, how could I expect you to trust me. How can something that could be so good start on a lie?" Nicole said, "How do you correct that?"

Ryan looked down at his lap that was covered by the duvet. As upset and disappointed as he had been feeling, her words swirled around in his head. They made sense. She was either a brilliant actress or she was telling the truth. "Okay." He finally said, "Let's say for one minute I was to believe you."

Nicole half smiled, not knowing where he was going with

this but hoping this would be positive.

"What if I didn't want to take the job? Where would that leave you and me?" Ryan continued, "Would you still want to see me? Would you be able to have a relationship with me?"

Nicole smiled, "I don't care if you take the job or not, yes I would still want to see you. There's nothing about my job that would prevent me from seeing you or anyone outside of MI5, any prospective partners have to have background checks run on them and we've already done yours. You would have to sign the official secrets act of course and swear to never tell a soul what I really do for a living. If you can do that then we'd be good to go."

Ryan stifled a smile, put his hands on his hips, looked up at the ceiling and pursed his lips, as though he was making a decision on what flavour milkshake to have whilst stood in a line at a burger bar. He looked back at Nicole.

"Okay then, where do I sign?" He said, with a soft smile.

Nicole bounced on the bed in her sitting position.

"Really?" She said, excitedly, "You believe me?"

"I do." Ryan said, and before he could continue with what he wanted to say, Nicole had jumped up from sitting on the corner and dived to land next to him on the bed.

Nicole wrapped an arm over Ryan's waist and kissed him on the cheek.

"I swear Ryan, I meant every word. I think I'm falling in love with you." Nicole said hurriedly, "You'll see."

"Hang on a minute." Ryan said, in a joking tone, "What do you mean, think you're falling in love with me? I thought you said you already love me?"

Nicole playfully slapped him on his tummy.

"No, I think what I actually said was, I think I love you. Get your facts right mister." and they both laughed.

Ryan tugged at the duvet that Nicole was laying on. She took the hint and moved up so he could pull the duvet down and allow her to get under it with him. She got into bed with him and they cuddled.

"You must be a little warm, wearing all those clothes in here like that." Ryan said with a cheeky grin on his face.

"Now you come to mention it, I am starting to feel a little warm." Nicole said, with an equally cheeky grin.

"So, if we are going to do this." Ryan started and they both laughed at the other possible connotation of his sentence, "I mean, if we are going to resume seeing each other, there is one rule you have to know and follow when you are in my flat."

Nicole looked at him thinking he was being serious and she was about to be berated for something she had done before.

"No clothes in bed." Ryan said sharply, "Unless of course you are dressing up for me. Princess Leia's slave girl costume, a naughty nurse, a police woman, or a street hooker. Any of those would be acceptable and in fact quite likely rewarded.

He laughed, Nicole smiled.

"Well we'll have to wait and see wont we." She replied, as she started to unbutton her blouse.

Chapter Twenty One.

It was twelve thirty when Ryan and Nicole eventually got out of bed and showered together. They hadn't spent all that time making love, there had been a few moments of just cuddling and talking. They both agreed it was this moment that they would consider they met for the first time, albeit with the hindsight of having known of each other before. This would be how they would start their relationship. Ryan ran downstairs with just a towel around his waist while Nicole returned to the bedroom to dry and dress. He came back to the bedroom soon after, with a tea for him and coffee for her. He placed them on the cabinet by the bedside.

"Coffee for you miss." Ryan said, smiling broadly.

"Why thank you kind sir." Nicole replied, as she walked over to him and hugged him.

Nicole had done her makeup with the few things she carried with her in her bag and was letting her hair dry naturally into the soft curls that Ryan knew and loved. She was only half dressed, wearing her blouse and panties. Ryan hugged her back and couldn't resist squeezing her bottom with both hands. He pressed himself against her.

"Easy tiger I have places I have to be, we can't start that again." Nicole said and laughed, "Besides, aren't you worn out yet? Where do you get your energy?"

"Okay, I guess so." Ryan said, playing the disappointed child, "You, you give me my energy. Look at you. Look how bloody sexy you are. I could spend days, if not weeks in bed with you."

"Maybe we can take a holiday together sometime and you can prove that to me." Nicole said, with a smile.

"Oh count me in." Ryan replied and smacked her bottom gently, "I guess for now though I should get dressed. I have somewhere I need to be too."

"Oh, and where are you going?" Nicole questioned as they broke from their embrace.

"To see a man about a job." Ryan said with a rueful smile, "Blue suit or grey?"

"Blue, with a white shirt and have you got a light grey tie?" Nicole responded, as she pulled on her trousers.

"I do as it happens. Have you been in here going through my stuff?" Ryan joked.

"Yes." Nicole joked in return, though Ryan wondered if she was indeed joking or not, "I'll take you in to the office myself then if you like."

"Oh, that's a point." Ryan said, "Where is the office?"

"Thames house. I'll take you there." Nicole replied, as she finished getting dressed.

It wasn't long before they were in her car and heading for Thames house. When they had parked, Nicole led Ryan to the building and on entering, took him to the security desk to get him logged in and the necessary pass to access parts of the building he would be going to see Mr Edwards in.

"Are you going to take the job Ryan?" Nicole asked.

"We'll see what Mr Edwards has to say, I have a few questions." Ryan replied.

Nicole took Ryan up to the top floor. On exiting the lift, Mr Edwards was already there, waiting for them.

"Good afternoon Ryan." Mr Edwards said, as he extended

his right hand.

"Good afternoon to you too." Ryan replied, and this time shook Mr Edwards' hand.

"Nicole, will you give us a while. Right this way Ryan." Mr Edwards said, as he beckoned Ryan to follow him.

As Mr Edwards turned, expecting Ryan to follow him, Nicole took her phone out of her bag, shook it and mouthed the words, "Text me when you're done."

Ryan nodded, smiled and turned to follow Mr Edwards. He was led down a corridor and turned left at the end. At the end of this corridor was a teak door. Mr Edwards open it and invited Ryan in. The room was on the rear corner of the building. It had white walls and was pretty bare except for a large conference table with eight chairs around it. There were large windows all along the rear wall that looked out onto the Thames River.

"Take a seat Ryan, anywhere you wish." Said Mr Edwards.

Ryan sat at the end chair on the left of the table closest to the door. He was sat facing the windows. Mr Edwards walked around the far side of the table and sat in the chair opposite him and crossed a leg over the other one.

"So, have you any questions?" Asked Mr Edwards.

Ryan asked several, pertaining to pay, amount of holidays, the usual things you would want to know before taking a job. Mr Edwards answered them all having expected to be asked them. Ryan went on to then ask about the job itself and what would be expected of him. He asked what sort of training there would be and how soon would he be expected to start. Once Mr Edwards had answered all of those to Ryan's satisfaction, Ryan thought for a moment.

"Do you have any other questions Ryan?" Mr Edwards asked, finally breaking the silence of the last few minutes.

"Yes, just three. I have no investigative training, what made you think I would be able to find Stephanie in the first place?" he asked.

"We were aware of that, and you could be given training in that area if you have an interest in it. To be honest that's why we had Nicole steer you towards the ex-boyfriend. With enough reasoning and talking most people will be quite easily led into someone else's way of thinking. We weren't interested in your ability to investigate anything we just needed to know how you act given certain situations. We didn't want you wasting time following red herrings, so we made it as easy as possible for you to find her, easiest way to do that, was make Nicole's suspicion of the ex being involved as strong a case as any." Mr Edwards replied, "What are your other two?"

"If Oliver was not really a thug how come he had a police record? When I hacked into the Police's national database, though the first search didn't return anything, my second attempt found a record of him. Same for his driver's license details in DVLA systems." Ryan quizzed.

Mr Edwards chuckled a little.

"Yes, you nearly blew the whole thing out of the water there with that little move. We had been monitoring your internet traffic coming out of your house. We soon realised what you were looking for and one of our tech guys had to create something on the fly really fast. We weren't ready for you to go looking that quickly. If you had have looked closer, you'd have seen a few mistakes on that search result. Luckily you saw enough for what you were looking for and didn't look deeper into it." Mr Edwards explained.

"Okay, I did think at the time it was a little odd why the search came back with nothing the first time." Ryan said, contemplatively, "Sorry I just thought of another question."

"That's ok." Mr Edwards retorted, "Ask as many as you like. I understand this is a big decision you are making here. For the record Ryan, I understand you were rather upset, especially with Nicole. Don't feel bad, don't feel like a fool. You were fooled yes, but you were by us, professionals at fooling people. Nicole has been with us a while now, I think of her like a daughter to me. She confided in me that she felt bad towards you. Don't hold it against her."

"Thank you, I won't." Ryan responded, "How did you know I was going to go to that tube station that night, and find that I.D. badge?"

"Your friend, Justin? He's been with us since before you met him at that place of work. I told you we've been interested and watching you for some time." Mr Edwards replied, "We didn't know if you would see the I.D. card, it was placed there ten minutes before you got down to the platform. We had to clear the station of any other members of the public in order to increase the chance of you doing what we wanted you to do. By the way, there was no actual abduction, even we would have struggled to pull that off, though I suspect if we really had to we would of. So when you hacked into the London Underground's C.C.T.V. storage facility the other day, one of our team cut a bit off of one of the video files to give you something to think on. Truth be told, it's the main reason I called an end to the scenario and had you pulled in. You were getting too close to discovering something was amiss."

"Jesus, Justin? Is there anyone in my life that doesn't work for you or that hasn't been surveilling me?" Ryan asked, not in an angry tone but slightly shocked.

Ryan stood from his chair and walked over to the large windows. He looked out across the river. Looked out over London stretching toward the horizon.

"You said at the warehouse, certain matters had escalated your need for me to join you." Ryan said, still looking out of the window with his back to Mr Edwards.

"Yes, something to do with the Chinese." Mr Edwards replied.

"Okay then." Ryan said, as he slowly turned to face Mr Edwards who had turned in his chair to face Ryan, "What do you need from me?"

The End.

Richard J Coley

Printed in Great Britain
by Amazon